# SHADOW OF DOUBT: A CHRISTIAN ROMANTIC SUSPENSE

SHADOW LAKE SURVIVAL
BOOK 5

SUSAN SLEEMAN

Published by Edge of Your Seat Books, Inc.

Contact the publisher at contact@edgeofyourseatbooks.com

Copyright © 2024 by Susan Sleeman

Cover design by Kelly A. Martin of KAM Design

# 1

Her gun was out of reach when she needed it most.

Brooklyn kept an eye on the security camera feed for her front door, the pounding of her heart sounding in her ears and overpowering her earbuds.

A man in a black cap fumbled with her lock.

Kane? Could it be Kane?

*Oh, God, no. Not this. Not again.*

Had he found her? Come to exact his revenge and end her life?

No! She wouldn't let that happen. She'd planned for this. Drilled it. Experienced it before. She could do it again.

She tossed her earbuds to the desk and rolled her chair to the side drawer. She slid it open. Reached inside. Picked up the Glock. The cool grip icing her palm. She flicked off the safety.

*Yes. Good. This is good.*

She could protect herself. Couldn't she?

She studied the video, her heart racing. The tall guy's head was down, his face out of sight. The warm weather didn't warrant a stocking cap, but he wore a black one pulled low. A disguise or fashionable? Either way the guy's build fit Kane.

Kane Tarver—the man who'd become the unethical hacker he'd set out to be and bilked honest, hardworking people out of their money. But worse? She'd been in love with him when they'd worked together as white-hat hackers. At least she'd thought she loved him until he turned to the dark side of hacking for money. She discovered the real Kane then and doubted he'd ever had any genuine feelings for her.

The door flew open and slammed against the wall, reverberating as it bounced back.

Hands trembling, she lifted her weapon and sighted it on the dark figure looming in the opening.

"I have a gun, and I'm not afraid to use it." Bravado in her words, but her voice trembled, giving away her anxiety.

*Please don't let him hear my fear and rush me. Please. I don't want to shoot him.*

"You're not going to use that thing on me, are you?" Her buddy Nick Thorn stepped inside and marched toward her. His usual dark eyes were a deeper brown and filled with an intensity Brooklyn hadn't seen since he'd married Piper and mellowed a bit. "Power down your computer. We're leaving now!"

Releasing a long breath, Brooklyn flicked on the safety and returned her weapon to the drawer, giving her heart rate time to start settling down. "You scared me. I could've killed you."

Nick peered at her as if she were a virus he'd discovered in a coding review. "Sorry, but it's not half of what Typhon will do if he arrives before we get out of here."

"Typhon." The mention of Kane's online nickname sent her heart plummeting. He'd chosen the handle for the father of monsters—a Greek mythological giant with a

2

hundred snake-heads. Based on his actions from that day forward, he'd picked the perfect nickname.

She blinked up at Nick, her mind racing. "He found me again?"

"Yes. Lucky for you I was at a nearby work thing when it happened, and I can get you out of here before he shows up."

This wasn't happening, was it? Typhon? Here? Tonight? She'd settled into her cute studio apartment in the Portland burbs just two months ago. He couldn't be coming for her this soon. Could he?

Sure he could, if he'd indeed located her online. But had he? "I didn't see any evidence that he found me."

"Then you're losing your touch." Nick frowned. "My alert kicked off fifteen minutes ago. Been trying to call you to warn you."

She pointed at her earbuds laying on the desktop. "I was listening to music. Didn't hear the phone."

"But you have online alarms set too," he said. "So why are you just sitting here?"

"Clearly they failed to activate and warn me." Failed big time. The warning system she'd created should've sent an alert of Typhon's handle appearing online in relationship to her, like Nick's had done.

So why did it fail? Were her skills not current enough or her equipment not robust enough to run her algorithms on a speedy basis?

"I'll show you. Scoot over." Nick shoved her chair out of the way with his hip, and his fingers flew over her keyboard, entering lines of code as fast as one of the latest computer processors could work.

"There." He pointed at the monitor and leaned back.

She squinted at the screen as if seeing the details might make it untrue that the world's most unethical hacker, who held a grudge against her and threatened to kill her, had found her.

She blinked at her screen glowing green in her dark, one-room apartment. Blinked again.

Yeah, there he was. His handle, Typhon, in plain sight. The day he chose the handle was the day she'd fled from him with Nick's help.

Even if the code wasn't on the screen in front of her, Nick was a world-renowned cyber expert working at the equally renowned Veritas Center here in Portland. If he said Typhon found her online, then it was inevitable that Typhon would locate her physical address too.

Question was, how much time did she have before she had to leave? Or had he already found her address and was on his way?

Nick eyed her. "Either he doesn't bother to hide his nickname anymore because he's desperate to get to you, or he figures he's untouchable."

She shook her head. "It's hard to believe he was once one of the good guys and we all used to work together."

"Well, he's not a good guy anymore, and we have to leave now."

He was right. No waiting. Better to flee.

She powered down her computer and mentally ran through her checklist of To-Do items that she'd followed too many times already. She would complete the essential items now, then go with Nick. When they were safely away, she would implement the plan she'd made for disappearing. She always had an escape plan at the ready. Always would as long as Typhon lived or continued to escape incarceration.

Her computer monitor went dark.

Nick started jerking out the plugs. "I'll take this to my car and come back for you and your personal belongings."

"Thanks," she said and meant it. She appreciated his friendship all these years and his legit concern for her wellbeing.

She got up to pack the few items she didn't keep at the ready, allowing her to take off with her important items at a moment's notice. How many times these past three years had she run from Kane and had to leave things behind?

Four? No five. She was starting to lose count.

She emptied her desk drawer containing her valuable papers into her backpack and went to the closet at the far end of the room. In her safe, she removed her backup gun and ammo, shoving it all inside her pack along with her laptop and tablet computers.

A quick shrug of the pack onto her back, and she grabbed the handles on two suitcases she kept filled at all times and rolled them to the front door.

Nick stepped inside. "Just need to get the printer and network devices."

"Take the printer, but don't bother with the network. I don't want to risk Kane tracking them again."

"Resetting them would work, but yeah, not using them again is ultimately the safest plan." Grabbing the printer, he glanced at her. "Ready?"

"As I can be." She retrieved her everyday carry from the drawer and followed him out the door. With a trembling hand, she twisted the deadbolt. She would drop the key in an envelope she kept in her suitcase, already set to mail to the leasing company, and send it from some obscure place that Kane couldn't trace back to her.

Nick jogged up the stairs through a blustery June breeze.

He took control of the suitcases. "Move it, Stick."

She wrinkled her nose at his use of her nickname. She possessed an usually high-functioning memory and recall, and he'd given her the nickname as a nod to a memory stick the first week they'd met.

He raced down the stairs at top speed. Her gut tightened more as she charged after him, fighting the wind with each step. She dove into the front seat of his SUV and settled her backpack at her feet. He slammed the hatch and got behind the wheel, not speaking but cranking the engine and roaring out of the parking lot.

She batted her windswept hair from her face and clicked her seatbelt in place. "You think Kane still lives in Portland and is nearby?"

"I think no matter where he lives full time, he's nearby right now." His dire tone raised her concern even higher.

"Why?" she asked as she searched out the windows for any sign of the creep but caught only the half-moon beaming down on the road and lighting their way.

"Because he's missed catching up with you, what? Four times now, and this will be the fifth. And he's got to be freakin' angry about it. He knows we have the skills to run algorithms that pick up his name, so I don't think he would release his name again unless he was close by to scoop you up."

"He would just let the information be out there long enough to scare me before he comes to my door."

"Exactly."

"Well, it does. Scare me, that is." She circled her arms around her stomach and felt the car rock under the windy night. "I have no idea what he'll do to me for turning him in to law enforcement."

"He had a thing for you, big time. I mean, I could say he loved you, but can a sociopath actually love? More like he thought you belonged to him, and he couldn't abide you choosing to leave him. So predicting his behavior is nearly impossible."

*Sociopath.* Described Kane to the letter. How had she not seen it when they were dating?

Memories of their time together played like a newsreel in her brain. Good times. At least she'd once thought they were, but now she could see beneath it all, and his duplicitous behavior came rising up and taking over the images.

She shuddered.

"Sorry." Nick took a sharp left turn, the car rocking before it righted itself, and he made another left. "I don't mean to scare you more. But I need to make sure he doesn't find you."

"Where are you taking me?" she asked. "I mean after you finish your defensive left turns to be sure we're not followed."

"Not sure. I'd let you stay with me and Piper, but now's not a good time. You'd be safe there with our top-notch security at the condos, but I have to think of my family. Carter's almost two now, and Piper's expecting again. I don't want to bring danger to any of them."

"Congratulations!" The word burst out, and she grabbed his arm. This was the first she was hearing of a second child on the way. "Boy or girl? Due when?"

A grin spread across his face. "We don't know the gender yet, and Piper's three months now, so do the math."

Ah, good news in the midst of all the mess in her life. Really helped her hope for a good future for herself too. "You really are living the dream, my friend. I'm so happy for you."

"You deserve to have the same thing." He looked her way, his expression gloomy.

His gaze held his sorrow. Not new. He hated the way she was forced to live on the run from Kane and that a dream of a family was out of her reach as long as Kane was alive and free. "I've got some friends in Cold Harbor that you might be able to bunk with for a short time."

She shook off her sudden sadness to focus on her safety. "Cold Harbor? Never heard of it."

"A small town down the coast, a few hours from here. Gage Blackwell runs Blackwell Tactical, and they have a secured compound. You'd be safe there, for sure."

"Sounds interesting." Her phone dinged, and she jumped. "It's my front door camera."

He flashed her a look. "It's likely Kane."

"This fast?" She refused to acknowledge Kane might be standing on the stoop. "I ordered a pizza. Maybe it arrived."

"You should ditch your phone. Kane will likely track the feed."

"I'll power it down now and remove the sim card, then trash it as soon as we're somewhere no one will find it. I have a new one in my backpack." She opened the app, and her heart fell.

"It's Kane." She stared at Nick. "He's at my..."

*Door. Her door.* Her breath left her body, and she couldn't finish the sentence.

A close call. Too close. She gulped air, but her lungs felt like bricks and didn't seem to fill.

Still, things were clear.

If not for Nick's quick thinking and rescue, she might already have been dead.

Colin Graham stared at his mother, fast asleep on the sofa in their cabin on Shadow Lake. Correction. Not really their cabin. The large, three-bedroom place belonged to the Maddox brothers and their business, Shadow Lake Survival, where Colin and his brother, Devan, taught wilderness survival skills. Russ, the middle Maddox brother, had moved out of the cabin after he'd gotten married and into a place his wife owned. He was kind enough to let Colin and Dev move in from the smaller cabin they'd each been occupying on the compound so their mom could join them and they could take care of her.

Take care of their mother. Made Colin's brain hurt just to think about. She had lupus, which the doctors had struggled to control over the years, and they'd always figured it was a possibility that she would require care with her day-to-day needs. But they'd all prayed it wouldn't come to that.

Not so. Her painful joints and extreme fatigue made doing most everything a challenge. She also experienced mild cognitive issues and forgot important things. Things like taking her meds on time. Or eating.

Dev walked up behind Colin and dropped into the chair at the table where his Glock and cleaning supplies sat. "Didn't think it would come to this."

Colin took a better look at his mother's face. Her body. She'd aged well on the surface, still a fit, beautiful woman with the same dark hair color shared with Colin and Dev. By looking at her, you would never know she'd suffered from lupus for so many years. But she *had* suffered. Majorly.

Still, she was a big-time believer in not letting her disease define her, and she refused to give in to it. Sure, she had a lot of days when the choice wasn't hers to make, but for the most part, she'd found workarounds.

Until now. Now her suffering had taken over. Colin hated to see her suffer. Would do anything to take it away. Scared him to see it. And her willingness to give in and come live with them scared him even more. She was far too self-sufficient to accept losing her independence unless she absolutely had no choice. Which meant she was even worse off than she was letting on.

9

Colin looked at Dev. "She looks just fine sleeping there. If only..." He let his voice fall off. "I don't know what I was going to say. There's no *if only*. With no cure for lupus, that's not changing."

"We can fix this," Dev said. "For now anyway. Keep working with her doctor and insurance company to get her back on the meds that work."

"Stupid insurance company, suddenly denying coverage." Colin gritted his teeth. "Hopefully her doctor's latest appeal will work, and they'll approve the right drug no matter the cost."

Dev slammed his fist into his other palm. "Give me five minutes with them, and I'd change their mind."

Colin rolled his eyes. "All that would result in is you going to jail, and then who would take care of Mom?"

"Too bad Jada just re-upped, or she could be here too." Their little sister had gone straight into the Navy from high school and, at the age of twenty-five, already had seven years in.

Colin nodded. "She was one of the last people I thought would make a career in the Navy."

Dev raised an eyebrow. "You don't give your younger siblings credit for growing up. You just see us as kids who always wanted to hang out with their big brother."

Colin winced. "There could be some truth there, but all I'm certain of now is that it's taking both of us to care for Mom, and we're failing on all counts."

"Not all counts. She's looked after."

"But what about all the hours we're missing at work? At this rate, the Maddox brothers can only keep us employed for so long."

"But they've been great about it."

"Yeah, while having to pick up our slack, and that's not fair to them."

Dev picked up the cleaning rod. "Too bad one of us can't afford to quit and take care of her full time. Or even pay for the meds ourselves."

"That wouldn't help Shadow Lake Survival. At least not right now We're in peak season, and classes are fully booked through August. The guys can't lose our expertise without losing revenue."

"You got a better idea?" Dev worked the rod through the barrel of his Glock. "We still can't afford to hire a nurse, and her insurance won't cover that either. And ditto on the home health care worker."

They'd looked into paying the cost themselves and were shocked at what a nurse was paid. Not that they should be surprised. Nurses were highly trained and worth the care they provided.

"Mom doesn't need a nurse," Colin said. "We can just keep trying to hire a caregiver with less training."

Dev blinked. "You losing your memory too, bro? We've tried that for weeks. Failed to get anyone to apply that we would even consider."

"Then we try again. Keep at it. I'll place an ad in the paper as soon as I can. I'm heading out now to do a joint class with Eryn Sawyer at Blackwell Tactical. I'll be spending the night in Cold Harbor at their compound, so you have Mom duty."

Dev increased the speed of his rod going in and out of the gun barrel. "I don't get it. Why do you need Eryn's help to teach a basic class on eliminating an online presence? Not when you were once a big-time cyber expert at the FBI and all."

"I don't need her help to do the training, but you know class participants can now choose to have us delete their online footprints, right?"

"Right. But it'll cost them."

"Money they appear willing to pay, so most of the participants sign up for the service. Means it takes two people to complete the work in the week we have them in our training program."

"Why can't Eryn come here?"

"She has more powerful equipment. Besides, she has little kids, and I hate to take her away from them."

"Even if Mom needs you?" Dev set down the gun and looked up.

Colin couldn't let Dev guilt trip him. He needed to make a living because he needed to support their mother too. Always had. Their dad tragically passed away when Colin was nine, and Mom's money had run out during his junior year of college.

Dev didn't know Colin was currently footing her bills. He thought their father had left plenty of money for her, but the medical bills ate it up at a record pace, so once Colin was out of college and employed, he'd stepped in. As an agent, he'd been able to afford it and didn't want to saddle his little brother with the costs, but with the survival business in startup mode, their salaries weren't high enough, and things were tight now. Financially, it was a blessing to have his mom under the same roof.

"I've already arranged with Barbie Maddox to take my day shifts with Mom while I'm gone," he said.

Dev tilted his head as he took in the information. Maybe looking for something to complain about since it was clear he felt like Colin was shirking his duties. But becoming members of Shadow Lake Survival meant they'd become members of the Maddox family, and that included being unofficially adopted by Barbie, the brothers' mother, and their father, Hank. So they had a support system, and Colin wasn't afraid to use it right now.

"Barbie works for me," Dev finally said. "Mom will like

spending time with her better than being with you anyway. She feels guilty about taking us from work, and Barbie is retired."

"Plus, Barbie's stories of living the flower-child life in the sixties are guaranteed to entertain her."

"Not to mention, going to the Blackwell compound won't be a hardship for you." Dev shoved his hands into his pockets. "I discover something new about the place every time I visit. Especially new weapons."

Dev was seriously into firearms, as was the Blackwell Tactical team.

Colin didn't have a collection of guns like Dev did. Still, he could appreciate how a firearm could be used to save lives. "They do have all the cool toys."

"I figure we will here someday, too, but Reid is just building the business."

"I'm glad we got in on the ground floor. It's rewarding to help build the business." Colin resisted frowning. "At least when we manage to get to work these days."

Their mom shifted on the sofa and guilt took hold of Colin. He shouldn't ever put his work first. Their mother had always been there for him and Dev, and he needed to be there for her as much as he could. Plus, as the oldest, she was his responsibility.

But that didn't preclude finding someone with the proper skills to stay with her so he and Dev could earn a living. Still, he wouldn't just settle for someone qualified. The caregiver had to be someone she liked and respected too.

*I know You haven't given us anyone yet, but I wouldn't be opposed to You letting the perfect candidate fall into our laps and making it happen soon.*

## 2

---

Brooklyn didn't pay any attention to Nick's driving as he piloted the city streets until they hit the highway toward Cold Harbor. No need. Serving in the army had taught him how to handle weapons and defensive maneuvers, and he would keep her safe.

Thankfully it had given her time to delete her home doorbell videos that showed Nick's arrival and their departure. If Kane managed to hack their account, she didn't want him to see that Nick had come to her rescue. She couldn't put his life or his family's lives at risk. Maybe it was time for her to cut ties with him. Change her identity. Move to another state. The best solution, of course, was to figure out a way to take Kane down. But no matter her desire to do that, she hadn't been able to find anything else concrete since turning him in three years ago.

Fat lot of good turning him in had done. He'd simply disappeared and vowed to get even with her, and now here she was homeless again. Now that she was safe, finding a home had to top her priority list. In a town or city where she could find another job and wouldn't need a car. Short of changing her name, she'd tried to eliminate her electronic footprint, and that meant not being in the state database for a car registration and being selective when accepting clients in her freelance business. She'd also gone to using cash as much as possible and did her best to find an apartment without needing to fill out automated paperwork.

Unfortunately, most of the places that fit her criteria were owned by individuals offering listings on Craigslist or online ads. When Kane located her again, and she fled, he could try to get information on her from these owners and hurt them in the process.

And he would. Find her again. That was a given.

She sighed.

Nick glanced at her, the dashboard lights reflecting the sharp planes of his face. "Thinking about Kane?"

"Yeah. I need to figure out a way to expose him, but I don't have a clue how to find him, much less get any evidence of his crimes." She tried not to sound so down, but she was feeling down. "My top priority right now has to be finding a more permanent place to stay."

"You heard Gage when I called, right?"

She nodded. "He said I can stay as long as I like."

"Which is good, but I've known you a long time and know you're far too independent to have to rely on him for housing for long."

"Exactly." Her stomach rumbled, and she wished that pizza had arrived sooner.

"I need to stop and feed you."

She wanted to eat, but she didn't like putting him out when he had a long drive back home after dropping her off at Blackwell Tactical's compound. "I can wait."

"I know you can, but you're a real grump when you get hungry." He pointed at a road sign that announced Gert's Diner. "We'll stop there."

The sign with old-fashioned lettering boasted the best

downhome cooking and baked goods in the state. Her stomach rumbled louder. "Ever eaten at Gert's before?"

He shook his head. "But it's open and nearby, and that fits my criteria."

"I was more thinking about the fact that Kane can't connect it with you."

"Oh, right. Makes sense. Nope. No connection." He exited the highway and took the access road for a mile. He cranked the wheel into the well-lit lot. Only two cars were parked near the large window, but an "open" sign flashed its welcome.

A red and white awning spanned the width of the building, and the signs in the window also foretold of downhome Southern cooking. Odd choice out in the rural Oregon countryside, but she was a big fan. Her granny had grown up in Alabama before moving to Oregon to get married. She made the best Southern dishes and had taught Brooklyn's mother how to cook them, too, so Brooklyn had her fill growing up.

Nick pulled around back. "Don't want my license plates in view of the road."

"Good thinking."

"Do you expect anything less?" He laughed. He'd never served in law enforcement, but his work at the Veritas Center involved working on law enforcement investigations, and he'd learned a lot about procedures and how to stay safe.

They hurried through a robust wind that smelled fishy and hinted at the coast not too far away from the front of the building. Inside, the sweet aroma of freshly baked pastries set her mouth to watering. The delectable treats scenting the air filled a large glass display case to her left.

An older woman, who had a single white streak like a lightning bolt going through the side of her short black hair, greeted them with a smile. Her nametag read *Linette.* "Welcome to Gert's. Are you here for takeout or would you like a table?"

"A table please." Nick smiled at her.

"Sit anywhere. Menus are on the table, but if you'll be wanting pastries, you might want to check out the case before you take a seat."

"Gladly." Brooklyn stepped up to the glass and drooled over rows and rows of donuts, cookies, muffins, and other pastries, but when her gaze landed on an individual pecan pie, her search was over. Her granny baked the best pecan pie ever, and memories flooded back of days spent in her kitchen, baking and cooking with her, before dementia took over and she passed away.

Tears pricked Brooklyn's eyes. She hadn't seen her parents since Kane started stalking her. She'd had to stop any communication with them then. She couldn't risk him hurting them to get information about her.

Oh, how she missed them. Tears ran from her eyes, and she angrily swiped them away.

Nick stepped closer. "What's wrong?"

"The pecan pie reminds me of my granny, and I miss seeing my family." She looked up at the fluorescent lights to stem the tears.

"Something else Kane's taken away from you." Nick gestured at the aisle leading to small tables with striped tablecloths that matched the exterior awning. "Let's sit. Go down to the end."

She strode down the aisle through tables on both sides of the room, past the only two couples in the room. Both were young and, from what she could see, in love.

What would it be like to come here with a boyfriend instead of a friend? To be dating? At her age, she should be settling down. Having a family. Most of her friends, who she no longer could keep up with either, already did. Nick was a perfect example, and with his work obsession, she'd always thought he was the most unlikely of her friends to get married and have kids. Yet he'd fallen hard for Piper, and now they were parents too.

He circled around the table and dropped onto a black wooden chair facing the door. She sat on the other side. He handed her a colorful menu in a plastic sleeve. "I had to bail on my event before dinner, but I guarantee whatever I choose here will be better than the rubber chicken dish they were planning to serve."

"Especially the dessert." Images of that pecan pie came back, and her stomach rumbled again.

"I'll get an apple fritter. I'm not a big fan of pecan pie."

She snorted.

"What?"

"The way you say it. Pea-can versus puh-con. Yours is how a lot of Northerners would say it, and if my granny was still alive, she would chastise you and say that's a can to pee in." She chuckled.

He smiled. "Not sure that's just a Northern way of saying it."

"Yeah, I heard that even pecan farmers vary on their pronunciation. Just saying." She opened her menu before they got into a discussion about her family and she started crying again.

She immediately spotted her dinner and didn't have to think twice. A vegetable plate that included fried okra, squash casserole, fat-back green beans, macaroni and cheese, and homestyle mashed potatoes. All dishes her granny had made and Brooklyn had never learned to cook. She would have to make it if she ever got to see her again.

*No. No. Don't think that way.* They would be together

again. Soon. She would find a place to live, and then finally find a way to take Kane down.

Their waitress strode down the aisle, her steps dragging, and her face tight with the end of the workday fatigue. She held out a coffee pot. "Looks like you could both use a cup."

They turned their cups over, and she filled them with steaming hot coffee. "Best coffee and vittles you'll find in these parts, as Granny used to say on the Beverly Hillbillies."

Brooklyn chuckled. "I was surprised to see downhome cooking here."

"Gert's a transplant from Georgia. Said the people of Oregon deserved to know real cooking." Linette laughed. "I hope you like it."

"My granny was from Alabama. My mama still cooks her recipes." Brooklyn's voice cracked, and she forced a smile as if she wasn't suddenly very homesick. She missed her parents. They'd been such a big part of her life before Kane. Sunday supper every week with those Southern dishes, games, and family fun.

"'Nuff said." Linette chuckled and set down her pot to get out a small order pad and pen from her apron. "What can I getcha?"

Brooklyn placed her order. "I'll have cornbread with that and sweet tea."

"Ah, yes, you know your way around a Southern cooking menu." Linette turned to Nick. "And you?"

"Don't know what I'm doing, but I'll take the roast beef dinner with green beans and corn. Biscuits and tea without all that sugar."

"Good choice." Linette jotted it down. "And did you decide on dessert?"

They gave their orders.

"I'd like to get a to-go box of pastries too," Brooklyn said.

"You can choose them on the way out," Linette said. "Can't go wrong with anything in that case." She picked up the pot and departed.

"Plan to feed your sweet tooth as usual I see." Nick put their menus back in the holder.

"No, I'm going to do that before we leave." She laughed. "Those I plan to give to Gage as a small thank you."

"Oh, right. Good idea. Not that he'll expect a thank you. He and his team help people all the time without expecting anything in return."

She still couldn't grasp the whole concept of a tactical team working out in the boonies. "A seaside town in nowhere seems like an odd place for a tactical team."

Nick poured a heavy dose of cream into his coffee and nodded. "Gage grew up in Cold Harbor, but he left for a time to serve as a SEAL. Came back home after he was injured and had to leave the team. He wanted to stay there because it's the only life his daughter knows. When his wife died and left him a huge insurance settlement, he started the business. He hires only people who are former military or law enforcement who lost their chosen jobs due to an injury."

"Giving them a second chance." She picked up her cup.

"Exactly, and they're all glad to help others who need a second chance too."

"Not sure I qualify for that, but then again, maybe I do." She sipped on the coffee, the dark nutty flavor perfect without any bitterness.

Nick stirred his coffee. "You deserve to catch Kane in an illegal act that would put him behind bars for years. I'll do whatever you want to help with that."

She met his gaze. "Don't think this will make me change my mind and take you away from your job or family to work on this for me. So many people are counting on you, and

20

now that Piper's expecting again, you'll have even less free time, which I expect you to spend with your family."

"It doesn't have to be that way." He frowned. "My past offer still stands. I'm glad to ask my partners at Veritas to take on your case pro bono. I know they'll say yes, and then it'll be part of my job."

She shook her head. She wasn't a charity case when there were so many other people deserving of their pro bono help. She would hire them, but she couldn't afford their rates.

"The Blackwell Team has an IT expert too. Eryn Sawyer. Top-notch skills, and they charge less than we do. Or at least they used too. Not sure what their rates are now."

She shook her head. "With always having to move and change jobs, I haven't been able to save much money. And I figure this time, I shouldn't take a white-hat job but steer clear of IT altogether. Maybe leave Portland and hole up in a small town. Then maybe Kane won't find me again, and I can build up my savings to be able to afford some help."

He snorted. "Leave IT? It's in your blood. And what would you do?"

"I don't know. Haven't thought about it." She took a moment to process. "I used to waitress in college."

He set down his mug. "I can't see it, but if that's your only option, it won't give you enough money to hire Eryn."

"Then I'll just have to find Kane on my own."

"I could lend you the money."

She wrinkled her nose at him. "No point in suggesting that when you know I'll say no."

"I know. But I just had to put it out there." He frowned. "Let me know if that changes or if you want the Center's help after all."

She nodded, but her pride wouldn't allow her to accept his charity. At least not yet. She would only change her mind if Kane upped his game and she didn't think she could stay one step ahead of him.

Linette delivered their food, and as they ate, Brooklyn turned the discussion to the latest technologies Nick was employing on the job. She enjoyed having a normal meal with a normal discussion and appreciated it when, on their drive, Nick talked all about Piper and Carter.

She loved seeing his devotion to his wife and how smitten he was with his son. The longing for a family of her own threatened tears.

*No, stop. Focus on being happy for him.*

Nick slowed the vehicle and flipped on his blinker. "We're here."

Brooklyn searched for a sign. Nothing. Just a small opening in a treelined road. He pulled onto the drive, and she leaned forward in eager anticipation of seeing her home for the next little while. A security light clicked on from the trees, highlighting the wooded drive. Several more lights came on as they rolled slowly down the narrow lane, the tires crunching over gravel until they reached a heavy-duty gate leading to an open area.

He pulled the SUV to the gate and pressed a button on the intercom mounted on the post.

"Nick, buddy." A deep male voice came over the speaker. "I'm on my way to the conference room. You remember where that is?"

"In the training building."

"Exactly. Meet me there."

The gate hummed open, and she scanned the area to see additional cameras mounted in various positions inside the compound. This place was protected like a fortress.

"Why all the security?" she asked. "Is Gage one of those former military paranoid types?"

"Nah, he's a regular dude." Nick pulled into the

compound, and the gate whooshed closed behind them until the lock hit the post and clicked closed. "They have a large cache of weapons on site along with other pricey equipment and had some theft attempts."

And protecting it made sense. "I'll feel safe here for sure."

"Just remember, no system is infallible. Especially when we're dealing with an IT wiz like Kane."

"You think he could penetrate this network? I mean, I'm assuming this Eryn person you mentioned set it up, and you seem to be impressed with her skills."

"Given enough time, I'm sure he could hack anything, but if he does, he'll face an armed response for sure." Nick fixed his gaze on her. "Still, an armed response takes time to muster, and it doesn't take long to scale the fence, even if it's reinforced with barbed wire at the top, and get to the cabin you'll be staying in."

"So don't let down my guard and keep my gun close." She sighed as she'd hoped to count on the protection of this team and live a more peaceful existence here. But no. Right now, if she wanted to stay alive, she had to sleep with one eye open and expect the worst.

In Blackwell Tactical's conference room, Colin stretched, while Eryn sat at the end of table, head down, staring at her monitor. He loved everything about information technology and was glad to be here working with an ultimate professional like Eryn.

Well, maybe he didn't love everything. Not when someone misused IT for their financial gain, which was far too prevalent these days and the reason he'd left the FBI. He couldn't handle seeing the abuse of anything and everything possible. Way too prevalent, and no matter how many creeps Colin put behind bars, they kept coming. One after the other. Like a barrage of bullets from a machine gun. Taking. Exploiting. Abusing.

Now he helped class participants avoid such scammers. Helped them eliminate their online presence so they couldn't be tracked or manipulated. Taught them how to avoid leaving any tracks online. How to spot scams and risky websites.

Colin tried to stifle his yawn but couldn't contain it. They'd had a quick microwave dinner and continued working for hours. It was getting late, and he wasn't used to sitting in front of computers for crazy long hours anymore. But if Eryn was game to keep working, so was he.

She looked up from her monitor. At some point, she'd sleeked back her long, black hair into a ponytail and flipped it over her shoulder. "This guy will take some time to finish. He's been very active online with pretty much every one of the socials."

*Odd.* "Most people who take our classes avoid social media like the plague."

"He used it for political reasons. Nothing personal. But man, the memes he's shared." She frowned. "He's definitely a socialist."

He didn't like the look of that frown. "Is there something else bothering you?"

"No, just wondering why I signed up to help with this." She laughed. "I mean, it's tedious and not very challenging."

"Oh, yeah, that." He chuckled.

"Doesn't seem like it bothers you, though."

"I get it, but tedious is just the thing I want to do these days."

She sat back. "Don't you miss being an agent at all? The excitement the job could hold. I know I do at times."

He shook his head. "Maybe I haven't been gone long enough."

"Yeah, time has a way of making us forget the hard parts and remember only what we enjoyed."

"Besides," he said. "We've had a few exciting months at Shadow Lake. Even had to dodge some bullets, so that was fun."

She blinked a few times and stared at him. "What kind of survival training are you teaching?"

He laughed. "We recently had a client who was being stalked and needed our help. And before that the Maddox brothers' significant others had some big issues that I helped with. You know how it goes. As the team's source of online information needed in investigations, you get pulled in all the time."

"Oh, I get it all right." She chuckled. "But I wouldn't have it any other way."

"Not sure how I feel about it when it comes a little too close to the reasons I left the Bureau. But I guess it does keep the job fresh and exciting." He tapped his monitor and yawned. "Especially when you have unending hours of this kind of thing in front of you."

The door opened, and Gage stepped into the room. He was dressed in his usual black tactical pants and a logo-embroidered team shirt. His dark hair was cut shorter than Colin remembered, and it was slicked back like he'd just taken a shower.

"Yo, man." He locked gazes with Colin. "Looks like you could benefit from a little more sleep. Those Maddox boys working you too hard?"

"Just the opposite." He explained about caring for his mother. "We need to find someone to hire soon or one of us will have to quit our job."

Gage tilted his head. "What kind of qualifications are you looking for?"

"Honestly, nothing much in the qualifications department. Just someone with a good personality who is kind and compassionate. Responsible and organized. Who can do basic things for my mom, like help her dress. Get her meals. Make sure she takes her meds. Basic common sense kind of things." Colin took a long breath. "And not offend her by treating her like a little kid. That's probably the hardest. Knowing when to step in without overstepping."

Gage nodded. "I don't mean to speak out of turn, but I might have a solution for you."

"You do?" Colin perked up, feeling as if he'd just downed one of his favorite espressos.

Gage perched on the side of the table. "You know Nick Thorn?"

"Are you kidding? Who in IT on this side of the country doesn't know about Nick?"

"Well, he has a friend who's a white-hat hacker, and she's looking to take a break from it. Not sure if she's interested in the kind of job you're offering, but she's going to stay with us until she finds her footing. So a live-in situation like you have might be perfect for her."

Colin tamped down his excitement as caring for his mother was a far cry from hacking. "Let's ask her for sure."

"Actually, she just arrived with Nick, and they're on their way down here. I'll go meet them and update her so I don't put her on the spot in front of you. If that's good for you."

"Sounds great."

Gage pushed to his feet and marched out of the room, his tactical boots thumping into the quiet, broken only by the hum of computer equipment. He still had his military-perfect posture and crisp movements of someone at attention. Gage had been on track to be a military lifer until the injury took him out and some things clearly carried over.

Colin admired what the man had built here and his family life. Not that Colin was ready for that kind of commitment in his own life. He had to recharge after his years chasing scumbags at the Bureau, only to have a long list of other equally or more notorious predators immediately filling the void. The child predators being the worst.

Colin fought back the shudder that wanted to take him and prayed for help. Help that God hadn't provided in the past, but then each day was a new day, wasn't it? And maybe the day that God said, "I got you."

Eryn's phone chimed. "That's a text from Trey. Lucas has a cold, and he's crying for me. I need to try to get him back to sleep."

"How old is he?"

"Almost five." She smiled, a dreamy one that lit up her face with happiness Colin only wished he knew as a parent. "But Lily is sick too. She's three, and Trey has his hands full with the two of them. I should be back soon. I'll let you know if that's not the case."

She rushed toward the door as if the kids themselves were calling out to her.

He couldn't imagine being the parent of three—she had an older daughter too—and still trying to work. But she loved her job, and she seemed to fit it in part-time.

Voices sounded outside the door. Male. Female. Calm, ordered tone. No excitement by the woman. He'd hoped she would be thrilled about the job, but maybe she wasn't interested. After all, she was used to something far more thrilling.

*Please. Mom's care is more important than me. I'll gladly deal with the residual trauma from my past work if You provide someone to care for Mom.*

The door opened, and a tall, curvy woman with flaming red hair in waves of curls down to the middle of her back stepped in. The sidearm at her hip surprised him. Didn't match the femininity she portrayed. Not that a feminine woman couldn't be a gun enthusiast, but in his experience it was more rare.

Why did she feel a need to carry? Was it because of what she'd learned in hacking? Learned that the world was a dangerous place and she needed to feel safer? He wouldn't doubt it.

She caught sight of him. Her eyes matched the shocking green accent light of his gaming keyboard. A jolt of interest hit him hard. He almost gasped, but swallowed it down.

She had to be the woman Gage mentioned. The one who might take the job as his mother's caregiver. If so, he would be glad to solve the problem. To have someone in the job.

But with her?

Could he live day to day with someone who made him forget everything in the room except her?

# 3

The job of caring for this Colin Graham guy's mother was simple. One Brooklyn could do. Would like to do until she decided what came next for her. But the intense study from him left her unsettled. It was like he was trying to read every single secret she held, and she had the bizarre urge to unburden herself to him.

Not happening. She couldn't very well tell him about the threat to her life. Not and work for him and live a normal life. He had "protector of the innocent" written all over his face. In his posture. In his assessing gaze. Just like all the other men in organizations like Blackwell Tactical and Shadow Lake Survival. Even Nick and his partners in the Veritas Center thought the same way.

"Will you excuse us for one minute?" she asked him. "I need to talk to Nick and Gage again."

She didn't wait for an answer but fled the room and hoped the guys would follow her. They did, but they didn't look happy about it. Or maybe they were more surprised.

She hit the cooling night air, bugs flitting in the light beside the door, and took a long breath before turning. It would take all her efforts to bring these two men around to her side. "I want you both to promise not to tell anyone about Kane."

"And by anyone, I'm guessing you mean Colin," Nick said.

"Especially not Colin, but no one in general."

Gage planted his feet, sending up a little pillow of a dust cloud. "Why?"

"I want to try to live a normal existence and not have every minute of every day a reminder that Kane is hunting me. If I tell guys like you and Colin about my situation, you all go into protective mode and get overbearing."

"I resemble that comment." Nick chuckled. "Seriously, though. I get it. I know I do it and some of the other guys do too. Just instinct."

"I know, and I'm not pointing a finger or placing blame. I appreciate the support, but this has been going on for years now, and I need a break from it." She rubbed her arms against the night chill. "I know I can't forget about it and have to keep my eyes open and watch, no matter where I am. But for the first time since I fled from him, I feel like this is an opportunity where he won't track me down."

"A reasonable request." Gage held her gaze. "But you're putting Colin and his family at risk. He should have the choice of hiring you under these conditions or not."

"I get that, I do, but I don't think he would be in any danger now. If I stay off the internet, Kane has no way to track me to this location. And I only plan to take on this job as a temp gig until I can find something more in line with my computer work."

Gage looked at Nick. "Is she right about that? About Kane not finding her?"

"Yes, in terms of an online footprint, but he could track her the old-fashioned way. On foot. PIs have been doing so for centuries."

30

"Odds aren't good, though, right?" She used her gaze to try to plead for agreement with Nick. "Kane won't have a reason to connect you with this town and especially not with Shadow Lake."

"She's right there," he admitted, but he sounded reluctant. "Other than a work connection, we really have no ties. He would have to look at everyone I worked with over the years and somehow suspect you or Colin above everyone else."

Gage's expression softened. "Can we keep an eye on him?"

Nick shook his head. "Only as much as I can track him online on the dark web. Which I can't guarantee. Unless he surfaces and leaves tracks for me to follow. If that's the case, he'll want to be found, and we would have to be very careful as he would likely be setting a trap to capture Brooklyn."

"So we avoid these traps, you stay off the internet, and Colin and his family should be safe." Gage met and held Nick's gaze.

"Theoretically, yes," Nick said.

Good. Gage was on the fence. Time to tip him to her side. "You said the Shadow Lake Survival compound is secure as well. He shouldn't be able to breach the fences and get to us." Brooklyn tempered her excitement and made sure her earnestness came through. "And I promise if there's any hint that Kane knows where I am, I'll notify Colin of the situation and leave immediately."

"I don't know." Gage bit his lip. He was waffling now for sure, something he seemed very uncomfortable with.

"I'll agree for now," Nick said. "But let me assess the situation when I get back to my main computer. If I see any risks, you'll have to tell him, or I will."

"Fine," she said, not at all feeling victorious because she did care about bringing others into her situation and the potential for them to be hurt. "If I get even a day of a more normal life, that's better than nothing."

"Okay," Gage said. "I'll go along with it, but Nick, you call me tomorrow with an update, or I go straight to Colin."

"I can do that," Nick said.

"Let's get back inside then." Brooklyn pushed past the two men, praying that their expressions didn't give away their concern to Colin. She really wanted to take this job if even for just a week.

One week of semi-normal life sounded heaven-sent, and she would live every minute of it to the fullest.

Colin bit his tongue against a need to know what the huddle outside was all about. Especially with Gage's and Nick's reserved expressions as they marched into the room behind the woman.

"So," Colin said and leaned back, acting casual when that was the last thing he felt. "I'm assuming that conversation was about the job taking care of my mom."

She nodded, but bit her lip.

Mixed message for sure. "And are you interested in it?"

"I am. Yes. Very." She ended with a satisfied sigh.

His pulse tripped. *Forget it.* Focus on the enthusiasm that she's showing now. He pointed at a chair across from him. "Take a seat, and we can discuss it to see if we're a good fit."

Now why did he say that when just the sight of her made him think of her as a woman not a caregiver? They were as far from a good fit as possible.

"I'll leave you two to get acquainted," Gage said. "And work out an employment plan."

Nick stepped closer to Colin. "Brooklyn and I once worked together as white-hat hackers, so if you want a reference I can give one, but don't count on it being good." He laughed and squeezed Brooklyn's shoulders.

She flashed a smile up at him, but rolled her eyes too. Clearly the two of them had a good relationship.

"Seriously," Nick said. "She's good people, and you'd be lucky to have her help with your mom. That is if you can put up with vintage movies. She's obsessed, especially with the sappy romance ones."

She shook her head. "You make that sound like a bad thing when it's anything but."

"Says you. Give me a Tom Cruise or Bruce Willis film over those any day." He stepped back. "I'll leave your things with Gage and call you tomorrow, Stick."

*Stick?* He sure couldn't be referring to her body as there was nothing sticklike about her. Soft curves all the way. So where did it come from?

"Later, man." She gave Nick a fond smile.

Yeah, the pair were good buddies. That was obvious. Completely. A pang of jealousy hit Colin.

*Seriously, dude. Jealous over a woman you just met? Unbelievable.*

Gage set keys in front of Brooklyn. "I put you in guest cabin three for the night. Just head back the way we came in, and you can't miss it."

"Thanks, Gage. I'll forever be in your debt."

"A bit of lodging is no biggie." He met her gaze. "Just remember our conversation and keep your word."

She looked as if she was fighting a frown over the sudden strain between them. "You can count on me."

He gave a sharp nod, and he and Nick took off.

"Seems like you're good friends with Nick," Colin said to break the ice.

"We are." A sweet smile found her lips. "He's a great guy and a wonderful friend."

The softness set off a bell of interest in Colin that he thought must sound like the cha-ching of an old-fashioned cash register. "Do you have any experience as a caregiver?"

"Not for pay." She twisted her fingers together on the tabletop. "But I used to help with my granny before she passed away. She had dementia. I helped with her meds, dressing her, cooking. That's when I developed a love for old movies. It was what she liked to watch. Especially when she was confused and afraid. Which was often. Especially near the end. But they made her happy, so I was glad to sit with her even if she didn't know me anymore."

Her story gave him a measure of confidence in her abilities. Too bad she'd had to experience such an ordeal. "Sounds rough."

"It's hard to see someone you love go through something like that. To be so terrified because they couldn't remember the basics." Her eyes glistened with tears. "I was honored to help her in any way I could, and I'm glad I could take some of the responsibility off my mom. She's an only child, and she took everything on."

"My mom has some memory issues but nothing to that level. More like forgetting to take meds or to eat." He tried not to sound worried and frighten her off. "She has lupus, and her needs are mostly physical due to joint pain."

She leaned forward. "I'm sorry to hear that."

He nodded as he couldn't trust his voice at that moment. He swallowed. Got a grip. "She has a really good attitude about her situation, but I don't at times. It seems so unfair that anyone as good as she is should have to suffer so much." He shook his head. "God and I've had a lot of talks about it."

"And what has He told you?" she asked, sounding honestly interested.

"Well, I don't know if He's so much as told me this, or I

have come to this conclusion after studying His word that He's all-knowing and what happens doesn't have to make sense to me. I just have to trust that He knows what's best. If He allows it in my life, it's for my or someone else's good, and I shouldn't question it."

She tilted her head, her thick hair swinging over her shoulder. "And does that give you peace?"

"When I'm actively studying His word and praying about the problem. Yeah, sure. But if I let it slide, then no." He clasped his hands on the table. "I have to admit to letting it slide too often. Waiting until I am at the end of my rope. When I see Mom really struggling. Then I let the questions fly again, and I basically start all over having to figure out the same thing." He shook his head. "I'm probably not making a lot of sense."

"Actually, you are. I see the same pattern in my life. Not about a physical illness but something else." She shook her head as if telling herself to stop talking. "I should let you know that this would be a temp job for me, and I will likely move on to something IT related if I find a good match. So if you don't want to hire me, I get it."

"I need someone right away, and if you can start tomorrow, I'd be glad for the help." He gave her a quick smile. "This would be a live-in position, but you wouldn't have to work when my brother and I are off work. We both live with Mom in a cabin on the Shadow Lake Survival compound. Unfortunately, we can't afford to pay much more than minimum wage."

"No worries. Oregon minimum wage is a lot better than the national rate. And I'd be glad to start in the morning. I don't have a car, so maybe I can get Gage to drive me over."

"I have a training to do here in the morning and can give you a ride afterwards."

"But your mom," she said. "Who'll take care of her?"

35

"Dev—that's my brother—will be with her."

"Oh, okay. Otherwise if it's better I can come with you tonight, but I'd like to decompress alone if that's possible."

He suspected what she had to decompress about was related to her secret conversation with Gage and Nick and that gun at her hip, but he wouldn't push her by asking because he didn't want to do anything to risk her not starting tomorrow. If there was a problem he needed to know about Gage or Nick would've made sure he knew.

"Take off," he said. "Decompress. We can work out all the details on the drive to Shadow Lake tomorrow."

She stood and held out her hand. "I look forward to working with you and your family."

"My class is from eight to ten, so if you could be ready to go by ten that would be great." He took her hand in his, the shock of her touch not a surprise for him, but the flicker of interest in those emerald eyes was. He ignored it.

A relationship was the last thing he needed right now with a career change and with all that was going on with his mother. Even if he did want one, he wouldn't go there with the woman who was going to solve his problem. At least in the short run, and if it worked out, maybe he could convince her to stay longer.

That is, if her secret didn't turn out to be a problem.

# 4

_____

Brooklyn opened the door to the conference room at precisely ten a.m. She wished she could say she'd slept the night and woke refreshed, but she would be lying if she did. The bed was surprisingly comfortable for a cabin, the bedding luxurious—which she credited Gage for providing for the people who enrolled in his classes—and the room was quiet. Maybe too quiet. Just a few hoots of an owl and the wind buffeting the thick walls.

But honestly, thoughts of working around others after such a long break from people kept her sleepless. That, and thoughts of Colin. She easily imagined him in one of the classic movies she watched. Suave, debonair, a real movie star of days gone by.

She glanced at him at the head of the classroom. He wore tactical pants that fit his trim waist to a T and a polo shirt with the Shadow Lake Survival logo embroidered on the chest. _Right_. Reality check, and time to let go of her very vivid imagination of him in one of her fave movies. This guy was more rough and tumble. An action star in one of the movies Nick loved. Still, if Colin were to pose for the old classic movie posters wearing the right clothing, his dark hair and intense look would have women flocking to the theater.

He shifted and caught her watching him.

The heat of a blush crept up her face, and she gave a little wave.

He acknowledged it with a quick tip of his head and continued on, wrapping up his talk by asking if anyone had any questions about protecting themselves online. A woman with sleek dark hair sat at the table in the front of the room. Her head came up, and she surveyed the group.

She had to be Eryn Sawyer, the Cold Harbor IT specialist who Nick had praised. Maybe she was teaching the class along with Colin. Brooklyn wouldn't be surprised if the two teams worked together.

Hands went up, and Colin called on a woman in the front row.

"I read that once something is on the internet you can't get rid of it. Is that true?" she asked. "I mean, you offer the service to help us clean up things, but does it even work or are you scamming us?"

Colin flashed her a professional smile. "I can assure you that we aren't scamming you. We can't eliminate things just by deleting them on your end. So for example if you have a Facebook account, we can delete your photos and posts, as it will stop other sites from picking it up in the future. But once uploaded, a digital file can be copied and stored in many locations. We have to find the sites that are storing the files and ask them to destroy them. They may or may not comply."

Eryn stood and planted her hands on the table. "Social media sites are very hesitant to help, but they are more apt to comply when the information was posted by you. If it was posted by a third party there is little chance to get them to take it down. Freedom of speech and all that."

"That said, there are tools to help us remove a lot of data like phone numbers and addresses," Colin said. "In fact, Google has a tool we use to do that, and in the future you can use it yourself."

"How?" The woman challenged with a suspicious look.

"Just search for your name," Eryn said. "Then in the pages that come up with data you want removed, click or tap on the three dots for the menu on that item. Next select remove result and Google will walk you through how to do it. They won't remove all items, but they will usually do addresses and phone numbers."

A guy with a shaved head perked up. "If this is so great, why don't they tell people about it?"

"That you would have to ask Google. Maybe search for an answer." Colin chuckled, then moved on to answer other questions. It took him and Eryn nearly an hour to take care of them all and for the class members to exit.

Brooklyn approached Colin, who'd started packing up his laptop. He looked at her. "Sorry that took so long."

She smiled at him. "No worries. It was interesting. I'm embarrassed to admit I didn't know Google had the removal tool. I did know you could have your home photo in their map program blurred by them, but since I don't own a home I never used it."

"It's good to see they're trying to help out this way." Eryn held out her hand and introduced herself. "Nick says you're one talented hacker."

"I do my best."

Eryn arched a perfectly tweezed eyebrow in the same rich black color as her hair. "And now you're going to help take care of Colin's mom."

There was a question in her statement, but Brooklyn ignored it and looked at Colin, who was zipping his laptop case closed. "We probably should get going, right?"

Both of Eryn's eyebrows went up this time. Fine. She got that Brooklyn was avoiding the question, but she wouldn't add anything else.

He looked at Eryn. "I'll be back after I get Brooklyn settled."

"I'll be taking a long lunch to spend with the kids while you do." Eryn glanced at Brooklyn. "Do you have children?"

"No. I've never been married. Not even engaged."

"Trey and I have three, but he wants five. I have not agreed." She laughed.

Brooklyn laughed along. Eryn was a very likable woman, and under any other circumstance, Brooklyn would continue the conversation, but not when she was on the run.

"It was nice meeting you." She didn't wait for Colin but rushed to the door and outside. She should probably be more aware of her surroundings, but for the first time in years she had a moment where she felt safe, and she wanted to embrace it before she left the compound.

She drew clear, crisp air into her lungs and admired the fluffy white clouds in the blue sky. Though in the low fifties at the moment, forecasters said they were in for a sunny day in the mid-seventies. A typical June day after a long, rainy spring, and the warmth of the sun on her face gave her hope.

Could she really find Kane, along with a reason that would stick for him to be arrested and convicted? To get her life back where she could follow her interest in a man like Colin or a friendship with a woman like Eryn?

Not as long as Kane was stalking her. Hunting her. But—

"The black SUV is mine." Colin's voice came from behind.

She jumped.

"Sorry. I didn't mean to scare you." He clicked the

remote for his vehicle, and the device beeped as it unlocked the doors.

"No worries," she said but hated that her brief moment of hope had ended so abruptly.

He strode ahead and opened the hatch for her suitcases and the passenger door for her, then walked around to the other side. She slid in, enjoying the soft buttery seats warmed by the morning sun.

Colin didn't speak but quickly got them out of the locked gate and on the road. When they were cruising on the highway, he glanced at her. "Sit back and relax. We have about an hour's drive."

She shifted to get more comfortable. "Tell me more about your mother."

"Are you familiar with lupus?"

"Not really."

He clicked on the cruise control, and the vehicle held a steady speed over the two-lane highway. "It's an autoimmune disease with no cure. In people with lupus, their body's immune system attacks their own tissues and organs. Causes inflammation that affects many things in the body."

"Things like what, specifically?" she asked, very interested now as she had no idea what parts of the body the disease impacted. She would need to know as she cared for his mom.

"Joints, skin, kidneys. Even blood cells. Heart, lungs. Brain." He took a long breath. "One telltale sign of the disease is a red rash over the nose and cheeks in the shape of a butterfly. The doctor who first diagnosed it thought it looked like a wolf's bite and named it lupus—the Latin word for wolf."

She had no idea. "I've heard of it. I think most people have, but I never knew it involved so much of the body. It sounds awful."

A deep frown marred this handsome man's face. "It really can be if the medicines don't control it. Mom had a long run of good health when they did work, but then her insurance refused to pay for the one that was working."

"How awful."

He gripped the wheel tighter, and even in the sunlight streaming through the window, his fingers looked white. "Her doctor is appealing the decision, but we haven't heard anything yet. Anyway, she's been tired a lot and has pretty severe joint pain. She's on high doses of steroids to make up for the loss of meds. That's worked in the past, but for the first time it's not working well."

Brooklyn couldn't even imagine seeing her mama suffer from a chronic disease. She was sure she would feel helpless as she suspected Colin did. Like she had felt with her granny. "I'll pray for her for sure, but specifically what kind of help does she need?"

"She needs assistance with anything that involves using her hands, which is pretty much everything. So dressing, cooking, cleaning, laundry, etcetera. Dev and I work odd hours sometimes—taking groups out camping for days—and we need to get back to doing that full-time. Our team-mates are picking up the slack for us, and that has to stop."

She had no idea they'd be gone for days. "Exactly what is it that you do?"

"We train people how to live off-grid. So how to live off the land. Things like hunting, fishing, gardening, foraging. Also building fires and shelters. First aid and weapon usage." He glanced at her. "As you heard this morning, I teach participants how to eliminate their electronic foot-prints and keep them gone, but I also do the basic introduc-tion class and camping trip."

Interesting. "So these are people who have had it with society and think they're better off alone?"

"Yes. Some are die-hard preppers, thinking Armageddon is coming, and others just want a simpler life where they don't have to depend on anyone else."

Sounded exactly like what she needed right now. "I can see the appeal."

He glanced at her again. She didn't meet his gaze. No way she would encourage him to press her for additional details. She couldn't tell him living off-grid would be the only way to completely hide from Kane, and even then, he could potentially track her to the property she moved to if it belonged to her or a relative.

"What did your mom like to do before she got so sick?" she asked, in order to change the subject.

"She was a big baker. Spoiled us rotten with baked goods." He grinned and rubbed his hand over his belly. "She was an avid photographer too. She continued to bake until the past few months but had to give up photography sooner when she lost her steady hand." He sounded so sad for his mom.

She ached with him. She couldn't see her mama right now, but she was healthy. Or at least Brooklyn thought she was as she hadn't been in contact for years.

"What about your mom and dad?" he asked. "Are you close to them?"

Ah, a question she didn't want to answer, and yet, she didn't want to lie or blow him off when he'd been so forthcoming. "They're very important in my life. I couldn't ask for better parents."

"I wish my dad hadn't passed away." He got a far-off look. "I think of him a lot but especially with Father's Day coming up."

"I can't even imagine. That would be so hard."

He nodded. "This year might be even worse. Reid—one of Shadow Lake Survival's owners—has daughters who are

43

planning a big Father's Day celebration on Saturday. They invited all the team members, but I'm not sure I'm up for it and might skip it."

"I could see that," she said. She wouldn't be able to attend an event like that and her dad was alive, just not someone she could talk to right now. She pointed out the window to change the topic. "Oh, look. A sign for the lake. Is it a big lake?"

"It's a decent size. Lots of good fishing." He clicked on his blinker. "You ever fish?"

"Plenty of times with my dad when I was little. Not as an adult though."

He made a left turn onto Shadow Lake Road. "I'll have to take you. My mom can do a mean fish fry. She might not be able to fry the fish herself, but she can instruct us on how to do it. And by *us*, I mean *you* because I can hardly make toast without burning the bread." He grinned at her.

She laughed. "What makes you think I can cook?"

"You didn't balk when I said the job included cooking, so..." He shrugged.

"As it happens, I'm pretty good in the kitchen but a bit rusty. I don't take the time to cook much just for myself."

He held her gaze for a moment before swinging his focus back to the road. "So no significant other then?"

"No, and you? Someone special in your life?" She held her breath in wait for his answer.

"Not besides my mom, my brother, and sister."

A horn honked behind them, and she jumped. She smoothed her hands down her jeans to try to hide her unease.

He eyed her as he slowed the vehicle. "Something wrong?"

She couldn't answer that for sure. "Tell me about your brother. You said you lived with him. I figure I should know something about the guy if I'll be spending time with him too."

Colin's eyebrow went up, likely at her sidestepping. She would have to get better at keeping her secret, or he would be questioning her before the day was out.

"Dev's two years younger than me," Colin said. "A former Clackamas County Sheriff's Deputy who specialized in water rescue. A real joker and pretty carefree."

"Sounds like a fun guy."

"He is." Colin frowned.

"Something wrong with that?"

"No. Not at all." He turned into a narrow opening in the trees that led to a dirt driveway. "I just wish I could be more like that, but I take things pretty seriously."

"Yeah, me too. Maybe I'll learn to lighten up from spending time with him."

"Maybe, but I sure haven't." He gave a wry smile.

"What did you do before taking your current job?" She leaned forward to search out the front window for any sign of the Shadow Lake Survival team compound ahead but saw nothing but evergreen trees and giant hostas and ferns growing below them.

"I was an FBI agent."

She whipped her head to look at him. "Seriously? FBI?"

"Yes. Is there something wrong with that?"

"No, but you don't seem like an FBI agent to me. Not that I've ever met one or know what they really are like. I guess I'm going on what I see on television."

"Well, I'm an IT guy through and through and just happened to apply to the FBI to use my skills with them. So I guess I'm more of a nerd than anything." He laughed, but it was a nervous laugh.

"I'm a card carrying nerd, too, so we should get along just fine." She smiled at him.

Their gazes connected and held. Something warm traveled between them, reminding her of a ray of sunshine breaking free and lighting up her world on one of the many gloomy, rainy days in Oregon, and compelling her to move closer to him.

She sat on her hands and didn't act. Not at all. She didn't want to get connected with a guy. Correction—she would love to start a relationship with a guy, but it was impossible now. Not without losing her focus, which had to be pinned on staying alive.

From her purse on the floor, her phone pealed in Nick's ringtone, and she jumped again.

*Stop it. Calm down.* If she didn't, Colin would soon figure out that something was up.

"Hey, Nick," she answered. "I'm in the car with Colin, and we're just arriving at the compound. Can I call you back?"

"Yes, but see that you do as soon as you can. It's about our mutual friend, and it's urgent."

Dev was teaching a class, and Colin stood back as his mother and Brooklyn sat together on the leather couch, getting to know each other. His mom was exhausted, but she didn't let it get to her and was still the warm and open person she usually was. Thankfully. She didn't want a caregiver, and he didn't want her to blow Brooklyn off before getting to know her. She said a helper made her feel even more powerless than normal and that the disease was winning. But she was practical too, and more than anything, she didn't like disrupting his and Dev's lives. So if they hired someone, that solved a problem for her.

Brooklyn was equally receptive to the conversation,

though she kept glancing at her phone. She hadn't returned the call from Nick, and she clearly wanted to. She'd been jumpy since Colin had met her and remained the same in the cabin, jerking at the slightest sound. Behavior that meant she was troubled or worried about something.

Was it the reason Nick called her in the car? Was it something Colin needed to know about? Should he ask?

Probably. But if he did, would it risk losing Brooklyn before she even got started?

Something to put aside now as his mom's shoulders were drooping, and she yawned. He crossed over to her and held out his hand. "Enough talking for now. Let's get you back to bed."

She looked at Brooklyn. "But I can't leave her alone when she just got here."

"It's fine." Brooklyn gave a genuinely warm smile. "I'll get some lunch ready so when you wake up, you can eat. Anything you're craving, Mrs. Graham?"

"If we're going to spend so much time together, you better call me Sandra...Sandy."

His mom offered her megawatt smile that always cheered him up as a child. "Tomato soup and grilled cheese sounds really good if it's not too much trouble."

"We have what you need to make it in the kitchen," Colin said.

"Then no trouble at all." Brooklyn returned his mother's smile with a wide one that could cheer up a child too. "Get some rest, and we can talk more over lunch."

His mother patted Brooklyn's knee. "You are a sweet thing for sure."

Colin helped his mom to her feet and handed her the cane she'd been using to take pressure off her knees. He walked with her to the bedroom. Her alarm, labeled "pain meds," sounded from her electronic communication device.

He silenced it, then while she climbed into bed, he got out two acetaminophen tablets and handed them to her with a glass of water from her nightstand.

"I have to go back to work, but Brooklyn will be here," he said. "I'll update her on your meds before I go and make sure she knows when you're supposed to take things."

"I have alarms set for the rest of the day." She swallowed the pills. "I do think she's going to work out. Seems like a real special woman."

"I agree, but it might be short-lived."

"Oh?"

He explained about Brooklyn's real career in IT, but he didn't mention that she might be keeping secrets from them. The last thing he wanted was for his mom to have something else to worry about. But he also didn't want her to get attached to Brooklyn only to have her leave in a few weeks for another job.

"Glub you, Mom," he said, kissing her forehead and using the phrase that had stuck since he was a toddler and couldn't say love.

She smiled up at him and squeezed his hand. "Glub you, too, and thank you for being such an awesome son."

Her words were filled with such emotion it almost closed his throat, and he couldn't speak. He couldn't let this moment get to him. He would have many more times like this to get through without breaking down, and he had to practice being strong for her in a way he'd never had to experience before.

His best bet was cracking a joke. "Hard not to be an awesome son when I'm overall awesome."

She swatted a hand at him and chuckled.

He left her laughing and wished he could do that more often. He silently closed the door to the main bedroom that had an attached bathroom. No question that she would have the main suite while he and Dev shared the hallway bathroom. Now they would be sharing it with Brooklyn too. Hopefully, they could make that work.

He stepped into the family room with a wall-to-wall stone fireplace and a large taxidermy salmon mounted above a thick wooden mantle. All the rooms held the fishing décor of days gone by, when the cabin was rented out as part of the family resort run by Barbie and Hank Maddox. Russ had lived here after the resort closed and never bothered to update the place other than the mattresses and living room furniture.

Brooklyn stood at the large picture window overlooking the lake. He approached.

She spun, and her eyes were wild before she connected gazes with him. Holding her phone to her ear, she let out a low breath. "Hold on, Nick. I have to finish this call in the bedroom."

She looked at Colin. "Can you tell me where I'll be bunking?"

"Down the hall, second door on the left."

"Thank you." She gave him a wobbly smile. "I'll just finish up my call and be right back, if that's okay with you."

"Fine," he said, not taking his eyes off her. "Just know that when you return, we're going to have a long talk about what's bothering you. And before you even consider it, don't think I'll let you get away without telling me what it is."

# 5

———————

Brooklyn stared out the bedroom window over a small clearing of lush grass to a forest of evergreen trees. She pressed her phone to her ear with Nick on the line. "And you're sure it was Kane who put the bounty out on me?"

"He didn't bother to hide it." Nick's disgust for Kane flowed through his words. "Seems like he's losing patience and willing to take more risks to find you."

The sun swept behind clouds, the dark sky ominous, maybe foretelling of Kane's advances, and she shuddered. "Not good for me, but maybe he'll get sloppy, and it'll help me find him."

"True, but what good will that do when we haven't connected him to any crime? For you to be safe, we need him to be locked up."

He had a point. If they couldn't get Kane arrested, then did they really want to find him? Maybe. "I guess if we located him, we would know where he was at all times. Good for my safety, but also gives us a better chance at catching him doing something illegal."

"True." Nick dragged the word out, and she knew a *but*

was coming. "But then what? We can't keep eyes on him twenty-four/seven for the rest of your life."

She released the curtain and crossed the room. "Maybe we can somehow ferret out what he's been up to."

"How?"

Yeah, how? "Someone could go undercover and try to friend him, but he's way too suspicious for anyone to succeed."

"Agreed."

"Maybe I need to let him find me. Tell him I've had a change of heart."

"No! That's not an option. Don't even think it, much less do it. Promise me."

She sighed but didn't want to promise.

"Say it, Brooklyn, or I'll drive back there and make you say it."

"Fine, I promise."

"And stay off the internet."

"Easy for you to say. Try it sometime."

He chuckled. "I'd rather not."

"I could use a VPN," she said, though a Virtual Private Network that handled login and internet activity by masking the actual IP address could be the answer for some people, it wouldn't be when a hacker like Kane was tracking you.

"You know that's not possible," Nick said.

As expected. "I know, but I'm having withdrawals and was hoping you might tell me it was okay."

He snorted. "Just keep your eyes open. I'll think on this development and get back to you. Call me if you see anything unusual. And I mean *anything*."

"Will do." She ended the call and stowed her phone.

She dropped onto the bed instead of heading for the door. She didn't want to leave the bedroom. Not because it was warm and cozy and begged her to stay. Nah, it was kind of dismal with an old quilt on a double bed, walls of pine paneling, and faded blue curtains on the small window. Not quite what she'd expected, but it was clean and that was all that mattered.

She didn't want to join Colin. Not when he clearly planned to ask why she'd been so jumpy and what was up with racing from the room to finish her call with Nick. Maybe even ask about her conversation with Nick and Gage yesterday. She'd hoped to have more time before having to tell him. To prove her value so he didn't give her the boot.

But if he asked outright, she couldn't lie to him. Not even to say she didn't know what he was talking about if he mentioned the items she thought he might bring up. So there was nothing for it but to tell the truth.

She took a deep breath and left the room. She found him in the living room, but another man of similar height, build, and hair color stood next to him, their backs to her. Likely his brother. Good. Maybe Colin wouldn't grill her in front of him.

She cleared her throat to let them know she was entering the room.

They both spun. The other man looked like Colin's twin, except he had a close-cut beard where Colin was cleanshaven.

"I'm Brooklyn Hurst." She held out her hand.

"Devan—Dev." He punched Colin in the shoulder before taking her hand and giving it a hard shake. "This bozo's brother."

"Like I told you," Colin said. "Dev's the family clown."

"So you talked about me?" Dev raised an eyebrow, looking darkly dangerous.

"For a few seconds is all."

He shifted his focus to her. "What else did he say?"

"Just that you were a former deputy, specializing in water rescue, and a carefree guy."

"Guess that's not bad then. Wait until you get to know us and the old stories start flying. You'll probably want to run for the hills."

"Hey, don't scare her off before she even gets started," Colin said.

Dev rolled his eyes. "Now who's the funny guy?"

"I wasn't joking."

Dev looked at Brooklyn. "Well, anyway, welcome. Colin is going to head out right now, but I have a couple of hours until my next class so I can fill you in on Mom's med schedule."

"I planned to do that before I left," Colin said.

"No worries, bro. I got it. You get going. Don't want to keep Eryn waiting."

Colin lifted his chin. "Since you seem to be directing my day, would it be all right with you if I grabbed some lunch before I go?"

"Sure. Might as well take a sandwich for the long drive."

Colin actually looked like he was getting mad.

She didn't want that to stop him from heading out the door so they didn't have to talk just yet. "I can make you a sandwich. Let's see what's in the fridge." She nearly ran to the attached kitchen and opened the older-model, avocado-green refrigerator in the small space with a matching oven and dishwasher.

She half expected Colin to come charging after her, but he remained with his brother, who he'd taken by the arm and led across the room to hold a hushed conversation.

Was it their turn to keep a secret? Something she might be interested in and would ask about except she wanted to keep Colin moving? She found ham and Swiss cheese slices and mayonnaise, mustard, and lettuce.

"Ham and Swiss sandwich okay?" she called through the cut out in the wall.

"Sounds good, but make it two of them."

"Mustard?"

"Just mayo, please."

She leaned further into the opening. "And you, Dev? Want a sandwich?"

"Nah, I'll eat with you and Mom when she gets up."

Brooklyn took the items to the small island with a worn butcherblock countertop and located bread in an old-fashioned, mustard-yellow bread box. The cabinets were flat-front oak, the countertop worn white laminate, and the room was painted a cheery pale green. Despite Nick's call, the cabin vibe relaxed her. It reminded her of a cabin her family rented on vacation when she was little, and she hummed as she worked.

Colin stepped into the room. "I know what you're doing."

"Making you a sandwich?" She batted her eyelashes at him as if innocent.

"Avoiding that talk I wanted to have, and batting those eyelashes at me won't change things. You're just postponing it to later in the day." He went to the refrigerator and grabbed a bottle of water, then to a basket on the counter to pick up a single-serving bag of potato chips.

She looked past him at Dev, who was assessing them with the eye of a former deputy. In case Colin didn't say anything, she didn't want to raise his suspicions too.

"Are you sure you don't want a sandwich, Dev?" she asked.

"Sure, why not? I could use a lunch appetizer." He laughed and slid onto a stool at the island. "Just mayo for me too."

"You know you don't have to wait on us." Colin grabbed

a zipper bag and bagged the first sandwich. "It's not part of the job, and we don't expect it."

"Speak for yourself, man." Dev laughed.

She laughed with him. "Colin is right. You do like to joke, and I for one like it."

"Most of the ladies do." He blew on his knuckles and rubbed them over his chest, then burst out laughing. "Seriously, haven't had a woman in my life for so long that I'm not sure what you all like anymore."

"I don't think things have changed much." She moved on to preparing Dev's sandwich. "Respect, being treated equal, and Christian values go a long way for me."

"Good to hear I'm still relevant then." He grinned.

She slathered mayonnaise on the thick wheat bread. "So why the break? Your choice?"

"Yeah, but unless you've got days to listen, I won't bother starting on that topic."

"Not that long of a topic," Colin said, but didn't elaborate as he shoved his lunch into a paper bag.

"Fine. Might as well tell you before he does. I got left at the altar, or nearly the altar, a couple of years ago, and I'm still not ready to get back on the dating horse."

"I'm sorry to hear that." She rested a hand on Dev's. "That's gotta sting."

"The sting is over, but yeah, well, you know." He shrugged, his expression the most serious she'd seen to this point. "At least I got into the game once. Not like this lunk." He jabbed a thumb at Colin.

"I've dated."

"Not seriously. I've heard of sitting on the fence, but he's been glued to it for years."

"No. Not seriously." Colin picked up his food. "I'll be back by seven. Big mouth here can cook dinner for Mom if you don't want to."

"Okay," she said, wanting desperately to ask why he was a fence sitter when it came to relationships. She could ask Dev, and he might tell her, but that would be going behind Colin's back. She didn't want to do that, because believe it or not, she thought she might have developed some feelings for him already, and she wouldn't do anything to hurt him.

～

In the fading light of day, Colin turned onto Shadow Lake Survival's heavily wooded driveway. He couldn't wait to get home, eat dinner, and kick back until bedtime. The class participants had asked question after question, each a personal thing they needed to eliminate on the internet, and he'd put them off by promising to look into it and jotting down a note to remind himself to do so. Still, it took valuable time when he could actually be eliminating the items.

And he was going to have that talk with Brooklyn. He prayed he could be tactful and not scare her off before they got started. A few times during the drive, he'd considered not bringing it up, but his gut told him to do so and his gut never failed him.

He reached the end of the drive and slammed on his brakes.

*Say what?* A vehicle he didn't recognize was parked at the gate, engine running. Colin eased his SUV closer. The driver's door opened.

A man stepped out and marched, head down, toward Colin.

Colin reached for his sidearm. The man stepped into a bright headlight beam. The light washed over his face.

*Nick.* It was Nick.

Colin let out a breath and released his weapon to lower his window. "What are you doing here?"

He scowled. "Something important has come up, and I need to talk to Brooklyn."

Colin didn't like the sound of that. "Couldn't you call?"

"It's not a calling kind of thing."

Colin eyed the guy. "What's going on that you're not telling me about?"

"Let's head to the cabin, and we can discuss it there."

Colin didn't want to wait, but he would respect Nick's wishes. "Step back, and I'll get out to open the gate for you."

Nick backed up a few steps. "Glad to hear you won't share your passcode for the gate with me. Some guys might, and that's how security fails."

"It's not that I don't trust you." Colin pressed past him and hurried to the gate.

"You shouldn't trust anyone when it comes to sharing passcodes or passwords."

"I work in the same field, remember? So I get it." Colin tapped in his code, and the gate swung open.

"Sorry. I'll get off my soapbox now, but people don't take this seriously enough. Or they use one password for everything. Odds are good one of their accounts has been compromised and their email and password for sale on the dark web. So they're just asking for their other accounts to be hacked."

"Trust me, I get it," Colin said again, knowing at times he'd participated in a similar rant.

"See you at the cabin." Nick climbed back into his SUV. He pulled through the gate.

Colin rushed back to his SUV so he could get onto the property before the gate closed.

He tailed Nick to the cabin and was out in a flash, then up to the door in front of Nick. No way was he going to miss a second of the conversation with Brooklyn. He stepped inside. She sat on the sofa alone, watching an old black and white movie on the television. Her head raised, and fear lit in her eyes.

"Colin. Oh. Good." She clicked the remote for the TV, and the screen went black. "You scared me with the way you barreled in here."

Nick stepped into the room.

"Nick." She lurched to her feet. "What are you doing here?"

He stormed across the room to her. "I have urgent news."

She looked at Colin. "Could we possibly talk alone?"

"No," Colin said. "I want to know what you're hiding from me."

"I..." She peered at Nick.

Nick eyed her. "It's time he knows."

"But I—"

"I know you'd rather that didn't happen," he rushed on, "but we need his and the team's help."

"We do? But..." Her fear was vivid in her eyes now.

Nick squeezed her arm. "They have former military or law enforcement skills, and we need their expertise."

Brooklyn clutched her hands together, her gaze flitting around the room.

Colin moved closer to Brooklyn but looked at Nick. "This sounds serious. Is my mother in any danger?"

"I don't think so," Nick said.

"'Think so'?" The words exploded out of Colin's mouth before he could temper them. "'Think so' isn't good enough. Either she is or isn't."

"She could be. So in your terms, yeah, she is."

Colin wanted to strangle Nick for involving his mother in something that could put her in danger and hiding it from him, but he couldn't very well do that. He shoved his hands into his pockets instead. "I thought we were buds. Yet, you clam up when you should be talking."

58

Nick continued to look at Colin but took a deep, exaggerated breath. "Let's all take a beat and sit down."

"Sounds like a good idea." Brooklyn dropped onto a lumpy sofa cushion.

Colin wanted to be close enough to see her expressions as she explained in the dim light, so he rested on the arm of the sofa. "Go ahead, spill, and don't leave anything out."

"Before I begin, just know I planned to tell you if Gage and Nick thought there was any danger to you or your family." She scrubbed her hands down her pantlegs. "I used to work with and date a guy named Kane Tarver. He was a fellow white-hat hacker. One day out of the blue, he decided he wanted to make more money and turned to the dark side, hacking and exploiting people. When I found out, I was shocked. Appalled. So I turned him in to the police, stopped seeing him, and changed jobs."

Not what Colin was expecting, but then he didn't know what to expect. "What happened to him?"

"There wasn't enough evidence to bring him to trial, and he got off." She gritted her teeth. "He's been threatening and stalking me since then. I've had to move several times so he couldn't find me. I've continued hacking, but change all of my email and online accounts each time I move. I don't do social media or anything that would put me on the internet, but he always finds me through my work."

"We have algorithms set so we can see when he discovers her internet presence," Nick said. "That allows her to flee before he finds her physical location."

Colin was getting the gist of the problem, and he didn't like what he was hearing. "And you're running from him right now?"

She nodded. "Nick got an alert on his phone last night and came to rescue me. We got out of there just before Kane arrived, but he didn't trail us."

"And it was convenient for you to hide out here, but not tell me. Why exactly?" His tone was testier than he planned, but come on. A stalker? His mom? The combination didn't sit well with him.

"I'm sorry. Nick, Gage, and I agreed that Kane couldn't possibly find me here and there was no danger. And like I said, if there was any hint that he did, I would tell you."

Colin jerked his hands from his pockets and ran them through his hair. "That's not a decision you all have the right to make for me."

"We—"

He flashed up his hand. "I'm right, and you know it. You just wanted a place to crash, and we were convenient."

"No, no." She shook her head. "I could've crashed at Cold Harbor until I found a job. But when Gage mentioned your situation, the job was something I could do, and I thought I could help too. I've pretty much decided to give up IT work so he can't find me, and this job with your mom sounded wonderful until I could figure out what I might do long-term."

He studied her, and she squirmed. He could be accused of being too intense and was probably badgering her right now just by the way he was looking at her.

"Stop being so hard on her, Colin." His mother's voice came from the doorway, and she stepped into the room, her cane clomping on the wooden floor. "I've been eavesdropping. Sorry." She smiled at Brooklyn. "But I know my Colin. He would've kept this from me."

"I... Yeah." He shook his head. "You're right."

She smiled softly at him. "You would've done the same thing you're accusing Brooklyn of doing."

Leave it to your mother to call you out in front of others. "Well, sort of."

60

She sat on the sofa next to Brooklyn and patted her knee. "I'm sure we'll be just fine together."

Colin met his mother's gaze. Glimpsed the affection for Brooklyn already residing there.

Well then. He'd lost his battle. Her expression said it all. But he had to protest anyway. "I can't risk it."

"It's my risk to take." She raised her shoulders. She might've lost weight and was a mere shadow of herself, but she looked strong and intimidating at the same time. "And I'm willing to take the risk so Brooklyn has a home."

"But things have changed, right?" Colin looked at Nick. "Something happened that brought you here tonight."

Sitting in the plaid easy chair, Nick uncrossed his feet at the ankles and planted them firmly on the floor. "Running my gazillion algorithms finally paid off. I located Kane's rental house. I was hoping you and some of your teammates would help me search it when he's not home."

Colin didn't need to give it a second thought. Helping to bring in a scumbag like this Tarver guy sounded like a no-brainer. "I'm in, and I'm sure they'll be onboard too. But I don't see how that would bring danger here."

"You never know what could go wrong." Nick gripped his knees. "He could show up while we were searching. Take someone out and ID him. Or he'll have security cameras, and we could fail to disable one, then he captures a picture of one of the guys. He has the skills to find the person's ID from that, and that brings him here."

A risk for sure, but one they could manage. If careful and thorough. "Then we just have to make sure we find all of the cameras, which shouldn't be impossible if we scan for his network and get a look at the Wi-Fi devices."

"Right." Nick rolled his eyes. "You make it sound so simple. You know he'll have employed top security features, and simply scanning his network could be an issue."

Colin sat forward. "Then we bring our A game. Me and you and Eryn Sawyer, too, for added IT experience and skills."

"Wait." Brooklyn's gaze shot from Colin to Nick and back. "I can't afford all of this. And I won't let you do it for free."

"Of course you will," his mother said. "I insist, and when I want something, I get my way."

"But I—"

"But you need help. These lovely men can provide it, and they're willing to do so without pay. Am I right?" She scanned the guys.

"That goes without saying." Colin peered at Brooklyn. "Now that I know what has you so jumpy, there's no way I won't help you fix it."

"I've always been on board," Nick said. "And hopefully tonight, you'll finally let me do something. All of us do something."

Brooklyn still didn't want to take their pro bono work from someone more needy, but this lead was too good to pass up, and she knew when to give in. "Okay, but I'll come along to help."

"No!" Colin's sharp tone made her jump. Surprised him too. "Tarver sees you, he could take you out on the spot."

"Then I'll have to make sure he doesn't see me." She clasped her hands tightly together. "I'll stay in the SUV, out of sight. Even sit on the floor if I have to."

Colin crossed his arms. "I can't—"

"I need to do this." She locked gazes with him. "He's controlled the last three years of my life, and if I sit here and do nothing, then you come back having been unable to hack the network, I'll always wonder if I could've done it. That we could've found something in his house that got him incarcerated and freed me from his tyranny."

"I don't know." Colin swiped a hand over his face.

"You have to let her come with you." His mom clutched his knee, her grip strength weaker than Colin would like. "She deserves to help bring this most odious man in."

"Odious?" Colin shook his head and laughed. "Where'd that word come from?"

"It's a good word for him," Brooklyn said. "So when do we leave?"

Yeah, when? "We need to get the men together to plan and drill, and we'll need surveillance footage for the property."

"Already got it," Nick said.

"Then let me get the guys to join us at the conference room." Colin stood and looked at his mom. "I'll find Dev so he can come stay with you."

She shook her head. "I'd feel better if he went with you. I'll be fine alone for now."

"I'll ask Barbie to come over," he suggested.

His mother sighed. "I hate to bother her, but I always love her company."

"Barbie?" Brooklyn asked.

"The Maddox brothers' mother." Colin's mom fished her phone from her pocket. "I'll call her while you get the guys together."

"I really appreciate this." Brooklyn pulled back her sweater to reveal a sidearm. "I can help if we run into trouble at Kane's house too."

Colin narrowed his eyes. "We'll have plenty of firepower."

"I'm a good shot and capable."

"She really is," Nick said. "Grady Houston, our weapon's expert, personally trained her. She has a wicked aim, and you'd be hard-pressed to find many people who can break down a weapon and put it back together faster than she can."

Brooklyn puffed up her chest, and she looked like an adorable young girl who'd just won the spelling bee. Still, as their eyes met, his heart took a tumble like a somersault that little girl might take.

Colin swallowed hard and smiled at her. "Not that I'm going to test you right now on the dismantling, but I can't let that pass without seeing it at some point."

"Bring it on anytime." She quickly drew her sidearm and put it back in the holster with precision movements only brought about by practice.

He was impressed, but it didn't matter how capable she was. He had no intention of letting her get into a shooting match with Tarver. In fact, he had no intention of any of them getting into a shooting match, but if Tarver showed up and drew down on them, Colin wouldn't hesitate to return fire.

# 6

Odd woman out. Yeah, that was Brooklyn right now in the small conference room with a large table and comfy chairs. Before she joined all male Shadow Lake Survival team members just a half mile from the cabin, she'd served an easy chicken bake for dinner, then tucked Sandy up in bed with her phone to call if she needed help. Barbie would come over to stay with Sandy when the team left the compound.

Eryn and team member Micha Nichols were the only missing people for this update meeting, but Eryn was at the gate and Micha had gone to let her in. Dev took a seat on Brooklyn's right side and Colin on her left. Sandwich filling described her right now. Colin had brought his brother up to speed, and both men had gone into a protective mode, much like Nick often did. He'd actually taken a seat next to Colin as if he needed to be close too.

Not unexpected. The other three men in the room would likely react in a similar fashion. At least from what Colin had said about them and the intensity in their gazes and posture. The three Maddox brothers took up the other side of the table. Reid, a former FBI agent, was the oldest,

Russ was the current county sheriff and the middle brother, and the youngest, Ryan, was a former deputy. Reid had darker hair and a more chiseled jaw, but Russ and Ryan resembled each in lighter hair coloring but not in build. Russ was very built where Reid and Ryan were more slender.

Eryn arrived, escorted by Micha, the last teammate and former Marine. He pulled out a chair for her on the near end of the table, then dropped into a chair at the end, leaning back and assessing Brooklyn with dark eyes.

Colin cleared his throat. "Okay, we won't waste any time. Brooklyn and Nick will fill you in on why we're here."

Brooklyn felt the need to stand and pace a bit, so she got up and launched into her story. When she reached the current plan to search Kane's place, she sat and let Nick take over. Though Nick was talking, the men continued to study her, making her uncomfortable. Were they thinking she'd put them all in danger and shouldn't have come here?

Reid was married with two children and lived in the big lodge that served as the company office too. He had to at least be considering that they could be in danger. Russ and Ryan had kids, too, but they didn't live in the compound so they might be more okay with her decision. Or maybe they were worried for their nieces and brother and sister-in-law.

"His house isn't in Portland as we expected," Nick said. "It's a little over an hour north of here." He tapped a remote, and the screen on the wall filled with a grainy satellite photo of a small, single-story house on a rural lot. "The good news is his rental house is on an acre lot, and he doesn't have any close neighbors to interfere with our visit. We should have free rein to determine if he's home."

"Have you thought about someone tailing him if we do find him home?" Ryan asked.

"Thought about it," Nick said. "It would be nice to have

66

eyes on him, but I don't want to risk spooking him and have him go underground. If we locate something that could help bring criminal charges against him, then we want the police to be able to find him."

"Good point," Ryan said.

"The real problem I see," Brooklyn glanced around the table at the others, "is that he's always been a hermit and doesn't like going out unless it's urgent."

Ryan leaned his elbows on the table. "Then we need to give him a reason to leave home."

"Like giving him a potential lead on Brooklyn's location," Micha added.

"My thoughts exactly," Nick said. "But we'll have to make sure that it's not obvious, or he won't fall for it."

"I can whip something up," Eryn offered.

"How do you know he didn't do the same thing here?" Reid asked. "Maybe he created a bogus address and he really doesn't live at that address."

"It could be a trap," Russ said, leaning back in his chair.

Nick rested his hands on the edge of the table and studied the men. "In my opinion, the lead was far too indirect for that. He's also turned into quite the anarchist, and he was protesting government interference in his life by shooting up a road sign. He posted a picture of the sign on a dark web forum. I used that photo to ID the location where it was taken. Guess he didn't think anyone could or would do that."

Russ raised an eyebrow, looking interested now. "But you did?"

"Would you expect any less from me?" Nick grinned and came to full height to pull back his shoulders, looking like the fierce contender she always knew him to be. "I ran a detailed algorithm to search for the photo. Got a match on Google Maps just down the road from this house. I still didn't know if he lived there or the name he'd been living under, but he's always been one to keep anything to ID him off the internet. That included banking. So I knew he had to pay his bills in cash."

Russ frowned. "Don't tell me you could find him based on that."

"I did."

Russ pursed his lips. "How?"

"I started by locating the utility companies for that property." Nick locked his focus on Russ. "You might not want to listen to this next part."

"Let me guess." Russ cocked his head. "You hacked into their files."

"You said it, not me." Nick smirked. "The electric company has a security camera at their teller window. So I downloaded those files and ran an algorithm to compare his photo to the feed until it found him, cash in hand. I zoomed in on the bill and read the property address and his bogus name."

"Which is?" Micha asked before Brooklyn could.

"Tom Bombadil."

"Of course." Eryn pressed a hand against her chest. "From Lord of the Rings."

Brooklyn had the same thought. "Kane's favorite book and movie series."

Colin shot forward in his seat. "And about the only semi-normal name in the series that he could choose without drawing a lot of suspicion."

"I confess I've never read the book or watched the movies," Dev said.

"Can that be true?" Eryn dropped her hand to the table and gaped in feigned horror at Dev.

He laughed. "I'm not one of you nerds who clearly all watch the same thing."

"I fall in the nerd category too. I loved the series."
Brooklyn smiled at him. He made a comical face, and she
joined in with his laughter. She was really coming to like
him for his humor. And his brother? Well, she was liking
him too, but for far different reasons.

He stopped laughing. "I suggest we take two vehicles to
the house. One with the assault team, and the other, the
nerd mobile. That way you all can figure out the security
cameras. Then once you clear us real warriors to go in,
we do."

Colin rolled his eyes. "It's hardly an assault vehicle."

"I know, but I sometimes miss my law enforcement days,
so humor me." Dev chuckled.

"He does have a point, even if he's calling us nerds."
Brooklyn ran her gaze over the guys to see how they were
receiving her comment. "I mean, we are nerds, but with
Kane's skills, we'll likely need to work together to hack his
network and not leave an obvious trail. The last thing we
want is to make one false step, raise his suspicions, and let
him know we're on to him."

"Agreed," Nick said. "It'll be a challenge, but I figure
between the four of us, the guy doesn't stand a chance and
won't know what hit him."

Brooklyn looked at Dev. "Same goes for whoever is on
your team. Kane will have an early warning system set up.
Something physical, like a thread or piece of paper on the
entry door. Probably additional items at his office where he's
bound to have a room full of pricey equipment, and you'll
have to avoid those."

Russ stood. "I obviously won't be on either team. In fact,
I need to step away before official plans are made, making
me complicit in breaking the law."

Reid looked up at his brother. "You can hold down the
training fort tomorrow if we don't get back in time."

"What's the topic?" His cautious tone and skeptical expression said he wasn't onboard yet.

"Newbie orientation." Reid clamped down on his lips as if he was stifling a grin.

Ryan snorted. "That's priceless."

Russ groaned and looked at Colin. "You're going to owe me big time for this, man. And you know I'll collect."

"Of course," Colin said as if there was no arguing with Russ.

Russ might be younger than Reid, but Brooklyn got the sense that he acted independently and pushed his older brother. It would be interesting to see the family dynamics play out as she worked there. If she worked there for long. She really did want to stay. Surprised her. Maybe because these guys were obviously a family. Not just the three Maddox brothers, but the other three too. A team, yes, but a family as well, and she was missing that so very much.

She waited until Russ exited, then turned back to the others. "What about a security system? Surely he'll have a top-notch system in place that we'll be facing."

Colin nodded. "But the four of us should be able to disable it."

"*Should be* are the key words here," Eryn said. "From what you say, this guy is crafty, and it's going to be a challenge to get in and out unnoticed. Especially without proper intel and time to plan."

"Should we hold off?" Reid asked. "Do more due diligence?"

"No time," Nick said. "This is the first lead in three years where we know his potential location, and we can't hang back. He could skate before we get there."

"So we're a go, then." Colin stood. "And we play it by ear, knowing every second that he could have a backup to his backup and probably another one so he can bring anyone down who dares to enter his property."

Brooklyn's gut tightened. She desperately wanted to find something that would put Kane behind bars. But would they also find something that might hurt or even kill one of these fine people?

That was her greatest fear right now. She prayed God was on their side and would protect each and every one of them as they entered a dangerously unknown situation.

Colin watched Brooklyn pick lint from her slacks and fidget in the back seat of Nick's SUV as they approached Tarver's rental house. She'd been jumpy and ill at ease since they pulled out of the compound. Not that there'd been anything unusual in the surrounding area to cause agitation.

A winding country road spread out before them with copious hills lined with typical evergreen trees and thick undergrowth made lush from all the Oregon rain. But that was it. That was all they saw out in the moon's bright glow.

Well, actually, he saw that *and* Brooklyn sitting next to him in the SUV that Nick drove with Eryn riding co-pilot. Colin had wanted to drive. To declare that he was in charge. But Nick had brought surveillance and other electronic equipment when he'd made the trip from Portland, and it didn't make sense to reload it all into Colin's company vehicle.

That didn't mean Nick was in charge. Not if Colin had his say. But Brooklyn's good buddy wasn't used to playing second fiddle, so Colin might be challenged. Didn't mean he would give in easily. Not at all. Not when Brooklyn's life was on the line. He would give his all to protect her even though she'd lied to him.

He sat back and eased out a slow breath of frustration. He hated that she'd lied. Well, technically, *withheld information* from him. But he could understand why she'd done it. She needed a safe place to land after being stalked by a lunatic, and their compound was a secure location for her. Plus, she was right. She hadn't put them in danger. At least not yet. And it also explained her need to carry.

But more important now, he couldn't look the other way and pretend she'd just come into his life to care for his mother. To ignore the threat. He felt compelled to find this Kane guy and bring him to justice. Colin had dealt with so many abusive people in his FBI career that he wouldn't let this go until he'd resolved it. Let Tarver keep stalking Brooklyn. She deserved to live her best life. See her family again. Get married and have a family of her own.

He glanced at her again. Did she want to get married? Want a family? He did, but not now. Not while he was still torn up inside over the things he'd seen in his IT job with the FBI. Kids. Women. All placed in horrific positions to be exploited, and he had to look at the photos to help find them. Horrible, terrible things he could never unsee. Never let go. Never forget.

Never.

For a time he could handle being exposed to it. They'd brought enough of these abusive monsters to trial and put them behind bars to help erase the images. But then the abusers just kept coming. One after another. Long line after long line. Relentless.

How could he get married and bring a child into the world when the world was so messed up?

His hands started sweating, and he focused on the road and mission to force the images from his mind. For now at least. They'd be back all too soon, of that he was certain.

Nick glanced in the rearview mirror and made eye

contact. "Get ready. We're about a mile out, and all cell phone Wi-Fi should be turned off."

"Already done," Brooklyn said.

"Did it miles back." Colin had made sure of that as their phones could appear on Tarver's network list and, if he was home, alert him to people in the area and put him on edge.

"Me too," Eryn said. "I only hope he picked up on and bought into the tracks I laid on the dark web. If so, he should now be on a wild goose chase to Portland to find Brooklyn."

Brooklyn leaned forward to face Eryn. "I've always wanted to leave him a false trail like that. But I'd have law enforcement waiting on the other end to arrest him. Couldn't do it. Not without just cause for an arrest. So there would be no point in it other than to mess with him."

Eryn glanced back. "I might've done it for that reason alone."

"Trust me," Brooklyn said, "I was tempted. But I figured if I did it too often when it really was time to trap him, he would be suspicious and run."

"Good thinking," Colin said. "I've tracked down my share of online criminals, and they're a suspicious lot. I can't tell you how many times we lost a suspect in the end due to minuscule things that they blew out of proportion."

He swallowed away the images from the last pervert who skated. A guy who'd abused twenty children. Mostly in his family. The day he'd snuck away from Colin's team and vanished for good was the day Colin put in his resignation.

This would not end the same way. Not if he could help it. He wouldn't let Tarver get away with stealing from so many people, but more importantly to Colin, he wouldn't let the creep skate on terrorizing Brooklyn.

He reached for his sidearm just to assure himself that it was on his hip where he'd placed it. Sure, he was tasked with hanging back and doing electronic work in the vehicle, but first he and Nick would form a recon team and approach the property on foot to assess the electronic surveillance. they both had to be prepared mentally and physically for an incursion onto Tarver's property.

"It's go time." Nick pointed ahead where Reid pulled the lead vehicle to the side of the road about a mile from Tarver's house.

A surge of adrenaline flooded Colin, and his hands started sweating. He scanned ahead for any threat, but the moon had moved behind clouds, and the pitch blackness of a country night was the only thing that greeted him.

Nick pulled in behind Reid and shifted into park.

Colin looked at Brooklyn. "Promise me you'll stay here, no matter what."

She hesitated but then nodded.

"I mean it, Brooklyn." He locked gazes with the woman who kept doing funny things to his insides. "I can't do my best on this recon mission if I have to worry about you."

"I won't go anywhere," she said.

Her tone was so earnest that he believed her and let out a breath. He tapped the seat in front of him. "Let's do this."

He and Nick got out. An owl hooted in the distance, and the scent of wood smoke drifted their direction as they moved to the rear of their vehicle.

Nick opened the hatch and looked at Colin. "Smell that?"

Colin nodded. "Could be a campfire or someone burning yard debris. It's still Oregon's open-burn season. Runs for another week or so."

Nick gave him a quizzical look. "A fact you just happen to know."

"Only because we've been doing that for weeks in our spring cleaning of the Shadow Lake Survival compound."

"They got you doing maintenance work, eh?" Nick reached inside for a backpack filled with surveillance items. "How the mighty has fallen."

"I don't mind. I'm contributing to the business, which is still in startup mode. Means we all have to be jack-of-all-trades kind of guys right now. A way to say thanks to the Maddox bros for giving us awesome jobs. Plus it keeps these guns in shape." He lifted a bicep and laughed to lighten the tension.

Nick quietly closed the hatch, and they started up the side of the road. They paused by Reid's door and he lowered the window. "You good to go?"

"Roger that." Colin reached into his pocket for a comms unit that would connect him with the team and pressed it into his ear. "Testing. Testing."

"You're coming through loud and clear," Reid said.

"So don't say anything dumb," Dev said from the passenger seat and laughed.

Colin rolled his eyes. Each man took his turn testing their unit, ending with Micha.

"You all should have your cell phone Wi-Fi turned off so he can't pick up on our signals." Nick glanced around the guys.

He got an affirmative nod from each one.

"Okay, then," Colin said. "We'll keep you updated on anything we find so we can start figuring out a work-around right away. Any questions?"

"Yeah, why you still standing there?" Dev chuckled.

Colin liked his brother's sense of humor most of the time, and usually when he offered something lighthearted in a really tense situation like this one, but tonight it grated on his nerves. "Then we're off."

He started out, traveling at a rapid pace, but cautiously taking in the area as he moved.

Nick came alongside him. "Dude. Slow your roll. We don't want to miss anything."

"Sorry." Colin eased up. "Just want to nab this guy, and the sooner the better."

"I get that." He shifted his backpack. "After all, I've been hunting him for years. But you've only known Brooklyn for like a minute, so what's behind this urgency?"

*Yeah, what?* "Past experiences on the FBI cyber squad."

"Ah, that," Nick said as if he understood. "You probably had to deal with some real bad actors."

"Indeed," Colin said and left it at that.

"It's hard to see the atrocities humans are capable of committing." Nick sounded like he spoke from a place of firsthand knowledge.

Colin looked at him. "You see it all the time in your job too, right?"

Nick winced. "Maybe not *all* the time, but enough to know the internet has made it easier for bad people to be even worse."

Colin wanted more information on how Nick dealt with this. Colin had burned out at the FBI, but they needed to keep their full attention on their search. They started off again, tiptoeing through pine needles, pinecones, and fallen crispy leaves and branches.

Nick grabbed Colin's arm and pointed through an opening in the trees. "You see that?"

Colin pivoted. "Flames on Tarver's property. The fire we're smelling."

"Could mean he's there."

Colin agreed, but he didn't want to say it aloud and make it true. "Let's check it out. Single file. I lead. You monitor Wi-Fi signal strength to see if we're in range of his network."

"Got it." Nick dug out his electronic meter from the backpack. "But watch for visuals on any cameras too."

"Roger that." Colin set off, plunging down an incline into the knee-high scrub of grasses and weeds until he reached level land and started moving under the trees. He had to skirt large ferns and other woodland plants but basically kept to a straight path.

The burning smell grew more caustic. "Not a campfire."

"Hold up," Nick said. "I'm picking up a Wi-Fi signal ahead. We need to take a good look for a hidden camera."

Nick passed Colin a night vision scope, and he scanned the trees, the green-tinged images reminding him of days at the Bureau when they'd surveilled properties before affecting an arrest.

He caught sight of an item that stood out, as there was nothing perfectly square found in nature. He zoomed in. "Found one. Dead ahead maybe three hundred feet."

"Let me look."

Colin handed the scope to Nick. "Top-of-the-line cameras have a range of around three hundred feet. Could be more."

"And you know he has the best cameras, right? So we have to expect coverage to at least that distance and account for it." Colin nodded at the backpack sitting on the needle-covered ground. "We're still out of range though. Grab a flag and mark this spot so none of our guys come closer than this."

Nick pulled out a blue flag affixed to a wire stem and inserted it into the ground.

"Follow me." Colin turned right to keep from triggering the camera. He counted his steps and stopped once he was sure he'd cleared the camera's likely max range. "Check for another one."

Nick lifted the scope and swung it over the area. "There's one about the same distance in. I'll plant a flag."

They continued moving until they found a safe gap and headed deeper into the property. Colin kept an eye on the area through the scope to be sure no camera recording lights activated. God was with them, as the devices remained dark. They inched closer, the smoke smell growing stronger and filling the air.

They crested a final ridge, and Colin dropped to his belly. He lifted the scope to take a good look ahead. "Whoa."

"What is it?" Nick plopped down next to him.

He took a longer look, and even with the night vision green tinge, the sight ahead of him was clear.

"Come on." Nick shoved out a hand. "Give me a look."

"Go ahead and take your look." Colin handed the scope back to Nick. "But you're not going to believe what you see."

# 7

_____

Brooklyn wanted so badly to get out of the SUV and pace away her nerves. Thirty minutes had passed, and they hadn't gotten a single update from Nick or Colin. Not even one. The guys could at least check in to say they were okay, couldn't they? She didn't know how recon missions like this one worked, but maybe they couldn't talk because Kane was home and could hear them.

She leaned forward to look between the seats at Eryn. "Is this normal?"

Eryn swiveled in her seat. "Is what normal?"

"Taking so long to do the recon and no word."

"Actually it's only been thirty minutes, which isn't long in a situation like this," Eryn said. "And not hearing anything is normal."

Brooklyn was trying to imagine Eryn as an agent on a stakeout and couldn't visualize it. "Did you do things like this all the time when you were an agent?"

"Not all the time, no. If you're thinking of TV shows or movies or even books, they often don't portray the real life of an agent. Far more paperwork than an operation like this one. And I'm not big on paperwork." She wrinkled her nose.

"Is that why you left?"

Eryn shook her head. "Had to leave due to an injury."

"Mind if I ask what happened?" Brooklyn asked because she was interested, sure, but also because she hoped it would help pass the time until the guys reported in.

"No problem," Eryn said, but her eyes darkened as if the memories were painful. "I was serving an arrest warrant. The guy answered the door, but as soon as I identified myself, he started to slam the door. Instincts kicked in, and I reached out to stop him. Dumb move. Really dumb."

She shook her head and took a deep breath. "I grabbed the edge of the door when I should have palmed it on the front. He slammed it on my hand, and it suffered some pretty extensive damage."

She stared at her left hand. "I don't have the ability to clench my fist or grasp an object very well."

"I'm sorry that happened," Brooklyn said, trying to uplift Eryn when there was so much angst in her tone. "But that was enough to sideline you?"

"Yeah, the FBI wouldn't risk the potential liability something like that raised." She opened and closed her fist, staring at it as if it didn't belong to her. "I could fail to be able to use my weapon or back up a fellow agent in a fight. So they benched me as an agent. I could've taken an analyst job, but I wanted at least the hope of some adventure. So I left to work for Gage. In many ways, I'm glad I did, and it's been a very positive experience."

"Really, how?" she asked, as Brooklyn couldn't see losing her calling as ever being positive. If she was forced to permanently leave IT, she couldn't think of anything positive about that.

"At the Bureau, it often took a long time to see that I was making a difference. With Blackwell, I see on a daily basis how I'm helping others." She paused, and a soft smile claimed her mouth. "The job also gives me a lot of flexibility with my work schedule, and that's great for being a mom."

Brooklyn could only dream of what being a mom might be like. Full-time or otherwise. "I imagine it was hard to balance being an agent and a mother at the same time."

"It was, and I was a single mom, so it was even harder. But I had my mom's help. She's the best." Eryn studied Brooklyn. "But you. You really can't go on with life until this guy is caught. I can't believe he's been after you for years."

"Me either, to be honest, but when it comes to IT, the guy has out-of-this-world skills, and he seems to be unstoppable."

"Don't give up." Eryn patted Brooklyn's knee. "One thing I learned at the Bureau is that someone might be a criminal mastermind, but everyone can be stopped. Just depends on the resources thrown at stopping them, and right now, you have a wonder team on your side. We will catch him."

The assistance from these fine people brought tears to Brooklyn's eyes. She looked up to hold them at bay. "I've been fighting this with just me and Nick for so long that you don't know what that means to me."

She squeezed Brooklyn's hand. "Well, now you have the resources, and if everyone we have working tonight isn't enough, I'll call in the rest of my team. Plus, I suspect Nick would call in his team too."

"He would, and he's offered, but I never felt good about taking him up on it."

Eryn blinked at her. "Why not?"

"I can't afford them, and they only have a limited number of pro bono dollars, so I don't want to take that away from someone really in need."

"Girl, you are really in need." Eryn's nostrils flared. "Trust me. This is no way to live, and I for one, am honored to help you get out of the situation."

Her fierce defense relieved Brooklyn's feelings of imposing. "Thank you."

Eryn waved her good hand. "A while back, I had a ransomware hacker threaten my life and needed the team to help me locate and bring him in. Means I know a bit about what it's like to be stalked. Mine was for a much shorter time. I can't imagine living under the strain and stress for years."

"I'm glad it all worked out for you." Brooklyn's attention was captured by movement in the scrub. She scanned the darkness. "It's Nick and Colin. They're back."

She wanted to race out to meet them, but lowered her window instead. "What did you find?"

"Hold on, and I'll be right there." Colin stopped to talk to Reid. His posture was rigid and stiff.

Her heart dropped. "It's not good news."

"How can you tell?" Eryn asked.

"Colin's posture. He's tense."

Eryn leaned over the seat to look out the front window. "He's definitely not relaxed."

He suddenly spun and marched to her open window. "You need to prepare yourself for some bad news. It's not what we expected to find. Not at all."

Colin stood by the guys near the burned-out shell of a building, the smoke still curling into the night sky. He'd pulled one SUV into the drive and pointed the headlights over the scene for a better look. Eryn and Micha volunteered to escort Brooklyn back to the compound and keep watch over her while the others scouted the property. The best plan in his mind when he couldn't be certain that Tarver wasn't hiding somewhere in the woods, waiting to strike. Even if Colin's brain continued to say keep her close at hand, he knew he'd made the right decision.

"You think he was on to us?" Nick asked. "Burned his own house down so we couldn't find any leads, then bailed?"

Colin stared at the ruins. "If so, it was effective. Looks like the fire burned hot, and we won't find much here to go on, if anything."

"We need to call the locals and report the fire," Ryan said. "But let's split up and take a quick look before we do."

"I'm not sure we need to call them," Dev said. "We don't know a crime was committed here. We can notify the landlord, and they can take care of bringing in the authorities if they want to. Or we just let it be and let them find it when they do."

Colin looked at his brother. "I'm with Dev on this. Keeps us out of it, and we won't be in any official reports. That way Tarver won't know we were on to him."

"Makes sense to me," Nick said.

"Then we won't see any of the sheriff's reports." Dev faced the house. "And we need to do more than take a quick look. We can do a grid search of the yard and house perimeter. With the heat, we'll have to wait on the house."

Colin agreed. They might've arrived at the tail end of the fire after it had died down, but the burning embers were still too hot to walk on. "If we don't find anything actionable, we get out of here. Then I'll find the landlord's name and make an anonymous call."

Reid firmed his shoulders. "So let's move. Hopefully, we'll be done in time to spare Russ from orientation duty."

Nick eyed Reid. "Is it really that bad?"

"Not if you don't mind teaching someone how to boil water." Dev laughed.

"Oh, right. It's bad then." Nick chuckled.

"Follow me." Colin led the men, then assigned coordinates to process the scene.

Carrying flashlights, they formed a straight line and marched forward as one, sweeping the beams over a yard littered with fallen debris. Every now and then, one of them paused to look closely at something, and they all stopped with him. But it turned out to be nothing, and they moved forward again until they reached the house without locating any leads.

"Fire was set intentionally." Reid held up his hand, and they all looked to where his beam was focused on the embers. "See the clear lines of accelerant residue? Indicates it was poured, not the pattern of a fire occurring naturally."

"And looks to me like the majority of the burning took place on the floor level not the ceiling in this area." Dev waved his light around an area where the structure still stood. Location said it was the entryway.

"Accelerant trail comes from there too," Reid said, moving his light. "Like he backed out dumping gasoline or another accelerant on the way out."

"Not surprising." Colin took a few steps closer to the section of building in front of him. He swung his light over the glowing embers that seemed to draw him in and came to a sudden stop, his heart wanting to stop too. "No. Oh, man. No. Is that a body?"

Dev added his light to the area. "Looks like it. Burned beyond recognition."

"Do you think Tarver got caught in his own fire?" Reid asked.

"Could be." Colin had to swallow hard not to want to hurl. He didn't want anyone to die, not even Tarver, but if this turned out to be him, Brooklyn's problems would be over. Would she leave then? Go back to Portland? Likely.

That didn't sit well with him, but a man had died, and

figuring out what happened here took precedence right now. Colin had plenty of time to think about Brooklyn leaving later. "We have no option but to call the locals now."

"Yeah, of course." Nick stared at the body. "But there's no way they're equipped to determine ID on such a badly burned body."

"They'll have to call in the state," Dev said. "I know they have at least one anthropologist on staff."

Reid shook his head. "Going to take some time, then. They're notoriously backlogged, and we won't get an ID for a while."

"No problem." Nick got out his phone. "I'll call Kelsey Dunbar. She's our anthropologist and can likely be here in an hour."

"An hour?" Ryan swiveled to gape at Nick. "From Portland? That's at least a three-hour drive."

"Did I forget to mention we bought a helicopter?" Nick grinned. "We're starting to get so many calls for our services from outside the city that we needed to quit wasting valuable time behind the wheel."

"Of course you bought one." Reid shook his head. "I'd like to have even a tenth of your budget."

If Nick was offended, his expression didn't show it. "We couldn't afford one when we were first starting out like you. You'll get there."

"I hope I'm around then." Dev rubbed his hands together. "Maybe I should start taking pilot lessons now."

The others laughed, breaking the tension as Dev was famous for doing.

"Hopefully, if Kelsey is called in, we'll at least be kept in the loop," Ryan said.

"Not if the local sheriff calls her," Nick said. "We'll have to contract with the county, and the findings will be private unless the sheriff is willing to share."

"Too bad we're not in Russ's jurisdiction," Reid said. "He would play ball for sure and keep us updated on what was going on."

Colin wished the same thing, but if he knew one thing about working an investigation, it was that it was rarely as easy as he would hope. "Nick, you go ahead and call Kelsey. We'll wait on making that call to the local authorities. That way when they do arrive, she'll be here, and they're more apt to use her services."

"On it." Nick stepped back and tapped his phone.

"I'd like to get a closer look," Colin said.

"We can't destroy potential evidence," Reid said. "We all need to back away."

"A zoomed-in photo won't hurt anything." Colin got out his phone. "You all light the area up best you can."

The guys swung their flashlights to flood light over the body, covering it like a blanket of light.

Colin focused on the victim and zoomed in to take several shots. The scorched remains turned his stomach. This wasn't the first time he'd seen a charred body, but this one was further damaged than the other man he'd seen. His camera displayed an accelerant trail leading to the space where the victim lay, so perhaps he'd been caught in the thick of the flames.

He snapped several shots and moved to new locations to take additional photos from different angles. Satisfied he'd recorded all he could with his restrictions, he stowed his phone.

Somehow stowing the phone removed the clinical feel from his actions, and the loss of life and the idea of someone's loss of a loved one hit him. Hard. Even bad guys had parents. People who loved them. "Would you guys join me in a prayer for the family of this person who perished in the fire?"

He didn't wait for an answer. No need. All the men were Christian. He led them in a prayer—the only thing he could do for the deceased right now—but he would also commit to finding his identity and give the family some closure.

He turned to wait for Nick, who sounded like he was ending his call. Brooklyn came to mind. How was he going to break the news to her? She would be distraught. Shocked. Maybe even more terrified. He wanted to break it to her gently.

He looked at the guys. "Keep this to yourselves for now, and I'll tell Brooklyn."

"You think it's Tarver?" Dev asked.

Colin shook his head. "From what she and Nick say about him, I can't see him getting caught in his own fire."

"That's the feeling I get too," Reid said. "After Nick is done making his call, we should search the rest of the property before notifying the locals."

Colin nodded, and they stood watching Nick until he shoved his phone into his pocket.

He stepped over to them. "Kelsey has to pack up the chopper with needed supplies. Figures she won't be here for ninety minutes. She's going to bring Sierra, our forensics expert, too. We hope the local sheriff will let her process the scene."

Colin nodded. "We should have Dev talk to him."

"The he is a she," Dev said. "Sheriff Abby Day. I went to college with her and used to know her pretty well."

"I didn't know that," Colin said.

"Lots you don't know about me. Especially my college days. Was safer that way." Dev laughed.

Colin rolled his eyes. "Good to hear you know her, if you have a good relationship. But I was thinking you should call because you were a former deputy and speak the same language."

Dev scratched his cheek. "You were law enforcement too."

"Yeah, but a fed. You know that can often bring tension with locals."

"Good point." Nick looked at the building. "Maybe Russ could run interference too."

"No," Reid said forcefully. "If this somehow blows back on us, we don't want him included in it."

"Okay." Nick raised a hand. "Point taken."

"Let's take a look around the rest of the property while we wait for your teammates." Colin turned on his flashlight again. "Line up for another grid search, but we'll head east."

They formed a straight line, and Colin fell in on the end. His nerves were on edge. Were they going to find another body? Some other evidence of a crime? Would it be bad for Brooklyn or help them bring Tarver in?

Colin cared an unreasonable amount for the little time he'd spent with Brooklyn. Was it just championing the underdog or one of those love-at-first-sight things that he didn't really believe in? But could he be wrong? Did it exist?

One thing was for sure, there was a connection between them. A strong one.

They inched forward picking their way through debris, the lingering smoke curling into the air was a reminder of the fatality.

"What's that?" Ryan asked, his light skipping ahead and illuminating a structure that hadn't been touched by the fire.

"Let's check it out," Dev said.

"We will, but keep to the grid until we reach it," Colin said. "Never know what we might find on the way."

They made their way toward the structure. Single story, the large box of a building was about fifteen feet square with concrete walls that had iron bars in the upper part of the front. A strong lock hung on a door on the side that also looked as if it was electronically controlled.

Ryan ran his flashlight beam over the area. "If the place wasn't so fortified, I'd say it was a kennel. But no chains or way to tie up a dog, and even the biggest dog doesn't need such a strong structure."

"Maybe the building was already on the property, then someone converted it to a kennel," Reid suggested.

"You all wait here. I'm going to take a look inside." Colin snapped on disposable gloves and opened a door as thick as the cinderblock walls. It held two locks. One was a simple metal hasp, the other electronic. Odd for an animal enclosure. The smell of feces and urine hit him hard, but his quick look with the flashlight didn't reveal anything moving. He did see plenty of animal hairs littering the floor among the large droppings.

"Whatever he kept in here was big. Scat is huge," he said. "And furry, but not furry like a dog, more cat like, I think."

"He didn't ever have pets when we knew him," Nick said.

Colin faced the guys. "I don't think this was a pet."

Nick's gaze narrowed. "Then what?"

Colin shrugged. "Hopefully Sierra can shed some light on what was housed in this enclosure. The animal could be loose now and wandering around the area."

He looked back at feces the size of a baseball. "I, for one, do not want to run into any animal in the daylight that could produce such large scat, much less the dark."

# 8

---

Colin had met Kelsey and Sierra in the lab and expected them to be sharp and scientific when in the field. He didn't expect them to be kind and compassionate too, but they were. They stood near a white van they rented after flying in. Both women were tall, but that's where the similarity ended.

Sierra swung open the back doors, and her stick-straight blond hair that hung down to the middle of her back slid over her shoulder. Equipment in tubs and boxes filled the back of the vehicle.

Kelsey slid a blue storage tub toward the door, and her shoulder-length black curls remained in place. Sierra wore khaki tactical pants and a polo shirt, but Kelsey had on a frilly blouse and black dress slacks along with dress heels. Not the way he expected her or any woman to arrive at a crime scene.

Sierra glanced over her shoulder. "Have you secured our participation with the locals yet?"

"Not yet," Colin said. "I'll notify them in a minute."

Sierra turned and locked gazes, hers intense and curious

at the same time. "Mind if I ask what you're waiting on? It's been some time since Nick called us."

He really didn't want to answer in case she thought he was manipulating them, but she deserved an answer. "We're hoping if you were on site when they arrived, they'd be more apt to let you do the work."

"Ah, yes. That's been tried several times." She chuckled.

"Successfully?"

"Depended on the officer in charge."

"I know the sheriff from college," Dev said. "She's a real stickler for rules, but she has an open mind too."

"Let's hope the open mind takes precedence with us," Colin said. "I wouldn't want to have brought you here for nothing."

"Never for nothing." Kelsey smiled. "If the temps have cooled enough in the house we could do a cursory look at the scene before they arrive and give you an overview."

Now that sounded like a plan. "Could you?"

"We'll do it while you call the locals." Sierra reached into a storage tote in the van and took out two protective suits. She handed one to Kelsey, who'd removed rubber boots from the bin she'd slid closer to her.

Practicality at last. He had to respect the fact that she liked to dress in a feminine manner. Maybe it was her way of saying she didn't deal with gruesome things. Either way, she sat on the bumper to slip into the legs of the white suit and put on the clunky boots.

Sierra looked up from pulling on her suit. "Nick said you saw an accelerant trail and suspect arson."

"We did and do," Dev said. "Looks like the trail leads from the door to the body."

Kelsey's delicate eyebrow raised. "So someone could've been trying to hide a homicide by starting a fire."

"Could be," Ryan said. "Or the fire was set to kill him."

"I don't much like that thought." Kelsey stood. "I always hope the victim died of another cause and not by flames. To me, dying in a fire is what nightmares are made of."

"Same," Colin said as he thought that had to be one of the worst ways to go. Horrific even. "We also located a fortified enclosure that held some sort of large animal. Sierra, might you be able to help us with identifying the animal?"

She slid her arms into the suit. "I can take a look."

"The enclosure is located on the east side of the house."

She gave a firm nod and put protective booties over her shoes. "I'll check out the house first. Then, if time allows, review the enclosure."

Kelsey handed a pair of disposable gloves to Sierra. "We'll get to it, but know that this will be cursory, as I said. We can't move anything to get a better look at something else or alter any evidence."

"Understood," Colin said.

"Then we'll check in when we're finished." Sierra slung the strap of a camera around her neck and led the way. Kelsey moved behind her as they strode confidently toward the burned-out shell of a house.

Colin turned to Dev. "You still up for calling this in and taking lead with the locals?"

"Sure thing." He dug his phone from his cargo pocket. "I'll start with 911, then ask to be dispatched to Abby or a detective."

"Sounds like a good plan," Reid said.

Dev nodded, then made the call on speaker and tapped his foot. Colin watched Kelsey and Sierra test the heat of the floor, then stand back. Too hot? Probably.

"Nine-one-one, what's your emergency?" the dispatcher asked.

"I'm Devan Graham, a former Clackamas County Deputy," he said. "I need to report a house fire and death."

His tone was clear, sharp, and filled with confidence as he explained the situation. "The fire is nearly out. Smoking embers. The body visible in the rubble and obviously deceased."

"Hold on." The sound of fingers clicking over a computer keypad filled the air. "I have a fire crew on the way, but all of our deputies are dispatched on priority calls. You can expect one in twenty to twenty-five minutes."

Murder, if this was murder, was a priority in Colin's book, but not in terms of saving lives, which dispatch had to consider. This victim was going nowhere, and they couldn't effect a rescue, so the other calls had to remain top priority.

"We have reason to believe this fire is a case of arson," Dev said. "And I was hoping you could dispatch me to the sheriff. I know she would like to get a heads-up as soon as possible."

"I can't do that, sir."

"Abby and I are friends from college. Give her my name, and I'm sure she'll talk to me."

"Hold on." The sound of those keys clicking again filled the cool night air. "I'll connect you to the department."

The phone rang, sounding through the still of the night. Colin shifted his attention back to Kelsey and Sierra. They'd moved further down the house rubble, but didn't enter at this location either. Kelsey shone a high-powered flashlight beam on the body, and Sierra used her camera to snap copious pictures. They continued further down the building exterior and followed the same procedure.

"Sheriff Day." The female voice came over Dev's speaker. Her tone was deep and sleepy, like she might be off duty and had been woken.

"Hey, Abby," Dev said. "Dev Graham."

"Dev! Dispatch said it was you, and you were a former

deputy, but I thought you were still with Clackamas County."

"Nope. Recently hung up my badge to join the team at Shadow Lake Survival."

"Right, I've heard of them. You train all the crazies in Armageddon prepping over there." She laughed.

He joined her. "Something like that, yeah."

"And you're reporting a deceased individual caught in a potential arson fire?"

Dev gave a clear and succinct description of what they'd found minus mentioning Kelsey and Sierra along with what they were doing on scene. Nor did he mention he and the team were here to break and enter—Dev would never be that dumb—but said they were surveilling Kane Tarver.

"Please tell me you haven't disturbed my scene." Ah, yes, the territorial tone that Colin had expected.

"Come on, now, Abby." Dev rolled his eyes. "You know me better than that."

"That's why I'm asking. Wouldn't be unheard of if you went barreling into a fire to try to save someone."

"No one to save." Dev frowned. "He was long gone by the time we got here, and before you ask, we did *not* go into the house at all."

"Good. Keep it that way." Her sharp tone said she was used to others following her directives. "But I need you to remain on scene to give me an official statement. See that you don't touch anything, and I mean anything, while you wait for our arrival." She let out a long breath.

"Something wrong, Abbs?" Dev asked. "I mean other than someone might've been murdered on your watch."

She groaned. "Way to point that out. But no, that's not it. A murder investigation is the last thing I need when we're already short-staffed. Hiring is a nightmare these days. Not

94

many people want to go into the field, and a lot of the good ones are leaving like you did."

"I'm sorry," Dev said. "I get it. Clackamas is having the same problem. I felt guilty going."

"You should." She let out a long breath. "I didn't mean that. It's just with the recent distrust of law enforcement, especially here in the PNW, it's hard to recruit."

Dev glanced at Colin but then turned back to the house. "I might be able to help."

"What? You want a job? 'Cause if you left Clackamas under good terms, I'd hire you on the spot."

"No, sorry. No job. What I was going to tell you is that we're working with the Veritas Center staff right now. Have you heard of them?"

"Who in this part of the world hasn't?" she asked, and thankfully didn't sound like she had a negative opinion of them, calling them boutique forensics only for the rich as many law enforcement officers did.

"They have a top-notch forensic staff and a forensic anthropologist who could handle the victim for you."

"Would love that. You don't know how much." She let out another almost endless breath of air over the phone. "But they're way too pricey for my blood."

"I'm sure we could persuade them to handle the investigation pro bono."

She didn't speak for a long, tense moment, and Colin had to wonder what she was thinking. So far she seemed to be accepting Dev and could go along with him, but then, he hadn't asked her to do anything yet.

"What's in it for you?" Suspicion lingered in her tone. "You hoping they'll share their findings so you can locate this Tarver guy?"

"Now that you mention it, that would be great, but I know that's not going to happen." Dev sucked in some night air. "They'll sign a contract with you to provide you the exclusive rights to their results unless you tell them otherwise. They have a reputation to uphold, and they won't violate that for anyone."

"So again, I say, what's in it for you?"

"If Tarver is behind this arson, perhaps your agency's collaboration with Veritas will find him and bring him to justice. Getting him off the street is all we're hoping for." Dev fell silent, but Abby didn't speak. "I can have them here before you arrive."

She snorted. "How's that even possible when they're out of Portland?"

Here was the tricky part, and Colin held his breath for Dev's answer.

"Like I said we've been working with their people. Give me the go-ahead, and you could have one of the world's top forensic anthropologists recovering the body tonight and giving you insights right away. This could go a long way with your constituents, who I know want to feel safe in their own county."

*Nice one.* Make her think about the people who elect her.

"Fine," she said decisively. "Make the call, but no one goes into the house before I arrive."

"Don't worry. We won't be sending anyone into the house or go in there ourselves."

A perfect answer from Dev because they'd already directed someone to enter and would not be asking anyone else to do so. Colin was most proud of his little brother. He was handling the sheriff without lying to her and while getting her to agree to accept help that would solve this murder, if indeed it was one, sooner rather than later. That was, if the sheriff and her team knew what to do with the data they received from the Veritas staff.

"I'm about twenty minutes out," she said. "Looks like I'll

arrive at about the same time as my deputy, but the fire crew has a head start."

"We don't want them busting into the house and destroying evidence, do we?"

"I'll get on the horn with the chief and tell them to talk to you and stand down until I arrive. I figure they'd comply unless a life is threatened."

Colin hoped the firefighters didn't consider a smoldering fire a threat to life, but it might not matter what he said. Sometimes when a first responder was called to a scene and adrenaline took over, it was hard to stand down.

Dev ended his call and shoved his phone into his pocket.

"Great job, man," Reid said before Colin could. "You handled her like a pro."

"Thanks." He wrinkled his brow. "But, honestly, it was all because I know her."

"No matter the reason, I've never been so proud of my little bro." Colin grabbed his brother and knuckled him on the head.

"And then you had to go and ruin it." He extricated himself and laughed.

Colin should probably have laid back, but it was hard to stop treating his little brother like anything but his little brother. "We need to get eyes at the road so we know when Abby and her deputy arrive and we can all be waiting here by the van."

"It's a good idea, but I assume they'll run with lights and sirens," Dev said. "This isn't a life or death situation, and they could cause an accident by running hot, but their adrenaline over a potential murder could overpower common sense."

"I have to admit I'd be tempted." Colin grinned.

"So will Abby, but I doubt she'll give in," Dev said. "She was top of all of our criminal justice classes in college, and it took self-restraint to study all the time when there were parties all around her."

"Then we need eyes on the road more than ever to know when she gets here," Colin said. "Who wants to head out there?"

Ryan pushed off the side of the van where he'd been leaning. "I'll do it."

"I'll go with my little bro," Reid said.

Ryan flashed a look at his brother. "Don't trust me?"

Dev locked gazes with Ryan. "Hey, I get that. We should compare notes."

Ryan laughed, but Reid planted his feet. "It's not that at all. I just need something to do instead of standing around."

"In that case, you're welcome to join me." Ryan plugged in his earbud. "I'll update you the minute I have eyes on them."

"Thanks." Colin pushed his earbud in, too, as did the others.

Nick dug out his phone. "Since we're on pause, I'll look to see if I can find any hint of Kane on the internet. Maybe he's already bragging about the fire. Or the victim. Would be like him to claim his superiority in outsmarting us, if that's what he did."

"Sounds like a plan," Colin said. He wanted to give Kelsey and Sierra a moment to take a look at the property and it would be a perfect time to follow up on his earlier conversation with Nick.

Colin joined Nick. "Before, when we were talking, you had mentioned handling the brutality that you see in your work. How do you go on doing it and still sleep at night?"

Nick didn't answer right away, but a pensive look took hold. "I guess I focus on the ones we put away and on my faith."

"I tried that. Failed." Colin bit his lip. "Big time failed. You have a verse or something that helps you?"

"Yeah, sure." Nick nodded vigorously. "Yeah, I do."

"Mind sharing it?" Colin took a step closer to listen more carefully.

Nick shoved his phone into his pocket. "Psalm 37:9 - *For those who are evil will be destroyed, but those who hope in the Lord will inherit the land.* I know that even if we don't find a particular bad guy or if there are more waiting in the wings, ultimately God will take care of them. I can only do my part and not let the garbage I see every day take over the life that God wants me to live."

Colin had hoped hearing Nick's verse would miraculously erase his angst, but it didn't. "I've tried that."

Nick tilted his head. "You're likely looking at things from the viewpoint of the victims. We have to do that while investigating, but not after an investigation concludes."

"Easier said than done."

"Yeah, man, I get it. Unfortunately, even when a case is closed and the bad actor is behind bars, the anger can remain. The images of their abuse remains too. We're indignant over the injustice. The harm done to innocents. I turn that lingering anger and disgust into righteous anger instead. You could try that."

That piqued Colin's interest. "What's the difference?"

"Righteous anger recognizes these offenses as against God or His Word. View these crimes as an offense against Him and His to deal with. Not yours. Never yours again. You did your part. Then, trust Him to have it and let go."

Colin had to admit that was an interesting take. One that might work. "I'll give it a try because nothing else has worked, and it's had a hold on me. You don't know how much I want to let it all go and move on."

"I do, man. I was there once. Not anymore." Nick took a

deep breath. "It also helped to meet Piper. It's hard to let those past memories take over when your current life is filled with goodness."

Brooklyn's face came to mind. "Yeah, yeah, I can see that too."

Should he pursue these feelings for her or would he just be using her to help him get over his issues? Could he ever tell if his motives were selfish? Until he could, there was no way he could move forward with her in any way other than boss and employee. Something to table for now as it would all be irrelevant if he couldn't protect her from Tarver.

"Thanks for the info, man," Colin said. "I'm going to check in with Kelsey and Sierra to see if they can give us something to go on."

Colin made his way through the fallen debris. Chunks of charred wood. Thick ash and smoldering items he couldn't identify.

Kelsey was looking at the camera display screen, the colors lighting up her face, and he caught a flash of sadness in her expression before she glanced at him and controlled it.

"I guess it was too hot to enter the house," he said.

"Way too hot," Kelsey replied but had gone back to looking at the camera. "So we took photos instead."

"Can you forward all of the pics to me before you sign with the sheriff?"

She nodded. "They onboard?"

"Sounds like it, but you might still need to assure them of the privacy of any forensics results you recover."

"We can do that." Sierra stepped over to them. "But before then, you should know I can confirm an accelerant trail. Also, if you get close enough, you can smell gasoline, so it was most likely what was used to start the fire."

Colin liked her straightforward approach. "Then we're looking at arson for sure."

"I can't say for sure." Sierra pressed her lips together. "Not until I take samples and analyze them, but first blush says yes."

Kelsey looked up. "The trail runs from the door to the victim as you said."

Sierra pointed at the enclosure area. "I'll go look at the enclosure while Kelsey updates you on her findings. I'll be taking the flashlight."

Colin nodded.

She took off, swinging the light in front of her, brightening what was now an ominous scene.

Kelsey turned with the camera and held it out. "A close-up of the victim. I feel certain he's male, but the only other thing I can tell you with certainty is that the fire burned hot. Very hot."

Colin held back a shudder at the vision forming in his mind and forced himself to ask questions that would bring additional details he knew would gross him out. "How do you know?"

"One of the great perks of working at such a well-respected agency is that we get invited to work on cutting-edge forensic studies." Her shoulders raised. "In the current study I'm working on, we've determined the heat of fires by looking at the bone discoloration patterns."

"Discoloration patterns?" To him, the body just looked white or grayish, sort of like charcoal ready on the grill.

She nodded. "Bones subject to temperatures below four hundred degrees are typically well preserved, and ones that appear yellow and brown in discoloration indicate temperatures between four to six hundred degrees. Ones exposed up to six hundred fifty degrees are black or smoked in appearance. Up to fifteen hundred degrees and above have a white or calcined appearance."

Queasiness set into Colin's stomach. "And the guy in this picture is whiteish."

"Exactly. Plus, gasoline fires can burn over three thousand degrees."

He shook his head. "Things that nightmares are made of."

That sadness Colin had seen earlier flashed for a moment in her expression, then faded. "Agreed. I always hope burned victims have succumbed to some other cause of death before the fire. Usually it's the smoke inhalation that causes death."

Colin could no longer hold back his shudder and didn't need to see additional photos. He handed the camera back to Kelsey and walked with her to the van. Dev leaned against the vehicle, and Nick sat on the bumper looking at his phone.

Colin recapped the information Kelsey and Sierra had shared.

Nick grimaced. "Kane is a true sociopath, and I wouldn't put it past him to set a fire while the guy was still alive but incapacitated somehow."

Colin didn't like hearing that. Especially since this was the guy who wanted to find Brooklyn more than anything.

Sierra hurried across the clearing to them. "You were right. A big cat of some sort was being kept in an enclosure way too small for it. No room for a large cat to exercise or even live well."

"Why have a pet, then abuse it like that?" Dev asked.

"Maybe it wasn't a pet," Sierra said. "He could be into wildlife trafficking."

Colin blinked at her while he gathered his thoughts. "Wildlife trafficking?"

Nick looked up from his phone. "Trafficking makes more sense than Kane having a pet. He never had pets or even indicated he liked animals, so I can't see him suddenly deciding to have a pet, much less a large cat. Plus, if there's money to be made at it, then he would exploit it to the max."

"Oh, there's money in it all right." Sierra frowned. "Twenty billion a year on the black market for illegal wildlife products. That can include the animals of course, but also medicine ingredients, exotic pets, jewelry, and accessories. It's the fourth largest illegal economy worldwide."

*Wow!* "I had no idea."

"And it's not just the money." She ripped off her gloves. "They're hunting, gathering, and trading endangered species and protected wildlife. That includes plants and animals, either dead or alive. Which is messing with our biodiversity. Currently more than five thousand animal species are threatened with extinction."

Dev shook his head. "That's a crazy number.

"I know, right?" She curled her fingers into fists. "But you can't stop there to get the whole picture. There's a human toll too. Illegal wildlife trade now includes armed violence, corruption, money laundering, and other forms of organized crime. And up to a hundred rangers a year are killed while trying to protect wildlife from poachers."

She stopped and tossed her gloves into a disposal bag. "Sorry. I'll get off my soapbox now. Can you tell I'm passionate about this?"

"Not the first time I've seen her on that soapbox," Nick shook his head.

She punched his arm. Seemed like their team worked much like the Shadow Lake team did with good-natured ribbing.

"What's being done to stop it?" Colin asked.

"Oh, no, back on that soapbox we go." Nick chuckled.

Sierra rolled her eyes. "The usual criminal investigations, but wildlife officers are running into problems identifying illegal furs and pelts with enough accuracy to succeed in court. DNA scientists like Emory are working on improving their odds. She's part of a group specializing in extracting genetic information from proteins that are coded for in DNA. They then compare the amino acid sequences of proteins to work back to DNA sequences."

"Why not just do the DNA?" Dev asked.

"It isn't always available, and these proteins are tougher and more abundant than DNA." Sierra unzipped the top of her suit. "It's all pretty complicated, but she's working with the National Fish and Wildlife Forensics Laboratory to build a database of proteins for the most trafficked species so samples collected in the field can be analyzed."

"Did you find anything in the kennel she can analyze?" Colin asked. "I didn't see any real fur, more like hair."

"I spotted some fur samples in the kennel. Not large, but we don't need a big sample, and Emory has a good shot at figuring out what type of animal he was keeping."

"That's great," Nick said. "My super team does it again. But how does that help us find Kane?"

Sierra frowned. "First of all, think of him being involved in wildlife trafficking. What if the victim was part of a trafficking ring that he participated in and for some reason Kane needed to kill him? If we find the animal type, we might find the ring that could lead to Kane."

Nick turned off his phone and darkness replaced the light illuminating his face. "Sounds logical, but there's something you don't know about him. He's never been one to join a group of any kind. He flies solo. So no ring. Just him. He has to be the best. Top dog. No matter who he steps on to get there. Unless that's changed, which I've seen no evidence of."

Dev studied Nick. "Do you think he would become a group player if it meant big bucks?"

Nick tapped his foot. "Could happen, I suppose. Although I think if he did, he would look for a way to eliminate his affiliation with the others and make those big bucks on his own."

Sierra perked up. "Then think about this. Organized crime is very much a part of wildlife trafficking. What if he cut in on their business, and they sent the victim to take him out of the picture, but Kane took the guy out instead?"

Nick shot to his feet and ran a hand through his hair. "Could be. Yeah, I could see him doing that, and now he's on the run. Desperate. Maybe even more willing to hurt Brooklyn. I'll get some searches set up on the dark web for Kane and any hint of wildlife trafficking."

Sirens sounded closer.

"Patrol car in sight," Ryan said over their comms.

"Officers are close," Colin told Sierra and Kelsey.

Sierra shrugged her shoulders out of her suit. "We'll get out of our protective gear. Don't want to look like we've been snooping."

"After that, can you send me the pictures you took?" Colin asked.

"Will do," Sierra said.

Colin wanted the photos. He really did. He had to search for any leads. But honestly, looking at photos that included the gruesome sight of a man burned beyond any recognition—perhaps on purpose by the man stalking Brooklyn— was the last thing he wanted to do.

The very last thing.

# 9

Brooklyn stared at Colin on the video call, pondering his question. How could she think about it and answer him when all she wanted was for him to be here instead of still at the crime scene?

Barbie had gone home, and Brooklyn had taken over Sandy's care, trying to get her to go to bed. No such luck. She curled up on the end of the sofa instead. They'd had *Breakfast at Tiffany's* on the television and had been chatting with Eryn and Micha while half watching the movie. More like with Eryn, as Micha was the strong, silent type. Not rude, just not one to engage in small talk or really watch this vintage romantic movie. Besides, he was outnumbered, and the topics often went to things women usually found more appealing.

Brooklyn had been pacing off and on. Until the call. Then she'd settled down. Kind of. She was glad Colin phoned with an update, but she wanted more from him. She wanted to see him in person. She'd never felt this way about a guy before. Not even after dating for months, and she honestly didn't understand it.

Then she also wanted to be at the scene. To help figure

out who died in the fire. Man, how awful. Someone lost his life in a horrific way. She prayed the reason he died had nothing to do with her. That Kane hadn't somehow done it to scare her.

Because she *was* scared. Maybe that's why she wanted Colin at the cabin. By her side. Sure, Micha and Eryn were with her, but despite their sidearms and extensive experience, she didn't get the same feeling of security from them. A silly thing. The pair of them were capable of protecting her and more.

"Did you hear my question, Brooklyn?" Colin asked.

"Sorry, I was zoned out for a minute," she admitted. "Will you repeat it?"

"I asked how Mom was doing and if I should come home to help out."

"Your mom is fine," Brooklyn said.

"More than fine," Sandy called out. "You found a winner in Brooklyn. I hope she stays for a long time."

Had Sandy hinted to her son to do something about that? Not as in extend Brooklyn's job, but maybe get to know her and develop a serious relationship? Or was Brooklyn just wishing for that? For something she couldn't have until Kane was behind bars.

"Glad to hear it," Colin said. "But don't stay up too late talking and wear yourself out."

Sandy frowned. Brooklyn suspected it had to be hard to have changed roles with her son where he'd become the parent figure.

"I'll keep you updated," he said. "Call if anything comes up or you need my help."

"Go," Sandy said. "I'm sure you're needed *there*."

Ah, yes, Sandy might as well have said you're not needed here right now so pay attention to where you are needed. But Brooklyn suspected she needed him too. Now for sure. But for how long? Maybe the next few days would tell.

The call ended, and Brooklyn set her phone on the table.

Sandy sighed.

Brooklyn swiveled to face her. "Everything okay?"

Sandy picked up a flowery pillow and hugged it to her chest. "It was hard enough to move in here, but to have my boys want to wrap me in bubble wrap is something they need to stop doing."

Brooklyn tried to put herself in Sandy's shoes and then in Colin's too. "I can see how you would feel that way. It's clear they both love you a lot and want the best for you. If my parents had a health issue, I could see myself doing the same thing."

"Oh, I understand it. Trust me. I've thought about it enough, and I should be thankful I raised them to be so responsible. I just don't want to ruin their lives by them thinking I'm top priority and require all of their attention." She rested her chin on the pillow. "I sure don't want them to put off their lives to be here with me. Which is why you're so important. You'll let them get on with things, and you could even help me encourage them to go about life as natural."

"I can do that for sure." Brooklyn would help, but if this turned into a long-term job, would she want Colin to go about his life? To find a woman to love?

"I can work on Colin too," Eryn said. "See if I can get him to relax a bit."

"Thank you," Sandy said, but kept her focus on Brooklyn. "Realistically, how long do you think you'll be here? Once this Kane guy is caught, will you stay or go back to your IT career?"

Brooklyn had to be honest. "Likely IT, but don't worry. If I do, I won't leave until you find someone to replace me."

Sandy frowned. "I don't know you well, but I suspect you're going to be very hard to replace."

"You'll find someone." Brooklyn let her thoughts wander to the future, but Kane came to mind, and she shut that down right away. "But then it's not an issue unless Kane is behind bars, and for that to happen, we have to find him."

"You will." Sandy dropped the pillow and leaned over to squeeze Brooklyn's arm, her face contorting in pain with the movement.

"And maybe I can help." Eryn got up. "My laptop's in the dining room. I can do some research on wildlife trafficking. Maybe figure out how to locate Tarver through that."

"Thank you, Eryn." Brooklyn smiled at her. "And for being here when I know you'd rather be home."

"No worries. A break from three kids can be a good thing." She grinned and went to sit at the rustic table that matched the pine-paneled walls.

Micha got up, too, and rested his hand on his sidearm. "I'm going to do a perimeter check."

Brooklyn didn't like his serious expression at all. "You think there's a problem?"

He shook his head. "I have the security app on my phone and would know if there'd been a fence breach. But my military days come back to me in situations like this. Gotta be extra careful when things are quiet. That's when things go south."

Could he be right? Was Kane outside the fence ready to penetrate their defenses?

Brooklyn's mood darkened even more. "I sure hope there's nothing wrong."

"Me too. Lock the door after me." He stepped outside, letting a cool wind drift inside.

Brooklyn crossed the room to turn the deadbolt and look out the glassy window to the dark night. She'd loved being in this remote cabin by the lake. The quiet. The peace. But now her stomach tightened. Still, stress wasn't good for lupus, and she had to remain lighthearted for Sandy.

Brooklyn had never been good at hiding her feelings. No matter how hard she tried they came to the surface and lived in her expression.

Well, starting now she had to learn how to conceal them. She took a deep breath, prayed she could pull it off, and swallowed every emotion that threatened to send her into a panic.

Colin stood with Dev and Sheriff Day, watching as the fire crew wet down the house's smoldering areas. Plumes of smoke rose up, and the sizzling sound snapped through the air. The crew stood down on arrival, watching the remaining hot spots until Abby arrived, but then the chief insisted on wetting down the hot spots. He said that ultimately it was his crew's responsibility to ensure the fire was out, and he didn't want a rekindle that could spread to the surrounding area. But, at the same time, he agreed to do his best to keep further damage to a minimum for the arson investigation.

This gave Abby plenty of time to sign an agreement with the Veritas Center and to question Colin and his teammates. The thirty-something woman whose serious expression spoke to the stress of the job seemed capable and knowledgeable. She was petite with near-black hair that hung straight to her shoulders, a cute nose, and big eyes, and she wore khaki tactical pants and a county logo shirt. If not for the way she carried herself, he could see the men in her department trying to walk all over her.

The two deputies on scene clearly respected her. That

said a lot for her in Colin's book, and he treated her with respect too.

Too bad she didn't reciprocate. She wasn't rude. Not at all, but her dislike or distrust of feds, and by extension former feds, was as clear as the night sky above. Nothing new for Colin, and no point in causing any issues. Not when Dev had a connection to her. So he'd stopped trying to communicate and took a back seat to his little brother.

"So tell me about Clackamas." She leaned against the Veritas van.

Dev narrowed his gaze. "If you're looking for dirt on the agency, I'm not one of those guys who kisses and tells."

"Nah, I actually want to hear about your experience. Especially your time with the marine unit. Figure there are times when we can learn from larger agencies, and I know we can step up our water patrols."

Colin liked her even more for the open-mindedness Dev said she possessed.

Dev launched into describing his time patrolling the rivers in Clackamas County. Abby pinned her rapt attention on him and seemed to drink in every word, but still, Colin saw her pull her gaze away to survey the scene too.

Colin should be glad his brother connected with the sheriff. Problem was, he wasn't used to playing second fiddle to his brother. Totally an ego thing. A thing he needed to get over if he wanted to find Tarver. And he did want to find the guy. Badly. Find him and help ensure a conviction for murdering this victim and put him behind bars for the rest of his life.

"Hey, watch it," Sierra said to the firefighter from where she was collecting evidence outside the house. "You're trampling all over evidence. Can't you see my marker?"

"Trying to do my job, lady, just like you," the tall firefighter dressed in full turnout gear snapped.

"Lady? Lady?" Sierra's voice rose an octave, and she clamped her hands on her hips. "I—"

"We appreciate any help you can give in avoiding these marked areas." Kelsey took Sierra's arm and tugged her to the side before she could finish her sentence.

"Grrr." Sierra glared at the firefighter's back. "Why do these macho guys think they need to call me lady? If I was a guy, they wouldn't say a word about my gender, and they'd give me more respect."

Kelsey released Sierra's arm. "I'm sure he didn't mean anything by it."

"You know he did and—"

"And if you let him distract you, you'll lose twice by wasting valuable time."

"Fine. Okay." Sierra took a long breath and let it out. "I know you get it. I'll move on to the kennel and come back here when they're done."

"Would you like me to take photos for you to speed things along?" Kelsey asked. "At least until I'm cleared to recover the body."

"That would be great."

"I'll grab my camera and meet you at the kennel." Kelsey spun and picked her way to the van, where Nick sat on the bumper. His attention was so focused on his phone he didn't notice her arrival. Or if he did, he didn't show it.

Colin didn't know him well enough to know which it was, but when he got bogged down on his phone or computer, he lost track of what was going on around him. They were actually lucky that Nick had taken a break to answer the sheriff's copious questions. But he didn't waste even a second before returning to his dark web search for signs of Tarver. Too bad he hadn't had any success yet.

The fire chief took off his helmet and ran a hand through sweaty gray hair as he stepped back to them. "We've wetted everything down, and you're clear to enter. If you want help in retrieving the body, we're glad to provide it."

Abby faced the van. "Hey, Dr. Dunbar," she called out. "You want help recovering the remains?"

"No!" She spun, camera in hand. "If we're clear to enter, then everyone stands down and no one goes near the remains. Including your men." Despite her feminine appearance in this heavily male-driven field of law enforcement, her tone carried authority, and Colin would never intentionally want to cross paths with her.

"We're glad to let you take lead," Abby said. "But I'll need to take a look at the crime scene before it's disturbed."

"Fine. You can follow me. No one else." Kelsey hung the camera strap around her neck and exchanged gazes with Abby. "But if you want me to help you solve this murder, please follow my directions to the letter."

"Of course." Abby tilted her head. "At least as long as other lives aren't at risk. In that case, you listen to my directions."

Kelsey nodded and changed her focus to Dev. "Could you go to the kennels and tell Sierra I won't be coming to take pictures for her and that she now has free access to the house?"

"Of course," Dev said.

She picked up a large bin and stepped toward the sheriff.

"Can I carry that for you?" Abby asked.

She arched an eyebrow, and Colin expected her to tell her she was capable of doing her own work, but she gave her the bin. "Thank you. Follow me."

She marched toward the house, Abby in tow. Colin was glad Kelsey had sent Dev to the kennel on the errand. Took Abby's attention off them and freed Colin up to fall in line behind the pair and travel at least to the edge of the house. He might not be on the official list to receive investigation information, but he could get close enough to listen in to their conversation.

"You can put the bin there." Kelsey pointed at a spot a few feet from the body.

Abby set it down and turned toward the victim. "Oh, man. Man. I..." Her throat seemed to choke off the words. "I've never seen anyone this far gone."

Colin had to give her props for being willing to admit her discomfort and not try to pretend she was okay with the gruesome sight.

"It can be hard to take in." Kelsey opened the bin and took out battery-powered lights. She set them up and focused the beams on the body, leaving a much clearer picture of the burned state of the victim.

Colin had wanted to join them in the house, but his queasy stomach thanked him for being at a distance. He focused on Sierra stepping out of the darkness with Dev.

Abby ran a hand through her hair and cleared her throat. "You do these retrievals all the time, but I guess you never get used to the sight."

Kelsey slid her fingers into a pair of disposable gloves. "You're right. I recover remains all the time, but not a lot of burn victims."

Abby looked around. "Nothing survived this fire. His ID, if he had any on him, couldn't either. And forget finger-prints, right? So how will you even identify him?"

"We start every investigation by completing a biological profile," Kelsey said. "Then we answer as many questions as we can to start. Our top-five list includes the victim's age, sex, ancestry, stature, and—if he's reported missing and we suspect it might be him—any individualizing traits that family and friends would know."

"Things like what?"

"Braces on teeth, healed or healing fractures, skeletal

deformities, amputations, and other medical and anomalous conditions of teeth and bones."

"If you can't complete that profile?"

"Then we have to use DNA." Kelsey frowned. "It's less likely to survive high-intensity fires, but it can, and that's a potential option. We could also get prints from other objects in the nearby area that can lead to a possible identity, and dental records, which we can compare to the teeth. That is assuming the teeth aren't too fragmentary for reconstruction and that good or reliable antemortem records exist."

Abby looked around. "You said this was a high-intensity fire. I didn't know prints could survive such heat."

"They can for sure. Many forensic technicians don't have the training or equipment to recover them. But if you have a skilled forensic team like ours with state-of-the-art equipment, prints can be lifted for comparison to databases."

Abby planted her hands on her trim waist. "Are there times when you just can't ID them?"

Kelsey nodded. "I've had times when I couldn't match remains to a specific individual. There weren't any medical or dental records for the living person, giving us nothing to compare the postmortem information against. Or there were times when the remains were so severely damaged or compromised by heat that it was impossible to extract DNA. Or the teeth were too fragmentary for reconstruction."

Abby frowned. "That occur often?"

She shook her head. "In my experience, it's rare when a forensic anthropologist can't reconstruct some living characteristic from bone, even burned bones. Though I have to say, wildfires can be particularly difficult when the victim is not in their home or vehicle."

Sierra stepped into the house but knelt by the door. "Speaking of prints, the front door knob looks good to lift prints."

"Great." Abby turned. "What about the accelerant used? Gasoline odor seems to suggest that."

"You're likely right," Sierra said. "Fortunately, the pour pattern is obvious. I'll take samples, and if you locate a suspect in possession of a gas can, we can match the gas used here to the cans."

"You can drill down to such a detail?" Abby asked.

"Yes," Sierra said. "And if you obtain samples from local stations, I can pin it to them, and they could have surveillance video showing your suspect buying the gas."

Abby frowned. "Wouldn't it be as fast just to go to nearby stations and ask for video?"

"You'd have to answer that, but when you take this killer to court, you'll want to forensically tie the gas to a local station if possible, so I'll still give you the data."

"Problem with either option is manpower." Abby looked at Dev. "You sure you're not wanting to get back in the game?"

Dev took a few steps closer to the house, glanced at Colin, then back at Abby. "I'm sure, but our team would be happy to help in this investigation in exchange for getting reports from the Veritas experts."

Abby frowned, and the shadows from the lights cast deep shadows over her face. "Tell you what. Let me deputize you for this investigation. I'll take lead on it, and you do the grunt work for me. If you do, I'll share the reports."

Dev didn't answer right away when Colin wanted him to jump on the offer. But he held his tongue and trusted his brother to handle this.

"That could work," he finally said. "But my team works with me."

"I don't know." Abby scrubbed a hand over her face. "It's one thing to bring in a temp deputy. Another to have the rest of your team horning in."

"They can all report to me, and I'll make sure they only work on what we need. No grandstanding."

Colin snorted.

Abby shifted her focus to him. "Not going to be easy to keep former feds in line."

Dev eyed Colin, reminding him of times they'd been caught by their father when they were up to their necks in mischief. "I can assure you they'll behave, if this is the only way we can get the information from you and help bring in a killer."

Colin gave a sharp nod of acceptance. Of course he did. No way he would antagonize the sheriff, but if he had to go rogue to find Tarver, he wouldn't hesitate to do so.

He'd do just about anything to give Brooklyn back her life.

# 10

Exhausted, Colin and the team piled into their vehicle to head back to the compound. Nick remained onsite with the Veritas team to help out with the investigation. But there was nothing the Shadow Lake team could do to aid in recovering forensics. Or the body. They were better off getting some shut-eye so they could be on their game tomorrow.

An ear-piercing alarm sounded on everyone's phone.

Colin had his in hand and looked at the alert. "Floor it. We have an attempted hack of the security system at the compound."

"A breach?" Reid pressed his foot to the gas pedal, and the vehicle climbed in speed.

"Not an actual breach. Let me look deeper." Colin dug into the log files. "Someone tried to disable the east gate camera."

"So they could breach undetected," Dev stated.

"No other reason to disable it," Colin said. "Unless we're talking about one of the class participants who wants to go AWOL without us knowing about it. But they could just ask to leave so that doesn't make sense. Unless, of course, they did something wrong, and they didn't want us to discover it while they were still present."

"Do we need to get Russ over there?" Ryan asked.

"Will probably take him as long to get there as us, but you never know," Reid said. "Call him."

Ryan made the call.

"I'm sure Micha got the alert, but I'm calling him, too," Colin said. "No way I want him to head out to the gate and leave Brooklyn and our mom alone."

"Eryn's still with them," Dev said.

"True, but not sure I'm good with that. I know her computer skills, but I don't know her defensive skills." Colin tapped Micha's number. He wished he could trust Eryn to be capable, but he couldn't. He wasn't one to trust without evidence. Probably the reason he was struggling with his faith. He couldn't trust God that everything would be okay with his mom when he had no evidence of it.

"I got the alert," Micha said in way of answer. "What's going on?"

Colin told him.

"Want me to check it out?" Micha asked.

"No. Stay with Brooklyn and my mom. Get them into the bathroom. It's in the center of the cabin and doesn't have windows."

"Way ahead of you. Eryn already moved them in there and is standing duty outside the door." Micha sucked in a breath. "I'll take the front door, but would be better if we had someone at the back."

Colin wished the same thing, but it was better to keep Eryn at the bathroom door where she could stop an intruder who got in from any direction. "Barricade the back door if you can. We're five minutes out. Until then, I'll monitor the camera feeds and let you know what I see."

The many cameras covered most of the property but not the back side of his cabin. Still, he could see most of the property and would be able to tell if the gate was indeed breached.

"Hang on," he told Micha. "I'll pull up the feed now."

He put Micha on speaker and switched over to the video feeds. He took some comfort that Micha was the guy back at the homestead, as he served as a weapons tech in the Army with Russ and was a top-notch marksman. If only he could clone Micha for the next four minutes.

He entered the security program, and the small screen filled with multiple camera angles. Too bad he didn't have a larger screen so he could see them all at once. He would just have to go through them one at a time.

He started with the east gate, spotted movement. "We've got action outside the east gate. Someone running away. Wearing camouflage. Ski mask. Headed for the road."

"Armed?" Reid asked.

Colin zoomed in. "Yeah, and looks like a closed laptop under his arm."

"So likely the person who tried to hack the system," Reid said.

"Likely."

"Any way you can trace him if he skates before we get there?" Dev asked.

"I might be able to get some data on his IP address. He would have to be using cellular data out here, and that could lead to his account and an address."

"I don't like this." Reid careened the vehicle around a curve and looked at his brother. "The lodge is too close to that gate. Get Megan on the phone. Tell her to be on alert."

Colin felt Reid's concern for his wife and daughters clear in the backseat. Like a physical cloud. The same cloud enveloping Colin for Brooklyn and his mom. And he wasn't married to Brooklyn. He barely even knew her. So how much more was this eating at Reid?

He shifted to the next camera and caught additional movement. "Vehicle driving off at the road. Looks like a jacked-up pickup. Oversized tires. High up. I'll try to get the plates."

He zoomed in. Nothing. Moved to the next camera. Caught the tail end of the truck. Zoomed in again. More nothing. He moved two cameras down the road. Grabbed a screenshot of the front of the truck. Then the back on the next camera.

He slammed a fist into the back of Ryan's seat. "No plates on the vehicle. None at all."

"Dude," Ryan said, ending the call. "Someone's sitting in this seat."

"Sorry, it's just—"

"I get it," Ryan said. "You wanted something. Maybe he'll turn off, and we'll intercept the vehicle on this road."

"Maybe," Colin said, not expecting to have such luck. "Megan have any problems?"

"Nothing," Ryan said. "But she wants Reid there now. She's worried about the girls."

"Understandable."

"And I want to be there"—Reid clenched the wheel tighter—"so it'll be my first stop. One of you can take over and drive down to the other cabin."

Colin didn't want to waste even a second of time before getting to Brooklyn, but he understood Reid's need and would respect it. "When we get closer, I'll open the gate remotely so we don't have to stop."

"Good plan." Reid glanced in the mirror and gave a tight smile.

Dev looked between the seats. "I'll take over driving to our place."

Colin nodded at his brother. "Any problems there, Micha?"

"We're good. I got this, bro." His confidence took away a fraction of Colin's concern.

Plan in place, they all fell silent. Colin continued to watch the feeds. The others were watching the road, looking for that jacked-up pickup.

"Get that gate open now," Reid said.

Colin tapped the right buttons. "It's open. No need to stop."

"You better hope you're right." Reid whipped into the driveway, tires squealing.

"I'll go in with Reid," Ryan said, his body bouncing over the rutted drive, "then head home to be sure this guy didn't decide to go to Pinetree."

"Go check on your family." Ryan lived at the next-door resort with his wife and young son, and Colin understood wanting to go home. If he had a family he would be doing exactly what Reid and Ryan were doing.

The vehicle bounced over ruts, and they flew through the open gate. Colin closed it behind them. Reid barreled ahead toward the large lodge that had been in the family for years and screeched to a stop out front, the back of the SUV fishtailing on the gravel drive.

He had his door open and was taking the wide steps two at a time, before the vehicle stopped rocking. Ryan slammed his vehicle door and charged behind him. Dev had bolted, too, and got behind the wheel, shifting into gear and winding their vehicle down the drive to their cabin. Colin prayed God had spared everyone from any harm.

∾

Brooklyn's body was tight with worry. Her muscles stiff and cramping. Tender to the touch. Stretching would help, but she wouldn't show Sandy any hint of her stress. At least, she would do her best not to. Sandy didn't need any additional tension, as it could further aggravate her lupus. Brooklyn would hate for this sweet woman to be penalized by Kane, who'd come after Brooklyn. Or at least it made sense that it was Kane who tried to breach the gate, as no one else in the compound had someone stalking them.

Sandy shifted on the closed toilet seat, her eyes glazed in pain.

"Is it time for more Tylenol?" Brooklyn asked.

She shook her head and put on a brave smile. "Don't worry about me. I'm fine."

"You're not." Brooklyn searched Sandy's gaze. "You're in pain. Where?"

Sandy held up her hands.

This wouldn't do. Not if Brooklyn could do something about it. "Would it help if I got a hot washcloth and wrapped your hands in it?"

"I've never tried that, but heat sometimes feels good, so it might work." Sandy gave a weak smile. "For a moment anyway until it loses its heat."

"I'll wrap a towel around the washcloth and can keep refreshing it too." Brooklyn jumped up and went to the small linen closet by the door. She took out several washcloths and a few hand towels to have them all at the ready.

"You're amazing, you know that?" Sandy said. "We're in lockdown, this creep who's been trying to kill you likely just tried to break in, and you're worried about me and ready to help."

Brooklyn got the water running. "It's nothing. I already think of you as family, and since I've been away from mine for years, it feels good to have a connection."

"Isn't it amazing the connection God can provide in such a short time?" Sandy smiled. "I think of you as family too."

Brooklyn let the water get as hot as she could take it, soaked the cloth, rang the fabric out, and then wrapped it around Sandy's hands.

"Ooh, this *is* nice." she gave a sincere smile.

Eryn knocked on the door. "Colin and Dev are approaching outside."

Sandy let out a breath.

Brooklyn wrapped a towel around Sandy's hands and held them. "Hopefully all is well, and we can get you to bed."

"I'm tired, but I'm not sure I can sleep after all the excitement." She leaned back. "Besides, I'd like to hear what Colin thinks is going on."

Brooklyn wanted to hear, too, but she didn't have a chronic disease that was in a flare-up. She wouldn't argue with Sandy now, but once they were safe, she would broach the subject again.

A loud pounding sounded on the door.

"Open up, Brooklyn. It's Colin." His deep voice sent a wave of relief through Brooklyn. She twisted the lock and pulled the door open.

He ran his gaze over her from head to foot. "You okay?"

"Fine, but your mom's fingers are painful, so I'm trying to warm them with a washcloth. Now that you're here, I'll get her to the couch and get the heating pad going."

He held up a hand. "Not quite yet. I need you to stay here while I check the fence perimeter for any damage."

"Damage?" She made sure to keep her voice down for Sandy's sake when it wanted to skyrocket. "Do you think Kane got in?"

"No. Just taking every precaution."

She let out a breath slowly so Sandy wouldn't catch it. "Then can you bring the heating pad in here?"

"Sure thing." He looked over Brooklyn's shoulder at his mother. "Anything else you need or want, Mom?"

"For everyone to stop worrying about me." She waved her wrapped hands. "Go do your thing. I'll be fine."

"I'll be back with the heating pad, and then I'll let you know when it's clear to come out." He spun and marched away.

"Such a whirlwind." Sandy stared at the door. "He's always been an intense person."

Brooklyn wanted to know more. "Even as a little kid?"

"No, not as a little kid." She smiled as if memories were assaulting her. "He was easygoing and so joyful. Until his dad passed away. Then he thought he had to be the man of the house."

"How old was he?"

"Nine, and Devan was seven."

"That must've been hard."

"I won't lie." Sandy rested her towel-wrapped hands on her knees. "It wasn't easy. Especially since it was so sudden."

"Do you mind if I ask what happened?"

"His dad was a firefighter." Pain contorted her expression, and she closed her eyes. "Got trapped in a building and didn't make it out."

"Oh, wow. Wow. I'm so sorry." Brooklyn rested her hand on Sandy's arm. "My dad's a firefighter too. Still active duty. He's a captain now, so he doesn't race into buildings as often as he used to, but I was always so afraid when he went to work and there was a fire."

She opened her eyes. "Colin was the same, but before every shift, when his father said goodbye, he promised Colin that he would always come home." Sandy bit her lip. "He shouldn't have done that because he couldn't promise such a thing. More than anything, it left Colin not trusting in others. Or trusting easily at all."

Brooklyn surely understood that. Kane had done the same thing to her. And it explained some of Colin's behavior. Maybe it could also explain why he wasn't involved with a woman.

He returned with the heating pad, and she saw the wounded little boy at his father's funeral. Oh, how she could imagine that loss. It had to hurt—cut him to the core. She wanted to wrap her arms around him and tell the little nine-year-old boy inside that it was okay, and he would be okay. She settled for offering a comforting look and squeezing his hand when he gave her the heating pad.

He studied her with concern at an intensity level she'd never seen someone direct at her before. "What was that for?"

She shrugged. "We just seem to have so much in common, I felt like doing it."

"Okay." He eyed her. "When I get back, you'll have to tell me about these things."

She nodded, though, honestly she didn't want to have a personal conversation with him. The last thing she needed was to connect even more and feel even closer to the man who was worming his way into her heart without even trying.

Weapons in hand, Colin and Dev split up. Dev headed west. Colin headed east, as he wanted a good look at the gate in question. He walked the fencing until he reached the location where he'd seen the man on video and searched the metal for any sign of tampering.

Nothing. Not even a nick, much less a cut of the fence.

He ran his flashlight over the ground looking for footprints. Nothing obvious. It hadn't rained in a few days, so the ground was dry. Still, he would check out the other side of the fence in the daylight when he could get a better look and not trample over vital evidence. Then if he found footprints or anything else, he would get Sierra to process it.

He continued down the fence until he met up with Dev at the far end.

"Anything?" Colin asked.

"No. You?"

Colin shook his head and started back for the cabin, Dev falling into place at his side. "Our would-be intruder didn't make it inside. He must've realized that he kicked off an alert, or he wouldn't have taken off like that."

Dev looked at Colin. "You think it's this Kane guy who's after Brooklyn?"

"Makes sense," he said, thinking about it. "But it also doesn't."

Dev flashed a quick look at him. "Why not?"

"First, how did he know she was here?"

"I don't know," Dev said. "Trailed her from her apartment?"

"Nick says that didn't happen. They didn't have a car near them much less a tail."

"Tracker then," Dev said.

"Tarver had no idea where she lived before now, so he couldn't have put a tracker on her phone or in her purse."

Dev stopped and stared at him. "Would have to be on Nick's vehicle, then. Tarver knows she's friends with Nick, and he could've found out Nick would be at that dinner. Then he put a tracker on Nick's vehicle while he was in the event and left the lead on the dark web that he knew would kick off an alert and hope it sent Nick to Brooklyn."

"And Tarver could follow him," Colin said, getting on

board with his brother's idea. "A good theory. Let's find out if it holds weight."

Colin dug out his phone and dialed Nick. "We had an attempted breach at our compound. Could be Tarver. Check your vehicle for a tracker."

"Hold up." Nick's testy tone came over the speaker and echoed into the night. "Not so fast. You're accusing me of leading him to your place."

"Accusing, no," Colin said, remaining calm and trying to diffuse the situation. "Suggesting it's possible, yes."

"Explain," Nick demanded.

Colin shared Dev's theory.

"Man, oh, man." A long breath hissed over the phone. "I don't want to think that happened, but it would make sense. Blake routinely checks our vehicles for tracking devices, but we haven't scanned it since the dinner. I'll check it and call you back."

Colin stowed his phone and wondered if he was off base here in suggesting someone like Nick could've brought danger to the compound.

"Our theory really does make sense," Dev said as if sensing Colin's uneasiness.

"Yeah, except Tarver is like this super hacker. I can't see him making a mistake like this."

"He's human." Dev started walking again. "He could've been overeager because he was so close to getting to Brooklyn."

"Right, but even if he *did* manage to breach the fence, he would've had to have gotten through all of us to get to her."

"Not if he managed a surprise breach."

"True." The mere thought sent a wave of panic over Colin as he reached the steps to the cabin.

Dev yawned. "It's late. We should get some sleep and debrief in the morning."

Colin glanced around the wide expanse of the property. "No sleep for me. I'll be carefully reviewing the security feeds to see if we recorded anything that can lead us to Tarver."

To lead them to the creep stalking the woman he'd come to care for.

# 11

Brooklyn prepared a lovely burrito bowl lunch for Sandy, who sat at the small kitchen table to keep her company. The recipe was healthy and packed with protein, so it shouldn't further set off Sandy's inflamed joints. The men—minus Micha again, who stood sentry at the front door—had gone to check out the fence and would be back as soon as the meal was ready. Brooklyn had chosen it for Sandy, but the recipe made enough for an army, so she couldn't very well exclude the guys from sharing the meal. Even if she really needed some time away from Colin to get her feelings under control.

She sliced the green onions and looked at Sandy. "I didn't even ask if you liked green onions."

"I do," she said enthusiastically. "What else is in the bowl? Other than the salsa and black olives on the island."

"Pinto and black beans, quinoa, corn, cheddar cheese, and avocado." Brooklyn tapped the oven. "And I'm grilling chicken in adobo pepper sauce."

"So that's the amazing smell that's making my mouth water." She inhaled and smiled. "Sounds heavenly. Are you sure I can't help?"

"Nothing but chopping to do right now, and your hands won't like that."

Sandy frowned and rested her cane against the wall.

"I'm sorry," Brooklyn said. "I'm sure it doesn't help to be reminded that you can't do it."

"I try to ignore what I can't do anymore and keep my spirits up, but I really don't like to impose on others." Her eyes glistened with unshed tears. "So I would've done just about anything not to have to move in with the boys."

"Boys." Brooklyn giggled, trying to keep this discussion light after the events last night. "Nothing boy-like about them."

Sandy smiled just as she had hoped. "They'll always be my boys."

"I'm sure they will." Brooklyn went back to chopping the onions.

"They shouldn't have to be saddled with me." She planted her hands on the table and stared at them. "I hear them talking when they don't think I do. Their lives have been upended. So I'm very thankful they found you."

"I'm thankful for the job right now." She smiled at Sandy. "I don't think of you as a job though. Like I said last night, you feel like family, and I really enjoy your company."

"Likewise." Sandy fell silent for a few moments. "Do you want to get married someday?"

*Oh, wow, where did that come from?*

Brooklyn stopped chopping. Wouldn't do to slice her finger. "I'd like that. Of course, Kane has to be arrested and be incarcerated for the foreseeable future before I could ever consider it."

"He will be."

"You sound so certain."

"One thing I know. If my Colin is motivated to do something, he won't rest until he succeeds. And, sweetheart, he is motivated to save you from this Kane fella."

Brooklyn had to smile over the thought of his care and drive to find Kane. "I can see that."

Sandy blinked a few times. "I think he has feelings for you."

"I think so, too, and surprisingly, I have feelings for him," Brooklyn admitted, shocking herself that she admitted it.

Sandy clapped but then winced and stopped. "How wonderful. I would like nothing more than for him to find a woman like you and settle down to have kids. You do want kids, right?"

"I do, but I don't think he's ready for any commitment."

"That's because of me." Sandy crossed her arms. "I applaud him for his sense of commitment to me. I am blessed by it, but I sure don't want him to put his life on hold for me."

"I don't think he has to do that, right?"

"Right."

"Then maybe in time if you're still living with him, he'll come to see that he can get married and still have you living with him."

Sandy tightened her arms. "If whoever he chooses as a spouse agrees to have me underfoot."

"You're so wonderful, she'll be bound to love you." Brooklyn scooped the onions into a small bowl. "Once she sees how much you mean to him, I can't see how any woman wouldn't want to help in your care."

"I hate to say this, sweetheart, but that's pretty naïve. Lots of women, especially new brides, don't want their mother-in-law in the same house."

"That's because they haven't met you." Brooklyn winked.

"Which is why you're perfect for my Colin." She held on to Brooklyn's gaze.

Brooklyn let her warmth linger until she couldn't handle seeing her own hope for her own future in Sandy's eyes and had to look away. She dumped out black olives onto the cutting board.

The front door flew open, and Brooklyn jumped, stabbing her knife into the board near her finger.

"It's just us," Colin called out.

She let out a breath at the shock and near miss of her finger.

He poked his head into the kitchen and locked his gaze on her. "Is there enough food for Ryan and Reid too? I'd like to do an update while we wait for Sierra and Kelsey to finish up. See if we can use the time wisely."

Brooklyn felt her face heat under his intense study. "There's plenty."

"Good because we brought them with us." He winked and left the room.

Sandy shook her head. "Just like my boy. Do, then ask for forgiveness. Sometimes it's endearing. Sometimes not so much." She laughed.

Brooklyn joined in, but the sound of the oven timer took her attention, and she got the chicken breasts out to slice them for the bowls. She liked to serve the burrito bowl with fresh bread, but hadn't been at the cabin long enough to get needed supplies to bake it. She hadn't asked, but she didn't think Colin or Dev would have yeast on hand. They could surprise her, but...

Brooklyn carried large bowls along with silverware to the passthrough and leaned out. "Would someone mind grabbing these to set the table?"

She didn't wait for an answer but turned back to get tortilla chips and the choices of fixings she'd prepared for the burrito bowls. She put them in a large divided platter that worked like a lazy Susan, which she set on the counter after Colin had taken the bowls to the table.

"You should go in," Brooklyn said to Sandy.

She frowned.

"What is it? Not feeling up to lunch with a crowd?"

Sandy reached for her cane. "No, I'm good with that, but I hate that you have to do all of this on your own."

"That's why I'm here."

"Not really. Not to feed an army of men."

"It's really no more work." Brooklyn started slicing the chicken. "There just won't be any leftovers, and we'll have a few more bowls to wash, which the dishwasher will take care of."

Sandy struggled to her feet. "Well, don't let us take advantage of you."

Brooklyn nodded, but honestly, it was just the opposite. She was feeling useful and connected for the first time in a long time, making her even more resolved to do whatever she could to locate Kane.

Colin's mom hobbled into the room, her cane thumping on the thick pine floorboards with a rhythmic thump, thump, thump. He pulled out a chair for her at the head of the long, rustic dining table. She grimaced when sitting. He gritted his teeth. They needed softer chairs for her to sit in than the matching log style. When this was all over and Tarver was behind bars, he would remedy that.

Colin went back to the passthrough counter to retrieve platters of food. The chicken smelled out of this world. Spicey and tangy at the same time. He wasn't quite sure what the meal was, but he was a fan of all of the ingredients. Well, maybe not the yellow stuff he couldn't name. Looked kind of like rice except rounder, and he had no idea if he liked it or not. He was generally a meat and potatoes kind of guy. Oh, and pizza—'cause what guy didn't like pizza?—but he didn't mind trying new things.

The other guys came into the room and settled at the table, their conversation filled with this week's NBA final games.

His mom plugged her nose. "So who smells like cigarette smoke and why?"

"Sorry, that would be me." Ryan stood behind a chair. "When we canvassed the route we thought the potential intruder took, I went into a convenience store where the owner smoked. I'll go take my jacket off, and that should help."

"That would be good," Colin said. "Mom's lupus makes her sensitive to all unusual smells."

"Just one more of the many perks of the disease." She laughed, but Colin caught the frustrated undertone.

How many times a day since she'd come to live here did he wish he could take this disease from her and take it on himself? Sure, he would hate having it, but he hated seeing his beautiful, wonderful mother suffering even more.

"Could someone grab the iced tea and glasses?" Brooklyn called out.

Dev dropped into a chair and stared at Colin. "You've been doing such a good job of helping I wouldn't want to deprive you of the final steps."

"You know what I'm going to say to that, right?" their mom asked.

"Don't let your big brother do everything," Colin and Dev said at the same time, then Dev laughed.

"Yeah, you can laugh 'cause you're the one sitting on your butt." Colin rolled his eyes. "But it's no biggie. Brooklyn's the one who got the wrong end of things."

She entered the room and swiped a hand over her forehead. "I like to cook, and I don't get to do it often for others, so it's my pleasure to make the meal. I'll be able to plan ahead for the next one and have all the ingredients to make something special."

"In that case"—Dev jumped up and pulled out a chair for her—"sit next to me, and we can talk about a menu."

She laughed, the delightful sound rising up and filling the room. Colin couldn't help the happy smile that crossed his face, capturing his mother's attention and gaining him a knowing look. So, fine. She knew he was attracted to Brooklyn. What red-blooded male wouldn't be?

He grabbed the iced tea and filled the tall glasses, handing them down the table.

"The tea isn't sweetened." Brooklyn picked up the sugar bowl from the tray and held it up. "My granny would be disappointed in me. She always said sweet tea was the only tea, but I didn't think you all were the type to want sweet drinks. The sugar's here if anyone wants it."

"I'm not too proud to ask for it." Dev reached for the bowl and started spooning sugar into his glass.

"And not too proud to consume the whole bowl." Colin shook his head as he took a seat. "Wait until you see him in the morning with his sugar-filled breakfast cereal."

"Hey, you gotta start your day out right."

Brooklyn laughed again, and Colin wished he'd been the one to make that happen, to make her happy. But he seemed only to bring her down with his serious nature. Or scare her. He had to change that. Make a point of it, or she was going to fall for Dev. Nothing worse in Colin's book right now than that happening. Seeing her dating his brother. No, he couldn't let that happen. Not at all.

Ryan came back and took the furthest chair from Colin's mom as possible.

"You don't have to exile yourself," she said, smiling at Ryan.

Colin didn't notice an odor this time, though.

"Don't worry, Mom," Dev said. "He doesn't smell anymore. At least not any more than usual."

Ryan rolled his eyes.

"So what is this great looking meal we're having?" Colin asked to change the topic.

"Burrito quinoa bowl," Brooklyn said. "So basically the same things you might find in a burrito but in a bowl with quinoa. Has a lot of good things for your mom, like multiple protein sources and the oils in the avocado."

"Ah, yes, quinoa," Dev said. "The grain that's so small, you wonder if ants are plotting to infiltrate our meal."

Brooklyn grabbed his forearm and chuckled.

"A seed." Colin suddenly felt very grumpy, and he wanted to rip her hand from his brother's arm. "It's technically a seed and part of the spinach family."

"Well, excuse me." Dev rolled his eyes. "I didn't think you knew so much about quinoa."

He didn't. Had never even seen it or eaten it, but he'd heard that little detail on a quiz show.

"Whatever it is," Brooklyn took her hand back, "it's the base of our meal. Put some in the bottom of your bowl and layer on any of the fixings you want. All of them make it super good, but choose only what you like."

"Never really been a huge fan of quinoa," Dev said.

"Maybe give it a try in this meal." Brooklyn handed the bowl to him. "You might find you'll like it."

"If you recommend it, I'm sure I will." He gazed into her eyes like a lovestruck little puppy, making Colin want to hurl.

"There was no sign of a fence intrusion today either," he

blurted out to stop the two of them from flirting. Okay, maybe not flirting, just getting along so well.

That did it. Brooklyn's cheerful expression evaporated, and Colin's gut clenched tighter. He might be filling his bowl with food, but he doubted he could eat a thing. Something new for him. Nothing much had ever stopped him from eating.

"Any evidence worth collecting?" Her expression filled with hope.

"Footprints leading up to the road." Colin's gut ached for the hopefulness that could be dashed at any moment until Tarver was charged and behind bars. "Sierra said she would stop by and cast them. Then do a more thorough review, just in case we didn't know what we were doing."

Dev shook his head. "We all know crime scenes and how to look for evidence, but she doesn't seem to give us credit for that."

"It *is* her field of expertise," Sandy said. "You all wouldn't stand by and let her tell you what to do in the law enforcement area."

"Point taken." Colin gave his mom a fond look.

Brooklyn took the quinoa bowl from Reid. "Is she done at the house?"

"No." Dev topped his bowl with ripe chunks of avocado. "She said she hopes to finish collecting evidence tomorrow."

Reid looked up from spooning black beans into his bowl. "I heard her mention that she'll be doing the fingerprints before starting on the recovered arson samples."

Brooklyn filled the bottom of her bowl with perfectly cooked quinoa. "Did she say why the prints take priority over those samples?"

Ryan nodded. "They hope the prints will lead to the victim's identity, which is the number one priority."

"Right," Colin said. "That makes sense. So I guess our footprints from last night are going to take a back seat too."

"She said she would put her staff on them." Dev stabbed a fork in a chunk of chicken. "But not to hold our breath on how helpful they'll be unless we find the almost intruder to compare to his footwear."

"Which, if it is indeed Tarver, we don't have a clue where he is," Reid said.

Ryan held his fork over a heaping full bowl. "Learning the victim's ID will do so much more for helping us find him than anything."

Everyone fell silent for a moment, likely thinking about the victim as Colin was doing. Thinking of the horrific way he'd died. If he was found in Tarver's place, he could very well be a criminal. Maybe another hacker. Or even a wildlife trafficker.

Colin couldn't let the fact that he was likely on the wrong side of the law sway him. No matter who this guy was or what he'd done, he deserved justice. Colin wouldn't stop until the man was identified and his killer brought to pay. If it turned out to be Kane Tarver, all the better.

# 12

---

Brooklyn poured a second cup of coffee and basked in the calm in the kitchen for a moment before rejoining the men in the living room. Colin had called a break after the meal so Sandy would take a nap, but the guys remained gathered around the dining table. Nick had arrived to join them. Dev unfolded easels, then added small whiteboards.

So the discussion was about to get more intense. Could she handle it? These guys seemed to take it all in stride. Except for Nick, they'd each lived a life where they hunted down criminals and dealt with all that entailed. Her, not so much. The closest she'd come to a crime was as a teenager, when she saw one of her classmates break into a closed store while she was walking home from piano lessons. She called the police and kept an eye on him until they arrived and arrested him. She even got her name in the newspaper for being a good citizen, but then her sleuthing days were over.

In her day, in her little hometown up the coast, that was a big deal. But today, it was nothing. A routine police call. Not as routine in her hometown, but elsewhere. She hungered for those simpler times. Until she thought about life without the availability of the internet and technology. Then she changed her tune. But today, she'd give just about anything to go home and not have to go back into the dining room because a man was hunting her, and they had to find him before he hurt her.

Colin poked his head in the door. "Joining us?"

She nodded, but couldn't seem to start in that direction.

"Something wrong?" He ran his law enforcement officer gaze over her. Probing. Demanding. And she could easily picture him as an FBI agent. "I mean, other than we don't know where Tarver is, and he might have killed someone."

She gripped her mug tighter. "I didn't expect to be in this situation. Not at all. I'm thankful for your and your team's support. I really, really am. But when you all get together, it can be a bit overwhelming for someone who's used to being alone with her computer most of the time."

"Yeah, I get that. I do. Even experienced it when I was a code crusader." He paused and grinned. "But I've come out of my bat cave, and now this chaos seems normal."

"I think I can get used to more people around. That's not the problem." She bit her lip before going on. "But I'm not sure if I'll ever be able to handle so many extremely intense guys in one place."

"We're only intense when working an investigation. Otherwise, we're pussy cats." He grinned, and he resembled Devan far more than when he was serious.

She liked this combo of intensity and fun as they seemed to balance each other out. "I'll believe it when I see it." She laughed and pointed at the door. "Lead the way. I'm ready to rejoin the guys, but I'm hoping it's the kitty litter crowd."

He laughed and turned back. His tone warmed her through. This was the good humor he was talking about. If everyone lightened up, she could see being part of such a group. Alas, the fun-loving guys weren't sitting at the table. The fierce group had shown up big time. And that included Nick, who was head down working on his laptop. He hadn't stopped searching for any hint of Kane online. No success yet, but if any data could be found, he would find it.

"Good," Dev said from where he stood by a whiteboard. "We're expected back at the crime scene soon and need to get started."

"Then let's get to it." Colin pulled out a ladder-back pine chair for Brooklyn, then sat next to her.

She set her mug on the scratched table that could tell years of stories about vacationing families, but they weren't there to hear fun camping stories. No, they were there to hear about Kane potentially murdering someone. She still could hardly process that, much less believe it.

Reid leaned forward and glanced around the table. "Anyone hear from Kelsey today?"

The men, except Dev, shook their heads.

"I talked to her," he said. "But nothing to report."

Colin sat forward. "She did say before we left last night that she thought it best to wait until today to remove the remains. She didn't want to miss anything."

"She still believe it's a male?" Ryan asked.

Dev nodded. "She's confident of that. Something about hips and bone structure of the eyes. We can proceed with looking for a male identity."

"Any other leads at all?" Reid asked. "From the Veritas staff or the sheriff?"

"A few things that we can help follow up on," Dev said. "Sierra says gas could very well have been the accelerant used to start the fire. To that end, I need guys to go to the local stations to collect samples she can take back to her lab."

"If we know the station where the gas was purchased, we can request their security footage," Colin added.

Dev nodded. "I don't mean to presume to decide who should do this, but Reid and Ryan, you're from the area and know all the station locations."

"Glad to do it," Reid said.

Ryan looked at his brother. "I'm on board if you take Gladys Miller's place."

"She's not *that* bad." Reid explained to Brooklyn. "Gladys is our town busybody. She'll talk your ear off."

"She means well, but she'll waste hours of your time." Ryan grimaced. "But yeah, I'm in. And I'll even take Gladys if I have to, but if so, you can call Mia and tell her not to expect me home until next week."

Dev rolled his eyes and got out a blue marker to write the item on the whiteboard and add Ryan's and Reid's names to the task.

"Micha." Dev turned back. "Sierra recovered a Sig P320 compact along with a silencer in the house. The weapon still has the serial number on it. Her team will be analyzing it when she gets all the evidence back to the lab, but before then we could be checking with local gun dealers to see if any of them sold the weapon and get the name of the person who purchased it."

Micha specialized in weapons in the military, so to Brooklyn, this seemed like a good fit.

"I'll make the calls." He ran a hand across his face. "But I'm not law enforcement, so even if they sold the Sig, they're not likely going to give me a name."

"True," Dev said, not seeming daunted by Micha's comment. "But if they admit selling it, I can then follow up for a name. And if any shop owner refuses to give you info, those are the ones we want to focus on."

"Okay, sure. I'll start on it after my class." He glanced at his watch and stood. "Which is in ten. Someone still has to take care of our guests."

"Now that's the attitude I like to see." Reid laughed.

"Any signs that this gun was used to take out our victim?" Ryan asked.

Dev shook his head. "Kelsey didn't see anything last night that would point to that, but last I talked to her, she hadn't turned the body. Or moved it at all, actually. Maybe she'll know more when Colin and I go back."

"Any chance I can go with you?" Brooklyn asked, despite knowing how Colin would answer.

"You don't want to go there," he said. "It's a horrible sight, and once you get a look at the victim, you can never unsee him."

"He's right, which you know I'd do almost anything not to admit." Dev smiled but firmed his shoulders. "But trust him. Us. This is a sight you don't want to see if you don't need to, and I don't think you need to. I can't see how you could help."

She sat forward and looked between the men. "What if something belonging to Kane survived the fire that meant something to me but not to you all? Or to Sierra and Kelsey? I might be able to find that lead we all want and need."

"She has a point." Reid glanced at each man in turn. "She could help, and with the police involvement now, odds are low that Tarver is in the area, and she should be safe."

"I don't like it." Colin clenched his jaw. "He could be hanging around out of sight."

"I doubt it." Nick looked up from his laptop. "Kane's known for cutting and running after he's broken the law. It's one of the ways he's escaped arrest. I doubt this scene is any different."

"I still don't like it." Colin stood and ran his gaze over the team. "We don't have eyes on him, and it's not safe."

"Not one hundred percent safe, no," Reid said. "But if we all go to the scene, we can eliminate pretty much every danger except a sniper shot."

"Right," Colin said. "The most deadly method to take someone out when they least expect it. You think that's an acceptable risk?"

Nick looked up from his computer. "Kane never had an interest in guns. He toured the Veritas facility after I left the company where we worked together. He didn't even ask to see the weapons lab."

"I remember that day," Brooklyn said. "He came back home saying he barely wanted to see anything other than the computers, but you were so stoked about the place that you insisted he see it all."

"I can't say it enough." Colin eyed them all one at a time. "He could've changed."

"Sure, it's possible he started liking weapons," Micha said. "But become proficient enough in long guns to take the kind of distance shot with precision that it would take? I doubt it."

"But it *is* possible," Colin said.

"Yeah, possible." Micha's skeptical look said it all for Brooklyn. He really didn't believe Kane had developed such skills, and as a weapons expert, he should know.

"We do what we usually do when we're at odds," Reid said. "We take a team vote and go with the majority."

Colin gritted his teeth but didn't argue. Brooklyn appreciated his concern for her, but she really believed he was being too cautious. And she trusted Nick's assessment. He knew Kane. Or at least had known him. She would pray that Colin was wrong and that Kane hadn't changed enough to become a proficient sniper.

Reid's phone chimed, and he grabbed it. "Front gate. It's a patrol car."

He lifted the phone to his mouth. "Can I help you?"

"Sheriff Day," she said. "I'd like a quick word with Dev."

"Sure thing," Reid said. "I'll open the gate for you. You'll find us all meeting at the last cabin on the left."

"Roger that."

Reid tapped his screen and stared at it. "Okay, she's in the compound and on her way to us."

"I'll meet her on the porch." Dev got up. "Hopefully, she has information for us." He strode for the door.

Brooklyn waited for someone to speak, but no one said anything. "I wonder if she'll update all of us or just Dev."

Colin's eyebrows knitted together. "Either way, we'll get the information."

"But wouldn't it be good to hear it right from the sheriff?" Brooklyn asked. "That way we can ask any questions we might have."

"True." Colin stood. "Let me tell Dev to try to get her to come inside."

He left the room, and Brooklyn immediately felt the loss of his presence. Like the force watching over her was gone, and she was vulnerable. That wasn't true, but she'd been so vulnerable for years and to finally have been able to let go a bit and have someone take care of her the past few days had been such a relief. Now, the way she felt before Nick came to rescue her had returned, and she didn't like it. Didn't like to think about a lonely life again.

*Oh, please let us find Kane so I don't have to go back to a solitary life. Living in isolation.*

The group fell silent, each of the guys taking a moment to look at their phones.

"Text from one of our guests." Reid looked at Micha. "Your group is waiting outside the conference room and getting antsy."

Micha frowned and got up. "Tell them I'll be right there before they start rebelling."

"They'd do that?" Brooklyn asked.

"Our participants are known for bucking the system," Ryan said. "So yeah. They'd rebel, and who knows what form that might take."

"Don't worry," Micha said, already heading for the door. "I'll jog down there so they don't get into any trouble."

He strode quickly out, passing Dev, Colin, and Sheriff Day as they entered the dining room. The petite sheriff had dark hair held back in a French braid and was dressed in khaki pants and a logo shirt. She had a gun at her hip and a badge on her belt, and she carried herself with an intensity that matched the men in the room.

She stopped at the end of the table to look at everyone. "Dev wanted me to include you all in the update."

"Thanks for agreeing to it." Colin took a seat.

She gave him a side-eye look but said nothing to him. Obviously, she still didn't like feds or former feds. She must have a reason, and Brooklyn would love to know what it might be.

"We haven't had a chance to meet." Brooklyn extended her hand. "Brooklyn Hurst."

"Ms. Hurst." Abby grabbed it and gave Brooklyn a bruising shake. "Sheriff Abby Day, but call me Abby."

"And I'm Brooklyn." She smiled. "I'm eager to hear your update."

"First." Abby planted her feet wide and placed a hand on her sidearm. "An alert was issued for Kane Tarver as a person of interest in this investigation. Driver's license has a bogus address for a vacant field as his address of record, and DMV only has one vehicle registered in his name. A pricey Hummer."

Brooklyn had known both of those details as Nick had

located that information when he hacked the DMV some time ago, but since his actions weren't legal they hadn't been able to mention it to the sheriff. She could comment though. "Kane liked to show off, and the pricier the item the better."

Abby shifted on her feet. "He may not have liked it so much. I just learned that it was found abandoned in McMinnville a few months back, and they have it in their impound lot."

"What?" Brooklyn shot up in her seat. "Abandoned?"

Sheriff Day nodded. "It was discovered by a neighbor when he was plowing a field. The photos in the file show the grass that had grown up around it. It had been there for some time."

He abandoned it? Seriously? Why would he do that, and why McMinnville?

The capital of the Oregon wine country, McMinnville was a city located near Portland. Some said it was a suburb, but it was an hour away, and Brooklyn didn't really consider it a suburb.

Colin looked at her. "Does Tarver have any connections to McMinnville?"

"Not that I know of," she said. "You, Nick?"

He shook his head. "I've never seen it mentioned in relation to him, but I can run yet another algorithm to search for McMinnville in the data I have stored on him."

Colin looked at the sheriff. "Will you have Sierra process the vehicle?"

"I asked her about it," Abby said. "But she's still working the arson site, so it's on a flatbed on its way to their lab, where it can be dismantled by her staff in their garage."

"Doesn't anyone else find it odd that he would abandon such an expensive vehicle?" Brooklyn asked.

"Not if he thought it could lead to him." Dev sat and

leaned his chair back on the rear legs. "A vehicle like that would draw attention for sure, and he can't afford attention right now."

"But it's been there for a while," Abby said. "Doesn't make sense unless he was planning this murder for some time."

"Someone else could've done it," Brooklyn suggested without really thinking it through. "Like they borrowed the Hummer and didn't bring it back. Or it was stolen."

"No." Nick shook his head. "Not buying the borrowed part. Kane's not one to share his toys. The odds of him letting anyone drive a vehicle that set him back a hundred grand are pretty low."

"I don't care who drove it," Abby said. "It needs to be processed for a lead that we desperately need."

She was right. Of course she was. And everyone knew it. They did need a lead, because right now they had nothing to go on, and "nothing" wouldn't bring Kane to justice and give Brooklyn back her life.

# 13

The smell hit Colin before they reached the ruins. The air was saturated with a burned odor that seeped into their SUV, but not a pleasant campfire, fireplace, or woodstove aroma people, including Colin, loved to smell. Mingled with the burned wood were furnishings and other materials releasing unpleasant odors.

And coming along with the smell was Colin's unease in bringing Brooklyn here. The guys were likely right. Tarver wouldn't come anywhere near this place, and she would be fine, but there was no guarantee. Something Colin needed. Craved as much as air.

He'd never worried this much before. But then, working in cybercrimes, he didn't often see people in immediate danger. Still, it was more than that. She got to him in a way that he both liked and hated. Right now he hated it as it left him vulnerable and filled with concern.

Dev turned into the driveway and lowered his window to show his ID to the deputy securing the property.

*Good. Good.* A law enforcement presence would help.

"Glad to see Sheriff Day has the resources to be able to

secure this place," Colin said to Brooklyn from across the backseat.

She swiveled to face him. "Helps you know Kane didn't get back onto the property."

"At least not from this direction," he said. "But having a police presence lowers the odds of him trying it from any direction."

As did having Micha with them. Colin had convinced everyone to wait for him to finish his class so he could ride shotgun, literally. Dev loved guns and was an expert shot, but Micha outgunned him. As the team's weapons expert and best marksman, Micha had brought his favorite rifle and would take a stand in a nearby tree to be able to continuously search the area and the tree canopy for a sniper.

"Are you usually this cautious?" she asked.

He shrugged. He couldn't admit he had feelings for her when he'd just met her.

"Is there some reason you're more worried about me?"

Ah, right to the point, as he was learning she preferred. He liked that among so many other things he'd observed about her. "I feel a responsibility for you."

"Because I work for you?" she added.

"Yeah, that, and—"

"We're good to go," Dev said, saving Colin before he confessed his feelings for her.

The car pulled forward, and he glanced back to be sure that Ryan was jumping out of the other vehicle to take watch at the mouth of the driveway. He was, just like they'd planned. One thing about this team. They might disagree and even argue at times, but when it came time to implement a plan, they were like the proverbial well-oiled machine. No one strayed from their assignment unless a life was on the line.

The vehicle bumped over ruts, and Dev parked behind

the van, this one belonging to the Veritas team. Chelsea Vale, one of the Veritas crime-scene photographers, had driven through the night to bring additional equipment for Kelsey and Sierra this morning and to assist with photographing the crime scene.

She stood near the van, talking to two other guys in white suits. Techs who most likely came with her. She wore her hair in braids. That, along with freckles covering her face, left her with a girl-next-door look, not a forensic photographer, but her expression was all business.

Dev killed the engine and leaned over the seat to look at Brooklyn. "You stay put while everyone gets into position."

She gave him a sweet smile. "I can do that."

"I'll let you know when I've located a good stand." Dressed in camouflage, Micha slid out and disappeared into the wooded area aligning the drive.

"Let me tell Sierra and Kelsey what's going on and post the other guys. I'll be right back." Dev hopped out and talked to Reid and Nick, who'd parked behind them.

They marched across the lot and took stances near the house that looked even less like a house in the daylight. A few structural timbers remained standing, along with a small section of the roof. Colin would make sure that area was off limits to Brooklyn. All of the team really. Too dangerous. But he would wait to warn her until they were in the house where she could get a better picture of the destruction and realize his warning was valid.

"Not much left," she said, wringing her hands together.

Was she having second thoughts? Could he persuade her to leave? "You still want to go inside?"

"Want to, no. Will, yes." She firmed her shoulders.

"I doubt there will be anything the Veritas staff misses," he said, still trying to give her a reason not to stay.

"You could be right." She bit her lower lip. "But at least I can sleep better tonight knowing I tried to help."

*Sure, but you might not sleep when nightmares of a burn victim permeate your dreams.* He didn't say that of course. He didn't have the heart to. And for all he knew, Kelsey had removed the remains, and Brooklyn could be spared that sight.

Dev started back in their direction.

"Got a perfect stand, and you're good to go." Micha's deep voice came over the comms unit.

Dev opened Brooklyn's door. "We're good to go."

She slid toward the door.

Colin grabbed her hand. "Hold up until I get out. Remember. You stay between Dev and me the entire time."

"Right." She smiled at him.

A sweet, apologetic smile that melted any worry he had for her. Albeit for only a moment. A brief flash of a time while he imagined life with her when she wasn't under siege by some madman.

He pushed out of the SUV and made his way to her side, taking in every bit of the area around him. The two forensic nerds who'd been with Chelsea scurried like little bugs in different directions, large plastic cases in their hands. One headed for Sierra, who was kneeling on the left side of the building, the other to Kelsey, who knelt by the body.

Neither woman looked up. Not for the men or for the arrival of the vehicle. Clearly they were in the zone, and Colin hated to disturb them, but he needed an update to formulate a plan.

"Straight to the house," he said to Brooklyn, though he was sad to see that the remains were still on scene for her view.

The three of them crossed the area, now soggy and muddy from the water sprayed by firefighters' hoses. Brooklyn's boot caught, and she stumbled. Colin caught her arm and righted her.

She looked up at him. "Thanks for saving me from a mud bath. I've heard they can be good for the skin, but I don't have time today to think about my complexion."

She laughed, but as they stepped into the ruins and picked their way to Kelsey, her good humor evaporated.

"Oh. Oh. Oh, my. That's horrific." Her face paled, and she looked away from the victim to gulp in air.

Kelsey stood, a spray bottle in hand. "It is indeed horrific."

Colin continued to hope smoke inhalation had gotten this guy first, but the trail of gasoline straight to his body probably said otherwise. Colin studied the victim. There didn't seem to be any change or attempt to remove the remains.

He introduced Brooklyn to Kelsey.

"Nice to meet you," Brooklyn said but kept her focus in the distance.

"I'm sorry it's under such difficult circumstances," Kelsey said.

"How's your progress coming?" he asked Kelsey to move them along, yet try not to come across as judgmental.

"I get it, it doesn't look like I've done a thing, does it?" She wrinkled her nose. "But I assure you I've been busy. We've completed the photos, and I'm in the process of stabilizing the remains before moving and transporting them."

"Stabilizing?" Brooklyn asked, but looked at Kelsey instead of the victim.

She shifted the plastic bottle to her other hand. "As I mentioned, the person's fingerprints and DNA are often destroyed in high-temperature fires, which we have here. They're the most resilient part of the body. However, with victims this severely burned, the dental remains are the fastest and most reliable way to gain ID."

"I hear a *but* coming," Dev said.

"You're right." She compressed her lips into a flat line. "But incinerated dental remains can be fragile, falling apart in transport and leading to errors in ID. So if we can stabilize them before transport we have a better chance of being accurate. We have a new method to accomplish that. Special spray glue." She held up the spray bottle. "I'm setting a virtual cast over the victim's jaw, and we'll have better odds of finding his ID."

"Seems like you really are on your game," Brooklyn said.

"They're the best at what they do," Dev said. "And that includes using new and cutting-edge procedures. Super-human forensic staff."

"I assure you we're very human." Kelsey waved a hand. "We do our best and are fortunate that researchers like to partner with us to test new products and procedures."

"What about DNA?" Colin asked. "Do you still think that's a viable option?"

Kelsey frowned. "I don't know yet. I mentioned the heat factor, where there's an inverse correlation. The higher the burn temperature, the less DNA is maintained." She stared at the remains. "Emory's test group used two different techniques to obtain DNA on burn victims. Both worked well, one better in fires that burned with higher temperatures like we have here."

"But it's different than the basic DNA tests performed for crimes?" Dev asked.

Kelsey nodded. "This technique allows for the amplification of shorter DNA fragments. I know that means nothing to you, but it's useful in those hotter fires. So Emory has several methods she can use, and our chances of a DNA identity are better than if we hadn't been called in."

"I'm thankful you came," Brooklyn said. "I will forever be in your debt."

"Glad to do it." Kelsey gave a soft smile that she seemed to have at the ready at all times, even at a gruesome scene like the one surrounding them. "We would love it if you found a way to pay it forward but don't require it."

"I will." Brooklyn's firm tone said she fully intended to do so. "You can count on it."

Kelsey tipped her head at the body. "That's all I have for now, and I need to get back to it, but you're welcome to check in with Sierra."

"We will," Colin said. "Thanks for your help."

He escorted Brooklyn across the house, picking their way through rubble and debris. Chelsea had joined Sierra and was snapping photos of something by a marker.

Colin wanted to ask about the item right off the bat, but he didn't want to be rude, so he introduced Brooklyn.

They exchanged greetings, and Sierra introduced them to Chelsea, who cast a quick smile then went back to work.

"What have you found that Chelsea can't seem to look away from?" Brooklyn asked.

"Sorry, we all get like that on the job at times." Sierra cast an apologetic look at Brooklyn. "Nothing particularly unusual, but could be crucial to the investigation."

"Okay, now I wouldn't be able to look away either." Brooklyn's coloring started to return. "But your marker is hiding the item."

"Sorry," Sierra said. "It's a shell casing. Looks like a 9mm, but that's just a guess. Grady, our weapon's expert, will have to confirm. Regardless, it could be proof that a bullet had been discharged here. Or not. Just a casing dropped. Could've been left as a way to lead us off track. We won't know unless we recover a slug."

"Mind if we take a closer look at it?" Dev asked. "We all have weapons chambered for 9mms."

Chelsea let her camera hang from the strap around her neck, featuring the design of bright yellow crime scene tape. "I'm done with the photos."

Sierra bent to pick up the bullet casing and displayed it on her gloved palm. The brass had discolored but was intact. "Thankfully, this wasn't in the path of the accelerant or the extreme heat could've melted the brass."

"Looks like the casing for my Glock." Brooklyn tapped the gun she wore under an overshirt.

Sierra looked at her. "Ah, so you're a gun owner like most of us here. I'm not surprised, with this guy after you. It does appear to be a 9mm casing, the same caliber as your Glock is chambered for, so makes sense that you think it could be for your gun. Of course, that's just a guess based on years of recovering bullets, and like I said, Grady will have to evaluate it to be sure."

"Looks like a nine to me too," Dev said. "Good find. Have you located anything else of interest?"

"I told you about the Sig with silencer I located, which is chambered for a 9mm, so that could further suggest a bullet was discharged here."

"Indeed," Dev said. "Maybe our victim didn't die from the fire after all."

"If not, hopefully, Kelsey will be able to prove that," Sierra said. "In other evidence, I've recovered the main doorknob and will process it back at the lab to see if it holds any viable fingerprints."

"You can find prints even after the fire?" Brooklyn asked.

"Maybe. If I can clean it satisfactorily. The soot's minimal, so I don't think it'll be a problem. And we've gotten better results using a newer technique called vacuum metal deposition."

"Never heard of that," Colin said.

Sierra got out a plastic bag and dropped the casing inside. "The process involves the thermal evaporation of metals inside a special chamber. The controlled high-vacuum conditions cause the metals—mostly gold, silver, and zinc—to form thin films, developing any fingerprints present and making them visible."

Colin was impressed with her knowledge, even if he didn't really understand the method. "And you can use this process on burned items like the doorknob or casing?"

Sierra nodded. "I have to safely remove the soot first. It doesn't always work, but those cases are rare."

"How long before we'll get fingerprint results?" Brooklyn asked.

Sierra tilted her head. "It'll be awhile. I can't do it in the field. I have to use a custom-built chamber in my lab. I'll have to finish up here first, but once I return to the lab, it should move along fast. Will take longer if the cleaning process is more difficult."

"Can't someone else at your lab run the test?" Brooklyn asked, sounding impatient for results.

"Sorry, no." Sierra frowned. "Just me."

"And I don't suppose you want to leave here right now," Dev said.

"I wouldn't mind leaving a crime scene." Sierra gave a wistful look. "But never before the scene is thoroughly processed."

"Which will be when?" Brooklyn asked.

"Now that we have help"—Sierra nodded at her photographer—"I'd say it cuts our time down to a day or two."

"Man." Brooklyn bit her lip. "That long? Wait...sorry. I didn't mean to sound like I was complaining. Just coming to realize that this isn't a speedy process."

"It's an exacting science that will take as long as it takes."

Sierra locked gazes with Brooklyn. "Unless, of course, you're clairvoyant and can direct us to evidence."

Brooklyn laughed but looked around the ruins as if she thought she might be able to help. "Kane loved to hide things in his bedroom. Under the floorboards. Do we have any idea which room was his?"

Sierra shook her head. "Guessing by size, I'd say the large corner room in the back."

Colin studied the area where the celling remained hanging precariously over the bedroom. "I'm assuming with the structure partially standing, you've stayed away from there."

Sierra nodded. "Too dangerous. We're waiting for the fire department to come back and safely bring it down for us."

"But that'll just set things back further." Brooklyn looked between all of them, her frustrations so evident in her downturned mouth that she looked like a pouting little girl.

If the situation weren't so serious, Colin would chuckle. But it *was* serious, made more so by the status of the structure. "We'll just have to—"

"Sorry." Brooklyn flashed him an apologetic look and bolted for the corner.

"Stop!" Colin called out. Why he didn't know? She wouldn't listen. He raced after her, careful not to catch his foot in a hole.

She moved at a rapid pace, continuing ahead of him and reaching a section where a closet had likely stood. By the time he reached her, she'd dropped to her knees. She clawed at the floorboards and one lifted in her hands. Then a second one came up. A third one.

"See." She glanced up, a triumphant look on her face. "I told you he hid things under the floor."

She had indeed. "But is there anything in there?"

She reached into the crawl space, but the ceiling groaned and shifted.

The roof was coming down. Now! On top of them. Too late to move out of the area. He had no choice.

He dove for the floor, circled Brooklyn's waist with his arm, and took her down to the charred floor. He rolled on top of her and covered her as best he could. He spotted something black in the space she'd revealed.

Had she been right? Tarver had hidden something?

Didn't matter at the moment. Lumber came crashing down on his back.

Now his focus had to be on staying alive.

# 14

The lumber fell. Crashing over them. Around them. Like giant pixie sticks. The concussive force as it hit Colin's body pummeling into Brooklyn.

What had she done? Let her impulsive thoughts get to her, racing into an area that was off limits. Now she'd put Colin in danger. Maybe put his life on the line as he took the brunt of the damage.

Sooty dust rose up. She tried to cough. Couldn't get a breath with Colin's heavy weight pressing down on her. The wood continued to fall but slower. Nearer to the exterior wall.

Colin lifted up on his elbows and looked her in the eyes.

*Thank you, God that he can move!*

"Are you okay?" His voice was husky, and he studied her face, concern etched in his eyes.

"Me?" She got out between coughing fits. "I should be asking you that. You protected me and took the hit."

He cleared his throat. "I'm good."

"You were hit hard. We need to take you to the ER to be checked out."

"Just a few bruises. I'll be okay." He brushed her face with his thumb. "Soot."

"I'm sorry, Colin. I didn't listen to you, and look what happened. You could've been killed or seriously injured protecting me. You shouldn't have done that. I put myself in danger and didn't deserve your rescue."

"When I saw the ceiling coming down..." His voice broke, and he cupped the side of her face. "I don't know why, but you get to me in a way I've never felt and can't explain."

Her heart lurched. "Me too. You, I mean. You get to me too."

Footsteps pounded their direction and stopped next to them. Boards were lifted and tossed to the side, freeing up Colin's back.

"You guys okay?" Dev asked.

"I'm fine, thanks to Colin," she said. "But he took the brunt of the fall and needs to be checked out."

"I'm good," Colin said. "Honestly, if I wasn't fine, I'd say so and make an ER trip." He pushed off her, but he seemed to do so reluctantly.

She got it. She immediately felt the loss. Felt alone. Wished everyone else would go away, and he would return to her.

Seriously, what had become of her? Possessed her? A burned body lay half a building away. A lead that could find Kane was mere inches away in the crawl space, and she was thinking about romance. About her feelings for this fine man.

He offered his hand to her, but she shook her head and got to her knees to face the opening.

"Stop!" Sierra called out.

Brooklyn swiveled to look at her where she stood next to Dev.

"I need to retrieve any evidence you found."

"But I..." She wanted to be the one to pull out the box, but knew she had to step back. "It's a black metal box."

"All of you back away so I can get a photo of the location and map it on my diagram." She held a bright yellow plastic marker in one hand and her camera settled around her neck.

Colin offered his hand again and this time Brooklyn accepted it. Big. Strong. Chafed. He clutched hers and tugged her to her feet. Surprisingly, he didn't let go, but helped her move out of the timbers.

"Ever see Tarver with a box like that?" Colin asked.

She nodded. "It's fireproof, and he kept backup drives and flash drives with important information in it."

"I don't suppose he was kind enough to leave any of that in the box for us," Colin said.

"You could be right," Brooklyn said. "Just because the box is here doesn't mean he didn't empty it."

"He might not have had time to get to it if he took off in a hurry," Dev said.

"What might make him run like that?" Colin asked.

"The dead guy," Dev said. "Say we're right about wildlife trafficking, and this guy is part of an organized crime group that Tarver made mad. He ran because there was a second guy after him, and Tarver figured he could come back for the box later."

"Not sure I buy that," Colin said. "He had to know there was a chance law enforcement would find it before he got back."

"Which means it had to be a life or death matter when he took off," Brooklyn said. "No way he would leave it behind for any other reason."

"But that doesn't make sense," Colin said. "Not if he had

a big cat here. He would have to load it up and that would take longer than getting the box."

"He could've already had the trailer hitched," Dev said. "And then the second guy showed up."

"Yeah, could be," she said. "But trust me. For him to leave this, if it does contain his data, he would've had to think his life was on the line and that he could somehow come back for it."

"Which means we need to get you out of here before he does." Colin cupped her elbow. "Let's go."

She stared at the opening. "But the box."

"Sierra can open it and tell us what it contains."

"I can, but not here," Sierra said. "It's locked. No worries, though, I'm good at picking locks. It's just going to take some time to do it. I'll first want to swab for DNA and then print the box so any residual prints aren't smudged in the process."

"So there's no reason for us to hang around here." Colin gave Brooklyn a pointed look.

"Not unless Brooklyn has another idea of where Tarver might've hidden evidence," Sierra said.

"I don't," she admitted even though she wanted to remain on scene to see what this super team recovered.

"Probably a good thing as I don't think my back could take it." Colin laughed.

She wrinkled her nose at him, then looked at Sierra. "Could you call us when you're ready to open it? So we can be there when you do."

"I hadn't planned to process it until I got back to the lab. It's a sterile environment with better lighting and equipment, and I don't want to miss anything."

"Oh, okay." Brooklyn's disappointment knew no bounds, and she was unable to hide it from her expression.

Sierra took a step closer. "You're welcome to join me in the lab when I do open it."

She spun to look at Colin. "Can we go there?"

"Maybe. If at the time we think it's a safe thing to do. Then I don't see why not."

"Thank you. Thank you. Thank you." She flung her arms around his neck and hugged him hard. She hadn't considered her actions, especially in light of his confession earlier that she meant something to him, but now she did and clung longer than needed. He didn't push her away, but suddenly cleared his throat.

She let go, but had to admit to herself that it was with great reluctance.

"We should go now." He stepped back and pointed at the narrow area ahead of him.

She caught sight of the knowing look Dev cast at his brother, but ignored it for now to step gingerly through the newly piled debris and not make a further disturbance. Thankfully, Sierra hadn't read her the riot act for messing up her crime scene. True, firefighters would've brought the ceiling down later, but maybe they had a way of doing so that wouldn't have created such a mess. They would surely have done it without injuring anyone.

They reached the hallway, or what once was a hallway, then stepped into the foyer area. The smell of gasoline hit her, and she stopped to look at Sierra.

"Did you actually recover gasoline?" she called out. "Know that it was used as the accelerant or is it still iffy?"

Sierra stepped down to them. "Nothing is concrete."

"But we can all smell it," Brooklyn said.

Sierra nodded. "And the downward burning is producing a telltale signature of gasoline, too, but lab tests are needed to confirm. I took samples of the burned floor area *and* the undamaged flooring for comparison. Those plus additional material that appears to have absorbed gasoline at the edge of the burn pattern. All will be used in analysis back at my lab. I'll treat the sample with a strong acid that destroys everything except the heavier metals I would expect to find in gasoline."

"So these samples have to go back to the lab, too, then," Brooklyn stated as she hoped she'd misunderstood, and Sierra could test it here.

"Yes, I need to use the equipment like my gas chromatograph to extract the results," she said. "But my assistants and lab techs can process these samples. I'm kind of a control freak and would like to do them myself, but since you all want information fast, I'll let them handle the floor samples while I process prints."

"Thank you," Brooklyn said. "I really will get out of your hair now."

"No worries. I like it when people are interested." Sierra's expression softened.

Brooklyn left Sierra and stepped into the foyer area. She kept her gaze pinned away from the burned body, and the moment she hit the ground, Dev and Colin flanked her to the SUV like a protective sandwich.

She liked Colin's protection but didn't like the feeling of being smothered by it, but it could have saved her life a moment ago. And, after seeing what happened to the man in the house, she finally had to accept the fact that Kane might've ended someone's life and probably had no qualms about murdering her too.

In his cabin, Colin rested on the arm of an overstuffed leather chair as Barbie got up from the sofa, leaving his mother and Brooklyn behind. Nick had remained at the crime scene with his partners to help them out so they could get back to Portland faster, but he would still monitor the internet and dark web.

Barbie's long, granny-type dress—much like she must've worn in the hippie days of the sixties—whooshed as she passed Colin to head for the front door. She left a lingering scent of honey and vanilla. He often imagined the crazy life she'd lived in a commune back in the day, but she never shared much about those times, and he would never pry.

He glanced at his mom, whose dark circles under her eyes spoke to her exhaustion, then looked at Barbie. "Did Mom behave? Get some rest?"

"Hey," his mother protested. "I'm not a kid who needs babysitting and reports at the end of shift."

Barbie tsked and flipped her long braid over her shoulder. "In either event, I wouldn't tell, so you're safe with me, Sandy."

"Thank goodness," his mother said. "Someone he can't pressure into reporting in like he and his brother do with each other."

Heat of a blush rose up Colin's neck. "I only mean to be helpful."

"I know, son, but there's helpful and then there's *helpful*, in the Gladys Miller kind of way." His mother chuckled over her reference to the town's local gossip and all around busybody. "And you're approaching full-on Gladys mode."

"I concur, and your mom is too sweet to really call you out," Barbie said, "I would've read my boys the riot act if they tried to baby me like you've been doing."

"And they would've given it right back to you," Colin said.

"No doubt." Barbie chuckled. "But it wouldn't stop me from trying. If I didn't, I wouldn't have survived raising three boys. I gave birth to them, and I'm still the boss. End of story."

His mom laughed, and he enjoyed the lighthearted sound stretching to the ceiling. She might still be in a major flare-up, but the good humor she somehow located within her no matter how badly she felt was a bonus. She'd always been that way. Able to find the positive and joy even when she was hurting. She relied on her faith. Dug deep when the days were especially difficult and told herself that there were others suffering far more than she was, and she lived a blessed life. Reminded herself that she had her family surrounding her. Not only her related family, but her church family too. Both she believed to be blessings far outweighing her struggles.

Heading to the door to let Barbie out, Colin wished he could be as optimistic as his mom was. She set the perfect example, but he often fell short. Maybe it was different to be the one suffering than to be the one watching someone you love suffering. Or maybe he was using that as an excuse, and he could do better. Much better.

"Thank you, Barbie," he said. "We very much appreciate your help."

"Anytime." She looked over Colin's shoulder. "Nice to meet you, Brooklyn. Good luck in keeping this guy in line. His strong-willed nature must be tough in a relationship."

"Oh, I...I can't..." Brooklyn shrugged. "It's not like that. We aren't..."

"It's all business between us," Colin said before Barbie got the wrong impression. "Nothing more."

"Um-hm. Right. Funny business." Barbie giggled like a little girl and swept out the door.

Colin watched until she got into her small pickup truck and drove off. He couldn't even imagine what it must've been like to grow up with such an eccentric mother. His mom might've been different due to her illness, but she'd fit the normal school-volunteering, cookie-baking mother mode. Now here they were, mother and son, trying to navigate life as it had been thrown at them.

He glanced around for any sign of Kane. He searched the heavy tree line. The lake shore. Shrubs lining the driveway. The only movement were tree limbs and grasses gently swaying in the wind. He closed and secured the door, checking the lock twice.

He felt Brooklyn's gaze on him as he returned but didn't look at her to see if she was as uneasy with Barbie's suggestion as he was. He sat in the sagging leather side chair and shifted to get comfortable over the almost protruding springs. The brothers really should up their furniture game here, but Colin wouldn't complain about free housing. In fact, he would replace as much of the worn items as he could as a thank you to the guys.

His mother shifted to face Brooklyn, wincing as she moved. "So how did your visit to this awful man's house go?"

"It was horrible seeing the victim," she said, then shared details of their visit but nothing about the body. "The box will be brought back to the Veritas Center, and I hope we can be there when it's opened."

"If it's safe to go," Colin warned.

She flashed a hopeful gaze up to him. "Do you think it will be?"

"Yes, unless Tarver shows himself before then."

"Of course you'll go, then," his mother said. "It's too important to miss in case this Sierra person has questions."

"It will likely be an overnight trip." Colin met his mother's gaze. "I can't leave you alone, and I won't let Brooklyn go without me."

"I wouldn't expect any less of you, son." His mother smiled. "Barbie can probably come stay with me."

Colin slid to the edge of his chair and focused on his mom. "We won't go if she can't."

"I won't be the one to stop Brooklyn from seeing this most important evidence." She crossed her arms, and he knew he was in for a battle of the wills. "If Barbie can't come, then I can find someone else. Maybe Mia or Megan are free."

"They have children to care for," Colin said.

"And they also have capable husbands. I'm sure Reid or Ryan could step up, or if not, then Russ's Sydney might be able to do it. I'm sure one of them can. But let me start with asking Barbie." She got up slowly, wincing as the pain settled into her joints, and grabbed her cane. "I'll call her from my room so the two of you can keep on working on the investigation or whatever you might want to do."

She winked and started toward her room, the clip-clop of the cane echoing in the house.

"That was about as subtle as a sonic boom," Colin said.

Brooklyn looked down at her hands and started picking at a hangnail. "Guess we're not doing a very good job of hiding our feelings."

"Guess not." He didn't want to get into this discussion now. "I want to thank you for how well you've bonded with my mom."

"It's not hard to do. She's one of the sweetest humans I've ever met."

"Still, you somehow get her to do things that Dev and I only get a flash of irritation over."

"Not sure what I'm doing differently, but I always wanted to be a nurse, so maybe that's coming out in me."

"A nurse?" He tried not to gape at the information. "That's a far cry from being a hacker. How'd you end up in computers instead?"

"Long story."

"We have time."

"Okay, but don't say I didn't warn you." She grinned. "I had leukemia when I was a kid. Meant I spent a lot of time in the hospital and got to know the nurses pretty well. The doctors' expertise was needed, but the nurses cared for me day in and day out. I wanted to be just like them and give back. So when I went to college I declared nursing as my major."

"What changed that?"

She scowled. "I got into the nitty-gritty of the job and discovered that the sight of blood takes me out. Bam. I see it and hit the floor. Just like that. Not my own, but other people's. Doesn't make for a very good nurse."

"I would guess not. That had to be disappointing."

"It was. Very."

"How did you move on to computers?"

"The long part of the story." She took a deep breath. "I had plenty of time sitting around in the hospitals and spent a lot of it on a laptop my mom got me for playing games. After a while, that didn't seem to keep my interest, so I decided to find out how a computer worked, and I took one apart." She gave a wry smile. "I was home by then, and unfortunately, it was my dad's computer. That didn't go over so well, but I got it back together and it worked fine. So that led to me buying my own parts and building my own computer. And then I decided I needed to know how my games worked, so I learned some coding. I even designed a few video games and joined the computer club at school."

Sounded like a full-fledged nerd to him. "But you didn't want to do computers for a living?"

"Nope. The desire to be like the nurses that were taking care of me was too strong for that. I honestly thought it was my calling. But when I found out I couldn't do it, I looked for a way to help others using computers. Not in traditional ways, like programming or repair. That led me to white-hat hacking. I see it as a way to prevent problems and even stop ones that could potentially be very harmful to people."

"You do provide a valuable service, that's for sure," he said. "And your ability to hack into systems helps put security measures in place so real hackers can't break in. Which is becoming all too common these days."

"People like Kane have made millions on the backs of other people." She gritted her teeth. "Sure, I really want him stopped so that I can go about my life. More, I want him stopped so he quits taking advantage of innocent people. Often times elderly people who are less computer savvy."

"You have a very altruistic way of looking at life, and I find that admirable." Attractive even, but he wouldn't say that and take them down the wrong path.

"Just trying to do my part." She nibbled on her lip. "Do you really think it will be safe to go to the Veritas Center?"

"The safest thing to do would be to keep you under wraps here behind fortified fences. But I have to respect the fact that I can't wrap you in bubble wrap when you could be a valuable part of this investigation."

He made eye contact and locked on, feeling as if he were locking in a mortar round. "Just know, if we leave to go there, I need to be certain you'll follow my every direction every step of the way. No questioning. No fighting. No arguing. Just do as I say. Because, though I applaud your altruistic way at looking at making Tarver pay, your life means more to me than finding a hacker and bringing him to justice. Much more."

# 15

Brooklyn stared out the rear window of Colin's SUV at they pulled into the Veritas Center parking lot. Colin sat in the back with her, Dev behind the wheel, and Reid rode shotgun. She had no idea what to expect, but she never thought the building would be beautiful and look nothing like a laboratory. Two glass towers rose into the sky and were glowing under spotlights shining down on them. A building connected them on the ground level, and a skybridge at the top level, the glass walls illuminated from inside.

"Doesn't look anything like a lab, does it?" She looked across the seat at Colin.

"I thought the same thing when I first came here." Dev glanced back in the mirror.

"Me too," Colin said.

"Same," Reid said. "But then I was told the place was built by Maya's grandfather for mixed use, and he left it to her when he passed away. She's the toxicology expert here. So she took on several partners, built out the east tower as labs that were supposed to be offices, and the right tower was and is condos where some of the partners still live."

"Talk about living close to work." She laughed and

reveled in the good feeling when life had been so tense for so very long.

She was glad Colin was able to bring her here. She felt happier each time they left the cabin, and she was actively involved in doing something to find Kane. She thought Colin understood that. When a problem presented itself he didn't seem to be a do-nothing kind of guy.

"Pull into the parking garage, Dev," Colin instructed.

He got a roll of the eyes from his brother in return. Not surprising. They'd drilled this trip several times today before leaving, and Dev had to know his role. So, protocol would say that he would follow their security plan without deviating unless a problem presented itself, and Colin didn't need to give him directions at all. But clearly he felt the need to say it, so he did. That was, between his big visual sweeps of the property and his hand drifting to the butt of his gun.

"I'll need the passcode to get in," Dev said.

Colin rattled off the number he got from Blake Jenkins, the former sheriff who was married to Emory, the DNA expert. Blake took charge of all criminal investigations and would be waiting at the door to let them in.

Dev ramped up the lot until they reached the top floor and parked near the entrance. The door opened, and a dark-haired man, who obviously worked out and carried himself with authority, stepped out to hold the door open.

"That's Blake." Colin looked at her. "Dev and Reid will go first just as we planned, then you and me. Got it?"

She, too, wanted to roll her eyes, but Colin was just being extra careful for her safety, so she nodded instead.

She followed directions and quickly got inside the building, where Blake handed out security passes for each person. "You'll need to wear these badges whenever you're out of your condos and will have to be escorted by a staff member at all times too."

"You take your security seriously," Brooklyn said, very impressed.

Blake's sharp nod fit his demeanor. "We're aware of law enforcement's skepticism in our ability to secure our evidence. Of course, we have better security measures than they often do, and we aim to take it even one step higher."

"Which is one of the reasons your lab is world-renowned," Colin said.

Blake flashed a short smile. "I wish I could take credit for that, but all these procedures were in place before I came to work here. I just make sure to abide by them and that our visitors do too."

"Don't sell yourself short," Colin said. "You have a strong reputation both in law enforcement and in your work here."

He waved a hand. "If you want to step out to get your luggage, I'll get you settled into your condos for the night."

Reid circled an arm around Dev's shoulders. "C'mon. We can handle all of it."

Blake had to enter a code for the door to open. Even from the inside. Even more impressive to her.

They exited, whisking quickly through the door, but Brooklyn's mind wasn't on them. It was on the living arrangements. Blake said *condos*, which meant they would be staying in more than one. Would she be alone or would Colin be with her? Or Dev? Reid?

Could she trust herself to be alone with Colin and not let their conversation travel to the personal realm? She could stay in her room, she supposed.

"You mentioned condos as in plural," Colin said. "Any way we can all bunk in one?"

Was he thinking the same thing?

Blake locked gazes with him. "You worried about security for Brooklyn and want everyone in one place for added measure?"

Colin didn't respond right away but then nodded. "It would be safer."

"All our condos have only two bedrooms so it would be more comfortable to have two units. Plus, this place is locked down tight with security cameras and alarms. We also have an armed guard on duty all night." Blake rested against the wall. "Pete's on duty tonight. He's a former law enforcement officer and quite capable. I assure you that Brooklyn will be safe here."

"We'll go ahead and take one unit anyway." Colin didn't consult Brooklyn and kept his focus on Blake as if he didn't care what she thought. "Brooklyn can have one of the bedrooms. I'll be bunking on the couch, giving Dev and Reid the other one to share."

Blake eyed Colin. "I don't think that's really necessary."

Colin firmed his stance, looking on the verge of turning combative if needed. "I do."

Blake let out a breath. "Then one condo it is."

Colin relaxed his shoulders. "I know it seems like overkill, but put yourself in my shoes. You'd do the same thing."

"You're probably right." Blake gave a wry smile.

Reid and Dev returned carrying suitcases and duffle bags. Blake tapped a code in the keypad to open the door, and the guys filed in.

Reid held up a plastic bag. "Can I give these gas samples to you so the lab can start work on them as soon as possible?"

"I'll drop them off at Sierra's lab as soon as I get you settled in the condo." Blake took the bag.

Colin took his bag from Dev to shoulder it and her overnight suitcase, which he set down to pull up the handle.

"Follow me," Blake said. "We'll cross over the skybridge to the condo tower."

Reid shifted his bag and stepped ahead. "I heard the Veritas partners lived in the condos."

"Most of us did at one time," Blake said. "Until we got married and started families, then needed more room. I like having a house for our family, but I have to say I miss the convenience of being so close for when nighttime duties call."

"Sorry about keeping you here so late," Brooklyn said as she stepped onto the glass-enclosed bridge.

"No worries. That's my job." He cast her a smile over his shoulder and stopped. "You'll want to take a look at the view. On clear nights like tonight, the stars are spectacular."

Blake went to a switch at the end of the bridge and dimmed the lights.

She turned to look outside, then bent back to look at the glass roof overhead. Stars glittered above, filling the dark sky and setting a peaceful tone and a very romantic view. One she could see sharing with Colin later. Alone. But not only was that a bad idea, it wasn't possible as they would need someone to accompany them. It wouldn't be very romantic with a chaperone.

He eased close to her, the wheels of her suitcase swishing over the smooth tile floor. Was he having the same thoughts? Thinking about her as a woman, not someone he had to protect? His breath tickled her neck. She held her breath to wait for him to say something romantic.

"As much as I would like to keep stargazing, this location is within rifle shot," he said. "Should Tarver have taken up weapons, you'd be exposed."

*Right. Way to be romantic, buddy.*

Her good mood evaporated, and she started across the bridge, picking up her pace to move away from him. He caught up, and she felt his penetrating gaze on her face. She wanted to tell him to back off, but he was just doing his job. Problem was, she didn't want to be his job anymore. She wanted him to be here because he wanted to be with her.

*Oh wow, when had that changed?*

She should only be thinking about staying alive. But then, why stay alive only to live as she'd been doing for the past few years? It wasn't even called living. More like existing. Surely not what God wanted for her in life. He wanted the best for His believers, and she hadn't been living her best life. Far from it. But what could she do about it until Kane was found and incarcerated?

Maybe it was time she started taking some risks. Letting Kane find her online so she could open a dialogue with him. Maybe there was something she could do to get him to leave her alone. She'd never asked. Just run and run and run.

She could use the center's Wi-Fi as she knew Nick had set the security at a level that would take superhuman efforts to track transmissions and hack it. She would wait to see if Sierra and Kelsey had located any solid leads first. But if not, she would put herself out there for Kane to discover.

They stopped in front of a condo, and Blake reached for another device by the door, this one a fingerprint reader.

"What are you so deep in thought about?" Colin asked. "Are you worried because I'm taking extra security measures? Because, as Blake said, it's probably overkill."

"I know you'll protect me, and I'm fine," she said. She was far from fine regarding these new feelings for him, but she *was* fine about his security measures.

She entered the condo first, and the others trailed behind her down a short hallway that led to a wide open space. The open kitchen with walnut cabinets faced a great room holding a large beige sectional. A stone fireplace with a big TV mounted above took up a full wall. A plush white rug covered the dark wood floor on that end of the room, and a large modern dining table and chairs sat on the other end.

"Make yourselves at home," Blake said. "Both bedrooms have attached bathrooms and there's a powder room down the hall to the main bedroom." He jerked a thumb over his shoulder at the end of the space holding the dining furniture.

Colin looked at Brooklyn. "You take the main bedroom."

"Okay." She didn't bother to argue as there was no point when she knew he would insist.

He gave a firm nod of acknowledgment and turned to his teammates. "You have the other room."

"Sounds good," Reid said, not seeming in the least bit interested in arguing about the decision to stay in one condo.

"The cabinets and fridge are stocked with food for snacks and breakfast," Blake said. "We'll do lunch as a group tomorrow, but if there's anything special you want, let me know and I'll get it for you."

"I'm sure what you've provided will be great." Brooklyn smiled at Blake. "Thank you for taking such good care of us."

"Glad to do it, but don't tell the other partners that I did so well, or they might assign me all guest duty." He laughed. "I'll be here to get you at eight a.m., and we'll head to the labs."

"Including the firearms lab?" Dev asked.

"Sure, yeah, if Grady asks to see you," Blake said. "But if not, I can do a tour for you if you want one."

"Want one?" Dev's eyes sparkled. "I *need* one."

"So you're a weapons guy." Blake arched a dark eyebrow. "You'll probably want to check out our firing range, too, then. I'm sure there are at least a few unique weapons in Grady's collection that he'll let you shoot."

"Count me in." Dev lifted up on his toes, then back down only to lift up again.

Brooklyn was surprised that he could wait until tomorrow and didn't ask to go to the firing range right now.

"See you tomorrow. Call if you need anything." Still holding the gasoline samples, Blake strode away.

Colin followed, and soon a deadbolt snicked into place.

He returned, going straight to his brother. "Let the firing range dream go now. I'll make sure we don't leave without you getting a crack at it, but I don't want your head in the wrong place tonight."

Dev lowered his heels to the floor. "Do you purposefully look for ways to ruin the fun or does it just come naturally to you? 'Cause let me say, you're a master at it."

Colin frowned.

"Since it looks like you'll be up for a while, does anyone want coffee?" Brooklyn asked to stop them from further brotherly sparring. "I'm sure there will be some in the cupboard, and I can make a pot."

"Sounds good to me," Reid said. "I'll just go drop my bag in our room and give Megan a quick call to let her know I got here fine. Don't want her to worry." he pivoted to leave.

"I'll text Mom," Dev said.

She watched Colin stare after Reid, a longing in his gaze. Was he wishing he had a wife to call? A family? Or was she just wishing that was what he wanted?

His mother seemed to think he wanted kids, but did she know her son's desires? She could very well be pinning her own desires on him.

"Brooklyn," he said. "Is there something wrong?"

"Wrong?"

"You're staring at me."

Facepalm. "Oh, right. Sorry. Did you want coffee?"

"Please."

"Let me drop off my suitcase, and then I'll get it started." She reached for the handle.

"I can take your bag to your room." He slipped his hand under hers, brushing against her.

His touch sent a tingle across her skin. She could hardly think straight. How embarrassing. She was acting like a teenager. She had to stop. Get away from him. Take a beat.

"Oh, okay. Sure. Thanks." She bolted for the kitchen and started ripping through the cabinets until she located a canister of coffee and filters that fit the pricey-looking coffee maker on the counter.

"I need a snack with my coffee." Dev came into the kitchen and jerked open the pantry door, putting the open door between them.

Good. He couldn't see her. She fanned her face and took several deep breaths.

"You okay?" Dev poked his head around the door. "You're not worried about Tarver finding you here, are you? Because even if he did—and he won't—he couldn't get into the building, much less past Colin on the couch."

"I'm fine." She lowered her hand. "Really."

"And then there's Colin." He pursed his lips, then turned to stare into the pantry. "I've never seen him this cautious and worked up. Me thinks it's personal. Like he has a thing for you, but as usual, he's not going to admit it. Not when he's so busy playing the good son."

"I don't understand."

"He thinks because Mom needs us right now that means his life has to end, and he has to focus everything on her care." He pulled out a bag of chocolate chip cookies. "He's always been like that. He attacks everything full-on. No halfway with him."

Guess that explained his intensity and drive to take care of her. Not that he was interested in her.

She inserted the filter and spooned coffee into it in a quantity she thought would work.

"Let me fill that for you." Colin returned and reached around her for the pot.

She almost argued but then just stepped back before they accidentally touched again, and watchful Dev saw her feelings too. She went to sit with Dev at the counter. He'd opened the cookie package and was chowing down on one.

"Mind sharing?" she asked.

He slid the container toward her, taking another one out before releasing it. "Thought these would go good with the coffee. If I don't wolf them all down before it brews."

She laughed. She loved Dev's fun personality. He continued to prove it was a contrast to Colin's serious intensity, but if she had to choose a life mate it would be the serious brother. Why, she didn't know, but she'd always been attracted to the more serious and brooding kind of guy. Like Kane. He fit that description. The crushed idealism Colin seemed to be fighting after his time as an agent drew her even more to him as he seemed to want to buck the system now.

He pressed the start button on the machine and leaned back against the counter. The pot kicked in, the dripping the only sound in the room.

"What's bugging you?" Dev asked his brother.

"Nothing, why?"

"You're kind of in a funk."

"Sorry if I'm not cracking jokes like you." He coated his words liberally with sarcasm. "Just trying to keep my mind on keeping Brooklyn safe."

"You can do both, you know? It's not all or nothing. You

can do your job and have a life too. Take care of Mom and have a life too."

Colin's eyebrow shot up, and he watched Dev. "Says the little brother who had a pass when Dad died."

"Pass?" Dev clapped his hands on the stone countertop. "He was my dad too, and I still miss him every day. No passing on that."

Colin's eyes creased as he ran a hand over his face. "That's not what I mean. As the oldest I had to step up. You got to keep on keeping on. Live your life."

Dev came to his feet and for the first time, Brooklyn saw a deep anguish in the guy. "That's not fair. I stepped up too. At home. With Mom. When you went to college. But you weren't there to see it."

Colin pushed off the counter as the pot beeped its completion behind him. "I came home almost every weekend."

"Yeah, rushing in and acting as if we couldn't survive without you. So we let you. It was easier for everyone just to let you take over."

Colin sucked in a breath. "Sounds like we need to talk about this, but not here. Not now."

"Agreed," Dev said and went to the cupboard to retrieve mugs. He held one out to Brooklyn, who felt like a fifth wheel and wished she could slink away.

Dev looked at her. "Oh, man, if you could see your face. This little argument is nothing for us. If you're going to be around us, you'll have to get used to it. We always kiss and make up in the end." He slugged his brother in the arm.

Colin grabbed him around the shoulder and knuckled his head, but he was grinning now.

She'd always wondered what it would be like to have a sibling, and she was learning quickly that it was a good thing. As good as a significant other? Maybe. At least that was all she could possibly experience, and she knew for sure she wanted to look into experiencing it with the brother who was now grinning at her and sending her heartbeat in a crazy rhythm.

～

The night ticked by like a slow clock struggling to keep time and nagging at Colin. Not that this place had such a clock. Everything was digital, and the equipment state of the art. Still, his brain heard the tick, tick, tick as he sat on the sofa, gun on his knees, foot tapping against the wood floor.

Movement to his right caught his attention, and he spun. Rubbing her neck, Brooklyn came into the room, her eyes tight.

He lurched to his feet and holstered his weapon. "You okay?"

"Headache." She winced. "Came in search of water and some aspirin."

"I saw a first aid kit in the cupboard. Bound to be something in there." He stepped into the kitchen and went straight to the upper cabinet, where he retrieved the plastic box from the top shelf. He located a packet of aspirin, handed it to her, and got a glass to fill with water.

"Thanks." She dumped the pills into her mouth and swallowed, then started rolling her neck.

"I'm pretty good at tension massages. At least my mom says it helps. If that's your problem, that is."

"It is, but I'll be okay once the aspirin kicks in."

"Why wait?" he said, a bit disappointed that she rejected his help again. "Allow me."

"Okay," she said, but with great reluctance.

He moved behind her and warned himself to be gentle

at first then gauge how much pressure to apply. She leaned forward and planted her hands on the island.

She'd clipped her hair up and her bare neck tempted him to plant a kiss there, not his hands.

*Focus.*

He gently began to massage, deepening it.

She groaned.

He paused. "Sorry, did I hurt you?"

"Sort of, but it's that pain that feels good because you know it's doing something to help alleviate your problem."

He continued on, finding the tight muscle and pressing his thumb into it. Her neck continued to scream out for a kiss. Or maybe his hands screamed to turn her to face him and tell her that he'd developed more than just a few feelings for her.

"Thank you," she said while his mind was busy waffling.

She turned, her back against the island, her face not more than two feet from his. A section of hair had escaped the clip, and he tucked it back in. She took in a sharp breath.

He locked gazes with her. "You don't like me touching you, do you?"

"It's just the opposite. I like it, but know it's not a good time for either one of us to get involved."

"Yeah, I have my mom to think about."

"Dev said you'd be thinking something like that."

He took a step back. "You and Dev were talking about me."

"Actually, Dev was telling me about you, and I was listening."

"I can only imagine what he said." He had to fight frowning and letting her know how much this impacted him. "We're kind of opposites, and he wouldn't just be standing here. He'd probably be kissing you right now."

"He has a fun personality, no doubt, but it's you I'm

interested in." She took his hand. "Even if it's not a good idea, could you be more like Dev for just a minute and be kissing me right now?"

Surprised, it took him a moment to respond. Before he could, she'd reached up to touch the side of his face, setting off a sharp laser of emotions, firing off all the nerve endings in his skin.

He reached for her hand to stop her, but she slid it up to his face and behind his head, lowering it as she rose up on tiptoes. He tried to back away, but only in his brain. He wrapped an arm around her slender waist and drew her closer, tight against him, and crushed his lips onto hers, the shock of contact taking his breath.

He could hardly think. But one thought made it through his daze. If kissing her was wrong, he never wanted to be right.

# 16

———

Brooklyn wished breakfast hadn't been so tense. But the kiss lingered in her mind. On her lips. Colin's touch was still a vivid memory in her brain, and she couldn't think of anything else. She should never have been so bold, but she didn't regret finding out if they would be well-matched. They were. For the brief moment he let go and let his emotions take him, she knew what being in a relationship with him would feel like.

She thought maybe the kiss would get these feelings out and she could forget all about any romantic feelings for him. Thought that he was a forbidden guy, so of course she wanted to kiss him all the more. But that wasn't it at all. The opposite had occurred. The kiss cemented in her mind that she wanted that relationship as badly as she wanted Kane brought to justice.

"Brooklyn, did you hear me?" Dev asked from the other side of the island. "Are you ready?"

"Oh, yeah. Ready." She pushed the counter stool back and stood.

Dev shook his head. "I don't know what's going on with

the two of you this morning, but you're both out of it. Something you want to share?"

"Blake is waiting at the door," Colin said. "Let's go."

She jumped up and raced for the door. She was all for moving on as she wouldn't tell Dev about the kiss, and the tension with Colin was too much for her to handle right now. She soon found herself in the elevator with four men discussing the investigation, one guy less familiar than the other three, but she hadn't known any of them for more than a few days. Just a few days. Hard to believe when she had such strong feelings for Colin.

She snuck a look at him, and her heart tripped into gear. There he was. Standing tall. Holding his own in the conversation, his rugged jaw set when he wasn't talking. His dark eyes were rapt with interest as Blake ran down the procedures the Center followed to secure evidence.

She had no interest in evidence protocols unless it involved digital evidence. She could get behind a visit to Nick's lab. She hadn't been able to take a tour because Kane knew of her friendship with Nick, and they never knew if Kane would track her here. But it was a certainty that she wouldn't be leaving this building without seeing it this trip. Plus, she might need to use a computer to tempt Kane to come out into the open.

Blake tapped the button for the lower level. "Kelsey has asked to see you right away, so we'll be starting with her."

"Did she say why?" Colin asked.

He shook his head. "No, but I believe she's discovered something of interest."

The elevator carried them to the basement, everyone falling silent and leaving the tiny space filled with a different kind of tension. Pondering-life-and-death kind. If the others were like Brooklyn, they were trying to figure out what

Kelsey might have discovered in the gruesome recovery of the body.

When the elevator stopped, Blake held up a finger. "Before we exit, just a reminder that you need a staff member with you at all times and you must always wear the security pass. Any questions?"

Brooklyn looked down on the white plastic badge hanging from the lanyard around her neck and shook her head.

"We're all glad to respect your rules," Colin said.

The doors split open to a brightly lit but windowless hallway holding several doors. An unpleasant smell permeated the air. Brooklyn hoped Blake would explain it.

He held the doors so they could exit the car. "The osteology lab occupies this entire floor. Everyone calls it 'The Tomb' for obvious reasons."

*Yeah. All the bones.* Brooklyn shuddered and stepped into the hallway with the others.

Blake let his hand drop, and the doors whooshed closed. "The odor is one of the reasons she has the entire floor when other labs share floors."

"I've been trying to be polite and not point it out," Dev said. "But it's been hard."

"Sorry about that." Blake glanced over his shoulder as he led the way down the hall. "Even though we have an industrial exhaust and clean air system installed, sometimes the odor seeps out when she cleans bones. We don't like to offend our private DNA customers, so we contain the odor down here."

"Cleans the bones?" Brooklyn asked, but the minute the words came out, she really wished she hadn't.

He continued walking. "Before bones can be examined or analyzed, the remains almost always must be macerated or boiled to remove any flesh and connective tissue."

Her stomach roiled, and she regretted asking even more. She had to change the subject before he shared additional details. "Do you know Sheriff Abby Day? That's who we're working with on the investigation."

"I know of her, but haven't worked with her." He stopped outside a door marked Osteology Lab. "She has a solid reputation in the law enforcement community though, and that speaks volumes to her skills and dedication."

"Good to know," Brooklyn said.

Blake pressed his fingers on a keypad on the door, and it popped open to reveal a well-lit room with several stainless steel exam tables. The back wall held a display case filled with bones that were labeled with their names.

A human skull sat on one table, and a full skeleton lay on another of the long, stainless steel tables. Kelsey stood over the skeleton, a long bone in hand.

Was this their victim? Had she already cleaned the bones?

As if she could read Brooklyn's mind, Kelsey held up the bone. "My latest investigation before I got called to your crime scene. I'm trying to determine a cause of death."

She set down the bone and stepped out from behind the table. She wore a frilly patterned dress in a vibrant fuchsia color under a lab coat and stunning black pumps with three-inch heels that Brooklyn would love to own. She seemed so delicate and fragile, and yet she worked in such a harsh field. Maybe she wore the dressy and feminine clothing as a counterbalance. At least Brooklyn could see that happening.

"Sorry about the odor today. We're working on several investigations, and my assistants have kept the wet lab running nonstop." She pointed at a glass-and-metal door, sealed tight.

Brooklyn took a quick look into the room that held similar metal tables, but these were connected to large stainless sinks against a wall. A huge burner and large pots sat on another wall. Tools took up yet another wall.

She looked at Kelsey. "That's where you boil the bones."

She tilted her head. "I'm surprised you know about that."

"Blake told us."

"Thank you for explaining." She gave Blake a smile. "It really is the most obnoxious part of the job. Well, some days maggots and other insects take top billing." She gave a nervous laugh.

Brooklyn couldn't laugh along with her.

"Blake said you wanted to see us," Colin said, thankfully changing the subject Brooklyn wished she hadn't delved into but somehow, like coming upon a car crash, she couldn't figuratively seem to look away.

Kelsey moved over to the skull. "This is the arson victim's skull."

She turned it over and pointed at a hole in the temple. "Do you see the beveling around the hole? A sort of cone-shaped bone erosion?"

"A gunshot wound." Colin blinked at her. "Our guy was shot?"

"He was indeed, and this is the direction of the bullet path through the cranial vault." She took a long metal pointer and stuck it through the entry wound and out a hole on the other side. "This is the exit wound, which you can tell by irregular and external beveling—the bone erosion on the outer part of the bony table."

"Any idea of caliber?" Dev asked.

"At this point I can tell you it was a low-velocity weapon, i.e., a handgun." She set down the skull. "But the good news is we recovered a slug containing tissue so I believe it to be the bullet that ended this man's life. We've taken our DNA samples from the slug, and Sierra has fingerprinted it, so Grady—our weapons expert—is evaluating it now."

"When we're done here, I'll give him a call to see if he has anything to report," Blake said.

"Is this the cause of death, then?" Colin asked.

Kelsey nipped on her lip. "Without any soft tissue or organs intact, I can't conclusively say it is, but few people would've survived such a trauma. Still, it is survivable. At least for a short time. So he could've died from smoke inhalation or the burns or something else that I haven't discovered yet. Sorry. I wish I could be precise, but assigning a cause of death in a trauma like this one will not be straightforward and will take some time."

"At least we know someone attempted to kill the victim by shooting him, even if he didn't succeed," Colin said. "Any leads on the victim's ID?"

"Too early for that as well, but I do have one additional thing that could be helpful in identifying him. He's missing the index finger on his right hand."

"Missing, as in totally gone?" Colin asked.

She nodded. "We searched the scene carefully for any of the bones we might have overlooked, and I'm confident we didn't miss anything. The fire was still too hot for scavengers to arrive before us and carry off a bone without burning their feet, so we know that didn't happen."

"Can you determine a time when the finger was severed?" Dev asked.

"The remaining bone shows no sign of remodeling, so very recent. But the area around the body hadn't been disturbed after the fire, so odds are good he lost this finger before the fire."

"Yeah, that could help," Reid said, finally breaking his

silence. "We'll have Sheriff Day ask local agencies if someone who recently lost a right index finger is missing. We can also plug it into ViCAP."

"ViCAP?" Brooklyn asked.

"The FBI's Violent Crime Apprehension Program," Blake said. "It's a database of unsolved violent crimes entered by law enforcement all across the country in hopes that other agencies will search the database and be able to match their crime to one already registered, and both will be solved."

Not something she'd ever heard of. "Sounds like it might pan out."

"It could indeed." Blake smiled. "If we're done here, I know Sierra is waiting to see you."

"I'm done until the rest of the bones are ready for examination." Kelsey rested her gloved hands on the table. "I'll put all of this information in an official report, and if I locate anything else, I'll contact you right away."

"Thanks for all of your help," Colin said. "We appreciate your expertise."

They all murmured their thanks before Blake escorted them out the door.

"Sierra's lab is on the fourth floor." He punched the four on the elevator number pad. When the door opened on their floor, he gestured with his free hand to step out ahead of him.

He led the way toward the lab that had a sign posting Trace Evidence outside a long window. He opened the lock, and Brooklyn slipped inside. She took in the large room with long stainless steel tables in the center and workstations to the left, where lab-coated individuals were busy working. Very few of them bothered to look up. Large pieces of scientific equipment she couldn't possibly identify ringed the room. The only things she recognized were stainless steel refrigerators.

Sierra stood behind one of the long tables covered with white paper. The black box from Kane's house sat on top. Its singed appearance looked more dramatic in this sterile environment, but Brooklyn couldn't wait to see what was inside and rushed across the room.

Sierra smiled. "Perfect timing. I'm about to open this. I just have one more fingerprint to lift."

She grabbed a roll of wide tape and pressed it on the top where she'd dusted it with some kind of white powder. Her eyes were narrowed in concentration, and she chewed on the corner of her lip as she pressed the tape onto the box and then lifted to hold it up to the light. "Perfect. Just perfect. A latent print that every trace evidence expert dreams of finding. Now all we need to do is find a match."

"And how do we do that?" Brooklyn asked.

Sierra pressed the tape on a white postcard-sized card and looked up. "I'll submit it to AFIS—the national fingerprint database—to see if there's a match in the system. If not, unless we have a suspect's fingerprints on file, we won't be able to match it to anything. Do you know if Tarver's fingerprints are in the system?"

"He was arrested several years ago for internet crimes," Brooklyn said. "But he was never tried due to lack of evidence, so would they have his fingerprints?"

"Depends on if he was actually booked," Blake said.

"He spent a few weeks in jail, so he was booked," she said, recalling his virulent email threatening retribution after he got out.

Blake gave a firm nod. "Then his prints should be there. Unless there was some glitch. Which you can never rule out when you're dealing with humans who can make errors and electronics that can fail."

Brooklyn didn't like the sound of that. "Does it happen often?"

"No, but more often than we would like."

Sierra held up the card. "If this *is* his print, which we can surmise at this time it could be, it matches the prints I lifted from the weapon, doorknob, and shell casings I recovered."

"So we have proof he fired a gun."

"No," Colin said. "If these *are* his prints, all the doorknob tells us is that he was at the house. And on the casings and gun, we can only infer that he touched them at some point. He could've loaded the weapon but not fired it."

"In either event, he most likely touched them before discharge, but definitely before the fire," Sierra said. "The prints were covered with soot, but he could've picked the items up to look at them before the fire started."

Brooklyn suppressed a sigh. They seemed to have a lead but not really have a lead. "How does any of this help us, then?"

"If he's arrested and charged with a crime," Blake said, "the doorknob placing him at the house could be important for prosecuting him."

"But not help in finding him," she clarified. Right now she wanted to find him.

"Right," Colin said. "Let's hope the box's contents will do that."

Brooklyn stared at the sooty container and couldn't help but compare it to Pandora's box, waiting to unleash untold miseries. "Can you open it now?"

"Yes. Time to pick the lock." Sierra took out a black leather pouch from under the table and removed a few slender metal tools. She inserted two of them into the lock and moved them around until it popped open, the sound reverberating around the quiet lab.

Brooklyn jumped. The sound felt almost like a gunshot

to her. Surely not as loud, but as sharp and crisp, and it warned her to take care.

Sierra rested her fingers on the lid.

An ominous feeling settled deep into the pit of Brooklyn's stomach. As Sierra slowly lifted up the top, Brooklyn had to fight not to look away from the lead she wanted, yet dreaded to see.

# 17

Colin couldn't take his eyes from the box. Waiting. Time slowing down. Anticipating the lid to clear. Seeing the secrets a sociopath straddling the line of sanity might hide.

Sierra flipped the top all the way open, then jerked back. "Oh! Oh, my!"

What in the world could it contain to make a seasoned forensic expert have such a visceral reaction?

Colin pushed forward to the table. Took a long look inside.

And then he saw the horrific sight.

His stomach roiled. Not what he expected. Not at all.

The thing that had her taking a step back. A human finger. Shriveled. Dark and smelly. The bone sticking out the end, and the skin curling toward the tip.

Brooklyn gasped and wrapped her arms around her body as she pushed away. "This is awful. Just awful,"

Dev and Reid each took a look.

"It could be our victim's missing finger," Reid said.

"We need to get Kelsey up here to look at it." Blake got out his phone and dialed.

As Blake talked, Colin moved closer to her. "Are you all right?"

"It's all a bit gruesome, right? I mean, I know Kane. Dated him even, and yet it looks like he cut off a person's finger." Her tone was intensifying with each word, headed toward panic. "And why? To shove it in a box and hide it under the house? Why do that?"

Colin wished he knew. It made no sense to him, and when a suspect began not to make sense, he became even more dangerous, as it often hinted at escalating in loss of control and added violence.

"That's a question we'll need to answer," he said evenly to help calm her down.

"Typically we see this in a kidnapping," Reid said, "where the kidnappers provide proof they have the victim. But they remove the finger and deliver it to the family, not put it in a lockbox."

"There's a burner phone in here too," Dev said from where he stood over the box.

"I'll take some photos, then print the phone and swab for DNA," Sierra said. "Then I'll need to get the phone to Nick to image it so we can see what it contains."

From the counter on the back wall, Sierra grabbed a camera and evidence markers.

"Why the image?" Brooklyn asked, seeming as if she was coming back to rational thinking. "Why can't we just take a look at it now?"

"Evidentiary procedures require the device to be in the same state as when discovered," Colin said as Sierra started snapping pictures of the box.

"And just turning it on to look at the files can change the state," Brooklyn said, catching on. "So you image it and work from the image instead of the phone."

"Exactly," Colin said.

Blake ended his call. "Kelsey's on her way up. While we wait, I'll call Grady to see if he has any information on the bullet recovered at the scene." He stepped back again and tapped his phone's screen.

"I don't mean to be rude, but would you all mind if I started processing the phone?" Sierra set down her camera on the paperless end of the table. "That way Nick can get to imaging it sooner."

"Please start," Colin said. "Ignore us."

She put on a clean pair of gloves, then laid fresh white paper on the table. Only then did she take out the phone and set it down. From under the table she retrieved a bin of supplies. Colin had seen prints lifted enough times to recognize the items as fingerprint powder and a brush, along with white swabs, sealed vials, and sterile water.

She adjusted a light over the phone. "Looks like some solid prints, which is where I'll start taking DNA samples."

She ripped open a swab package and released a few drops of sterile water onto the tip. She then rolled it over the phone, placed it in a vial, and continued to follow the same procedure a few times.

Blake came back to them. "Grady has an update, too, so we'll go see him next."

The door opened, and Kelsey clipped across the floor, her heels clicking and her pleated skirt swishing. The other staff paused to take notice, then returned to work, but Colin caught a few sidelong glances as if they were wondering what was going on to bring the anthropologist to their lab.

Kelsey took disposable gloves from her lab coat and slid her hands inside. "Where's the finger?"

"In the box," Sierra said. "No one has touched it."

Colin stepped aside to give Kelsey room.

"It's not fresh by any means, but has been in this box for some time." Kelsey picked up the digit and set it on the white paper. "It's from a left hand, that I have no doubt of."

She measured the finger through the bag and studied it, turning it several times. "Longer than a typical female's index finger. Still, could be a female with a long finger, but the nail and nailbed aren't well cared for. Also it's meaty and blunt. And the skin hasn't aged, so I'd say young male."

Kelsey looked up. "If I can get a clear print I could confirm that."

Brooklyn gaped at Kelsey. "From a fingerprint?"

Kelsey nodded. "Females have significantly higher ridge density. Meaning a finer ridge than males for both radial and ulnar areas. And eighteen-year-olds and younger have higher fingerprint RD than older males."

Brooklyn shook her head. "I'll pretend I know what that means."

"As long as we do is all that matters," Sierra said. "Something else that can help is that fingerprints contain certain amino acids, and levels of these acids are twice as high in the sweat of women as in that of men."

"So this could be the missing finger from our victim?" Colin asked.

"Could be," Kelsey said. "Something I can confirm as well."

Brooklyn stared at the finger. "But can you even get a print from this shriveled finger?"

"Unclear right now." Kelsey turned the finger to stare at it. "The fingertip is quite decomposed, desiccated. Plus, it's shriveling and rigid. This reduces my chances of obtaining clear prints."

"Chances," Dev said. "So it is possible?"

"Yes," Kelsey said. "I have a variety of methods I can use to try to rehydrate it."

"And if anyone can get a print from it, it will be Kelsey." Sierra beamed at her colleague. "She's tops in her field."

Kelsey's face burned bright red as she smiled at Sierra. "I appreciate your confidence in me, and you know I'll do my best."

Colin was surprised to see the humility in these professionals who were at the top of their game. They weren't anything like the cocky scientists he'd expected to encounter.

Sierra grabbed a tablet computer sitting at the end of the table. "Let's get the finger booked into evidence, and then you can take it to your lab."

"How long will it take to rehydrate?" Colin asked.

"Depends on how many methods I have to try." Kelsey retrieved an evidence bag from under the counter and started noting details on the bag with a black marker. "Investigation number?"

Sierra rattled off a long number.

Kelsey recorded it on the bag, then deposited the finger inside. "I'll get back to you the minute I have something or if I fail."

"You won't." Brooklyn smiled.

Kelsey gave a sharp nod, then spun on her heels and exited the lab.

"Can you get that phone to Nick?" Blake asked. "Or do you want me to come back and deliver it?"

"We got it." Sierra looked up, the swab in hand. "And then, I'll get this DNA swab to Emory and let you all know what AFIS reveals on the prints if anything."

"Then we're off to the firearms lab." Blake pointed at the door. "After you."

They took the elevator down to the first floor and headed past a conference room with glass walls to the back of the building. Dev rushed ahead of them and stopped to peer into a long window.

"Eager much?" Colin laughed.

"Hey, if the door wasn't locked I'd already be inside." Dev laughed.

Colin glanced in the window, where display cases were filled with copious weapons and ammunition, all with neat labels below.

"Kind of like Kelsey's bone display, but this is much easier to look at," Brooklyn said.

Until you thought about what guns could be used for and that this lab existed to find murderers.

Like the other spaces they'd visited, long tables sat in the middle of the room, but no one was visible.

Blake opened the door and held it for them. "Grady's in the back with the bullet recovery containment system."

The sound of gunshots intensified until they abruptly stopped. They filed through a doorway to the next room. Wearing hearing protection, a redheaded man with a close-cut beard stood near a big stainless steel box filled with water. A table sat next to it, holding several weapons sealed in evidence bags. The caustic smell of gunpowder filled the air.

Grady caught sight of them. He set down the gun and ripped off his headgear.

Blake introduced everyone, ending with Dev.

"The weapons enthusiast." Grady held out a hand to Dev. "Hope the lab doesn't disappoint."

"Are you kidding?" His raised voice sounded like the eleven-year-old Dev who got a Red Ryder BB gun for Christmas. Their mom clearly didn't approve and worried he might shoot his eye out, like in A Christmas Story, but their dad had promised him the gun. She made sure to keep the promise, but only let him use it when supervised.

"This is amazing." Dev spun to take it all in. "And your collection in the other room. Wow. Just wow. I could spend hours looking at it."

"Someone's almost always here, so feel free to stop in anytime." Grady picked up a bagged weapon from the table.

Brooklyn pointed to the weapons on the table. "Is one of those guns from our fire?"

Grady shook his head. "I finished with the ballistics tests, so it's tucked up in a locker along with the slug."

"But you discovered something?" Colin asked.

"I did indeed." He tapped the stainless steel next to him. "The slug recovered from the victim is a match to the ones I fired here from the Sig recovered at the scene."

"How do you even figure that out?" Brooklyn stared at him. "If you don't mind me asking, that is."

"Don't mind at all, but let me warn you it can get a little technical and boring." He grinned. "Due to the way gun barrels are machined, each one leaves behind a distinct marking on the bullets they fire. So I take the recovered weapon, fire a bullet into the water bath here. Then, for both the bullets recovered on scene and the ones from the bath here, I digitally capture the surface in 2D and 3D. This provides me with a topographic model of the marks around the bullet's circumference. They can then be compared to each other. If they match, we can conclusively say the recovered weapon is indeed the weapon that fired the deadly bullet."

"So the recovered Sig was the weapon used to fire the deadly shot," she clarified.

Grady widened his stance. "It was indeed, but I'm sure Kelsey told you she can't conclusively say this was the cause of death."

"Right," Dev said. "But she said few people could've survived such a shot. Still, we'll for sure need to talk to

Sierra again about the prints she was going to submit to AFIS."

"Which will take her time to do," Blake said. "We can head to our conference room for a recap while they do. Then, I've arranged for lunch delivery so Brooklyn doesn't have to risk leaving the building and invited everyone who's working the investigation to join us. They can provide any additional updates then."

"Thank you, Blake," Brooklyn said. "That sounds perfect."

"Maybe thank me later if you're able to eat with the discussions that will occur." Blake eyed her. "We're used to such talk, but I know it can be hard on civilians."

Brooklyn paled, and Colin wanted to take her hand—to help her deal with all of these forensic details that were too gruesome for the average person to contemplate, much less see and hear the vivid details. But he doubted she would want him to in front of others. Maybe not do it at all. Of that, he could only hope he was wrong, as his need to take care of her was growing with every hour.

Blake had provided a hearty meal of large burritos, rice, and chips with guacamole and salsa. Colin was surprisingly hungry, despite the discussion. In addition to his team and Brooklyn, Nick, Grady, Sierra, and Emory had joined them. Kelsey was supposed to be there, but she called to say she was running late.

Blake gave them a bit of time to eat before starting the update, but he finally set down his drink and stood over his plate, still holding half a meal at the head of the table. "We'll start with Emory and the DNA."

"You would start with your wife." Nick gave an ironic smile.

"No favoritism here." Blake rolled his eyes. "She has a meeting in fifteen minutes."

"Now, boys." Emory laughed as she pushed her black glasses up her freckled nose and stood.

Colin wasn't sure if he liked their joking or if it annoyed him. His team would be doing the same thing to lighten the tense mood if it had invaded their conference room, so he would try to let it relax him.

"After all that, I really don't have much to report." She ran a hand over glossy red hair. "We're processing DNA from the front doorknob, the gun and silencer, the casing, the burner phone found in the storage box, and the box itself."

"So everywhere Sierra took prints," Colin clarified.

"That's right," Sierra said. "DNA and prints often live together on a surface, as we have touch DNA from the human hand."

"How long will that take before we know anything?" Brooklyn held on to her burrito, dripping with sauce on her plate.

"We've already isolated and quantified the DNA, which can be an unusually high time suck, along with finishing the PCR process. So that's good." Emory had gone from laughing to technical and professional. "And the genetic analyzer is running now. That'll take about twelve hours to complete. Then a few more hours for analysis, and we should have a match—if one exists—in law enforcement databases."

Emory stopped to take a deep breath. "I've also started working on DNA we extracted from the victim, and DNA from the finger found in the box to help Kelsey determine if it is from our victim. That also should finish in about the same time frame."

Reid picked up a chip. "Any other areas we should know about?"

She nodded. "We're examining the few scraps of the victim's clothing that survived the fire for touch DNA from his killer, but that will be very time-consuming and could take weeks before we find any samples of value or if we find any at all."

"Any questions for Emory?" Blake asked.

Nos were murmured, and shakes of heads traveled around the table.

"I'm only a phone call away," she said. "Nice to meet everyone."

She gave Blake a sweet look, then exited the room.

"Okay, next up, Grady," Blake said. "Do you have an update or did you just come for the food?"

"Food," he said around a bite in his mouth. He swallowed. "Not sure I can add any more, unless anyone came up with questions since I saw you."

Head shakes traveled around the table again.

"Then it's up to you, Sierra." Blake sat and grabbed his burrito.

She took a long sip of her drink, then got up to join Blake at the head of the table. She picked up stapled packets and started them down each side of the table. "The top report is a detailed analysis of the accelerant from the fire. As you can see we detected tetraethyl lead, which means it's gasoline, as suspected, but we also noted the properties of the gasoline in the report. My team is still comparing this to the gas station samples you supplied, but at this point we don't have a match to a particular station."

"If you don't find a match to a local station, could the gas have been sitting in a can on the property for some time so the station's gasoline might now be different?" Colin asked.

"Ooh, very good question." Sierra's eyes widened. "Yes, that's quite possible as is the possibility that it wasn't purchased locally. I should be able to get the final results on the local stations to you this afternoon. If we don't have a match, then if you want to expand your area of comparison, I'm glad to process additional samples." She tapped her packet. "Next, I think you'll be interested to see the analysis on the animal fur found in the enclosure, so turn the page for that."

Colin quickly flipped to look at the animal results, then flashed his gaze up to Sierra. "A jaguar? Tarver was housing a jaguar in his kennel?"

"Yes," Sierra said. "He had the big cat in conditions way too restrictive for such a fine animal, but yes, he was keeping a jaguar in that kennel."

"Or could someone before him have done that?" Colin asked.

"Good question, again," Sierra said. "We can't age the hair, so yes, it could've been there for some time. However, I can tell you the sample we took wasn't degraded. But fur, just like human hair, takes a long time to decompose. The caveat to that is, it all depends on the location of the fur and the conditions it's exposed to. A nice dry kennel like where we located it would aid in the fur surviving intact longer. But —" she paused, her finger raised—"we also recovered animal scat with a high moisture content."

"Which means it's fresh," Colin said, as using scat in tracking was their team's wheelhouse. "And if the scat is from a jaguar, it makes the fur likely fresh too."

"Exactly." Sierra smiled. "So, if your suspect has been at that house for more than a week, he was likely keeping the jaguar."

"We don't know how long he's been there, though." Dev looked at Nick. "You find any connection to Kane regarding animal trafficking?"

Nick set down his water bottle. "I've been searching for something to tie him to it, but haven't found anything. Doesn't mean it doesn't exist, but I suspect I would find it on the dark web, and it usually takes me longer to find data there."

Colin didn't have to ask about the dark web. Not when he'd spent years perusing the part of the internet where the average Joe didn't have any reason to access, but where criminals thrived. With much of the data encrypted and hard to extract, Nick had his work cut out for him.

"Sheriff Day might know about wildlife trafficking in the area where Tarver was living," Dev said. "I'll check in with her to see if she has any information."

"What about fingerprints, Sierra?" Blake asked. "Anything concrete yet?"

"Next page of my report." She turned the page on her packet and held it up. "I received results from AFIS. We found the same print on every item, and the database confirms it's a match to Kane Tarver."

"Not a surprise," Colin said. "But good to see it confirmed in black and white."

"Which means odds are good that he shot the victim." Brooklyn's voice was so low and strangled, Colin had to sit on his hands not to reach for her.

Sierra nodded. "Though of course we can't concretely prove that he picked up the gun and fired it. The forensic evidence would speak to that."

Colin scanned the page, disappointment settling in. "No other prints recovered, though?"

Sierra frowned. "I have one partial from the doorknob, but it's not enough for a solid comparison."

"So, no luck then on our victim's ID?" Dev asked.

"Normally I would say no, but we have been working with an engineering student to evaluate fingerprinting using AI. He developed an AI-based system that has learned to correlate a person's unique prints with great accuracy."

Dev's mouth fell open. "Artificial Intelligence in finger-printing. Is nothing safe these days?"

"How does it work?" Colin asked.

Sierra set down her papers. "The system analyzes the curvature of the fingerprint's center swirls rather than the minutiae or endpoints in its ridges. Of course, this is contro-versial at this point and not accepted at all, but it's possible I can get a lead for you. If I do, it most definitely won't be accepted as standard practice or hold up in a court of law."

Colin shook his head. "AI is taking over the world."

"I hear you," Sierra said. "Most disturbing about this student's work is that he claims to have proven not every fingerprint is unique. Something we've believed and lived by in criminal courts."

"Wow!" Reid slapped his hands on the table. "That could open a real can of worms."

"If it proves to be founded, it could indeed rock our system. Would give many inmates whose convictions are based on fingerprints cause for appeal."

Dev shook his head. "I've been glad to be out of law enforcement, but I keep learning even more reasons why it was a good decision."

"Amen to that," Reid said.

The phone sitting on the table near Nick rang.

He lifted the handset. "Conference room." He listened. "Oh, hey, Kels."

He listened again and frowned. "Okay. Sure. I'll tell them."

He hung up and turned to the group. "That was Kelsey.

She managed to plump the finger found in the box to get a print. She wants to see you in her lab as soon as you finish here."

Colin didn't care if he finished lunch. He pushed to his feet and started for the door. He had to think she wanted to see them because she had an ID. At least, that was his hope. Maybe the man's identity would lead to finding Kane Tarver and having him arrested for murder.

# 18

Blake and Nick joined Brooklyn and the rest of the Shadow Lake team for the trip to Kelsey's lab. Brooklyn wasn't surprised to see the anthropologist standing at the table near where the skull had been located earlier, but now additional bones for the lower part of the skeleton had been added to the table. The odor had improved, but Brooklyn's stomach still roiled around her lunch. She hadn't been very hungry and shouldn't have eaten a bite, which she now regretted.

"Oh, good." Kelsey cast them a ready smile. "Sorry if I interrupted lunch, but I thought you would want to be here when the results came in for the finger." She tapped a white bin with the plastic-bagged finger. "I was able to rehydrate it faster than I thought. I suspect it hasn't been separated from the body as long as I first believed."

"Were you able to generate a valid print?" Nick asked.

She nodded. "I already submitted it to AFIS and got a result back faster than I expected for that too."

"So you know who our victim is?" Brooklyn tried not to sound excited. After all, they were talking about a man who'd lost his life.

"I know who this finger belongs to, but that's all at this point, as I will have to clean it to compare to the hand and see if it was excised from these skeletal remains. And Emory's DNA will conclusively link it to this victim. Or not." She touched the skull with her gloved finger.

"For now," Blake said. "Share the name."

"Okay, here goes." She moved to the computer in the corner and started something printing, then snatched a page up from the printer to study it. "The deceased's name is Matteo Albertelli."

"Albertelli!" Blake's eyes narrowed. "As in one of the brothers heading up the Albertelli organized crime family. Wow!"

"Pretty much everyone in law enforcement in this state has heard of them," Colin said. "But what in the world does Tarver have to do with them?"

"When I was a deputy, they were mostly into prostitution and drugs," Dev said.

The others turned to Brooklyn. Of course they did. They wanted to know if he was connected to Kane. "Never heard of him. What about you, Nick?"

"No relation to Kane that I know of."

"They're involved in the digital world for their pornography," Colin said. "But are they into electronic theft and hacking too?"

"Not that I'm aware of," Nick said. "But I only know what I've run into in investigations and don't know all of the details of their businesses."

Blake scowled. "Matteo's older brother, Luka, is the head of the family and is suspected of several murders, but no agency has ever proved it."

"I'll dig into him," Nick said.

"Sierra mentioned that organized crime is involved in

wildlife trafficking these days," Colin said. "Could be their connection to Tarver."

"When I ask Sheriff Day about wildlife trafficking, I'll mention them too," Dev offered.

Colin looked at his brother. "Good plan. Unless anyone has the stomach to go back to lunch, we can head to the condo and regroup. You can make the call there."

"I could eat. Then I can always eat, but I'm good." Dev chuckled and faced Kelsey. "I'd appreciate an official report to give to Sheriff Day."

"Of course." Kelsey smiled. "I'll issue one after I'm able to confirm the finger belongs to this victim. I should be able to do that before the DNA comes in so you'll have an official answer to that as soon as possible too."

"Thank you for that." Colin gave a tight smile.

"And for all you do." Brooklyn squeezed Kelsey's arm. "I'm amazed and in awe of your skills and willingness to do such a difficult job. We're all better off for your dedication. Yours and everyone's here."

"Amen to that," Reid said. "If only we could clone you all and put you in every law enforcement agency in the country, far more crimes would be solved and so many perpetrators wouldn't go unpunished."

"I don't think the country is ready for that many Kelseys." Kelsey clutched her chest and laughed.

The others laughed with her, and Brooklyn appreciated how she'd lightened the mood so they could leave without such a heavy feeling deep inside.

"I'll head back to my lab to run a background check on Matteo Albertelli." Nick charged out of the room and the others followed.

At the stairwell, Nick waved at them and disappeared behind the door.

Blake strode to the elevator in his usual hurried steps and took them up to the skybridge. Brooklyn slowed to enjoy the warmth of the sun beaming in as she crossed the glass-enclosed space. She peered at the surrounding rural property laden with evergreens and grass green and thick from spring rains. The calming effect of the lush rolling hills belied the terrible things that were discovered in this facility.

Colin fell into step with her. "Nice view."

"I appreciate it even more today," she said. "The feeling is in such opposition to The Tomb."

"Kelsey's a saint to do the job she does and then to work in a windowless basement all day on top of it. I don't know how she does it."

She glanced at him. "You like to be outside."

"I do. All the guys on the team do, so our jobs are perfect for us."

She kept her focus pinned to him. "Do you ever miss being an agent?"

"Not really. Not with the things I saw and would still be seeing if I'd remained."

"Bad?"

He rubbed a hand over his face. "The kinds of things that rob your sleep and never let you go. Make you wonder if it's even wise to bring children into this broken world."

So maybe his mother was wrong, and he didn't want a wife and family. "I had no idea it was that bad."

"You might think Tarver is the worst of the worst, but he pales in comparison to the child predators I hunted down. Molesting or pimping out a child is the lowest of the low in my book."

"Yes, I would agree with that, and I'm sorry you had to deal with it." She slipped her hand into his and squeezed. "I hope someday you find a way to let it go. A reason to move on and believe in the good this world still has to offer."

He clutched her hand as if it were a lifeline and stared at her. "I'm starting to think that reason has recently come into my life."

They got lost in each other's gazes for a long moment. She heard one of the guys clear his throat, but she didn't know which one. She jerked apart from Colin.

"One thing that would be good about being an agent," he said as he started walking again. "I would have access to records and databases right now. We might find Tarver faster if I did."

She sighed. "I'm beginning to think we might not find him, and this will continue until he finds me again."

He studied her. "If for some reason we don't locate him, and I'm not saying we won't, but if that happens, will you stay on with my mom?"

Brooklyn didn't even have to think about that. "Absolutely. If you will allow it, that is. The danger and all. You know, with him maybe knowing I'm staying with you. I like her a lot, and it's more fulfilling than I thought to be able to support her needs."

He gave her a funny look she couldn't interpret and picked up his pace. A look almost as if something was strangling him. Maybe he was thinking about his mom's future and how she could very well go downhill from the lupus until she needed more and more care. Brooklyn hated the disease. All diseases, but the world was filled with them, and all they could do for the ones with no cure was manage the symptoms the best they could and support the person who suffered.

Blake opened the door for them. "Will you want to stay tonight?"

"If it's okay," Colin said. "I'd like to be here when the DNA results come in."

"Of course. I can arrange a dinner meal for you, if you'd tell me what you might like."

"You're quite the concierge," Dev said.

"Meals are simple." Blake planted his hands on his hips. "You'd be surprised what I've had to arrange for other visiting guests."

"What are our options? Because, a massage would be nice." Dev laughed. "I mean it would be nice, but kidding, of course. I'll go make that phone call."

"Just let me know about dinner." Shaking his head and chuckling, Blake headed down the hallway.

Brooklyn entered the condo, and Colin paused to secure the door behind Reid.

Dev plopped down on the sofa and called the sheriff with his iPad.

"I'm doing a video call. Helps to see her expressions." He held out the iPad for others, and they gathered around him.

Abby answered and immediately narrowed her gaze. "You've been quiet far too long, so you better have an update for me."

"I do and as you can see, I'm with my team and Brooklyn." Dev brought Abby up to speed on today's top developments. "I was wondering if you've had any issues with wildlife trafficking in your county?"

She cocked an eyebrow. "This about the possible big cat in the kennel?"

"Yeah. The scientists here have confirmed it was a jaguar."

"Oh, wow. Seriously?" She blinked rapidly. "I remember studying them in zoology class in high school, and they aren't common in the US. Definitely not common in Oregon."

Brooklyn didn't know that. "So Kane could've bought the cat with the intention of reselling it for more money."

"Sounds possible, but man, I wouldn't want to take the risks of having a live cat like that in my custody." Abby shuddered.

"Organized crime is often involved in wildlife trafficking," Reid stated.

She tipped her head. "And you're wondering if Tarver and Matteo Albertelli were working together, and that's why we found him in the house?"

"We are," Dev said. "You have any details on the Albertellis?"

"Sure, I'm familiar with the family, as are most law enforcement officers. But they're out of Portland, so I only know what I've heard on the grapevine. But hang on, and I'll go to my office to look up their rap sheets." The camera moved away from her face and was pointed down at the floor as she walked. Her booted feet thumped on white tile that was surprisingly clean for a public space.

She dropped into a chair and propped up her camera. Her fingers flew over the keyboard, and she leaned forward. "Let's see here. Matteo did some time for attempting to bribe a judge in a prostitution case. Not for himself, but the prostitute who was facing time. Otherwise his sheet is clear. Now, his brother Luka has a long list of charges, but nothing stuck. Human trafficking. Drugs. Money laundering. Counterfeiting. Even two instances of murder."

Dev gritted his teeth. "How does a guy get off on so many charges?"

"He has his flunkies do the dirty work for him, and they're too afraid to testify that he's the brains behind the crimes." She leaned closer to the screen. "I'd heard that in one of the murder cases, there was actually a witness willing to come forward, but he disappeared. They found his remains dissolved in a barrel."

Brooklyn's turn to shudder. "Not someone we want to have anything to do with."

A pounding sounded on the door, and Brooklyn's gaze shot to it, while her pulse kicked up.

Colin touched her arm. "Relax it has to be someone who works here. I'll get it."

He strode down the hall. Brooklyn couldn't relax. She had to know who it was, so she followed him to see Nick enter, his laptop under his arm.

"You learn something about Matteo?" Colin asked.

"No." Nick brushed straight past Colin and took Brooklyn's hand to lead her to a dining room chair, Colin keeping up with them. "You'll want to be sitting when you see this."

"You're scaring me." Her heart dropped as she sat, and Colin stood beside her.

"Sorry, but it *is* scary, and I can't sugarcoat it for you." Nick opened his laptop.

"What's going on?" Abby asked. "Show me."

"Sheriff Day is on the iPad," Dev said to Nick, then got up with his tablet, and he and Reid came to stand behind Brooklyn.

Nick clicked a button, and pictures of her family flooded the screen. Her mother. Father. All recent pictures of them going about their day.

Her gaze flew to Nick. "Where did you find these?"

"Dark web. Posted by Typhon."

"Kane? Kane posted pictures of my family on the dark web? But why? Why?"

Colin rested his hand on her shoulder, and the warmth from his touch was the only thing keeping her from losing it.

Nick clicked to a message board and opened a posting from Typhon.

*I know you're monitoring this, B. If you don't contact me by midnight, I'll be releasing biotoxins into the water supply for their little town, and there's no way they can stop me. I'm monitoring all communications, so don't try to warn them or anyone else.*

*Contact me and they live.*

*Don't and they die.*

If Colin could take the pain from Brooklyn, he would. She sat staring ahead in the same chair as if she'd lost everything. If he could make the decision of whether to contact Tarver or not for her, he would. If he could hold her in his arms, he would. But he could do none of these things.

Maybe holding her in his arms was an option, but would it bring her comfort or more stress? Probably stress.

Nick peered at her from his chair by the still-open laptop screen displaying the offensive message. "What do you want me to say to him, if anything?"

"Not so fast," Colin said. "Can you even reply without him being able to track the transmission? Because unless things have changed since I left the FBI, that's not possible."

"You're right." Nick shifted uneasily on his chair. "Not one hundred percent, but I can route it through so many hubs it will take him a lifetime to track."

"Then I'd like to ask him what he wants from me," Brooklyn said. "But not in this public forum."

"No worries," Nick said. "I'll set up a private message board using the data he provided."

Brooklyn glanced between Nick and Colin. "Do you think he's going to ask me to meet with him?"

"That makes the most sense to me," Nick said.

"But you won't agree to that," Colin stated in no uncertain terms, so she wouldn't even consider it.

"I don't think I have an option." Tears wetted her eyes.

"Not if I don't want him to poison my family or other people in my hometown."

Colin couldn't let her contact that creep. "All we have to do is warn your family not to drink the water."

"No!" Her anguished cry cut into him. "Kane said he was monitoring their communications. He would know."

He still wasn't going to let her meet with Tarver, so their only option was to make sure no one drank the water. "What if one of us went to visit your parents in person? He's not likely hanging out at their house but monitoring their calls and electronics."

"I can't risk that," she cried out, her agitation nearly at the breaking point. "He could be watching them, and we don't know it. Besides, what about the rest of the town? Would they warn all the people not to drink it? Could they shut it down? Could they do it in time?"

"At the very least we can warn the officials at the water treatment plant to be on the lookout for any tampering," Colin said.

"Come on, Colin." Nick shook his head. "You know this guy has the capabilities to electronically interfere with water treatment plants without the locals being any the wiser, even if on alert. The possibility of cyber-manipulation by him is quite high."

"I know he has the skills, but can he actually poison the water?" Colin met and held Nick's gaze. "It's possible, yes. Probable, no. I sat on task forces for the FBI where we studied the likelihood of such an attack. First, the plant would need to use a SCADA system—Supervisory Control and Data Acquisition—for there to be digital controls of pumps and treatment facilities."

"Which is possible," Nick said.

"Possible yes, but less likely for a small town like we're talking about. But even then, Tarver would need huge quantities of a biological agent to counterbalance the dilution effect of the large body of water, and he would have to somehow override the filtration too.

"I assume there's a local water tower." Sheriff Day's voice came from the iPad. "And could he target that?"

A question Colin didn't like, but had to answer. "A post-purification drinking water storage facility in a small municipality is likely to be more vulnerable to a hazardous attack. A water tower has smaller quantities of water, but, and I think you need to consider this, it would still be difficult to pull off."

"But no matter what we do," Brooklyn said, her voice holding real sharp hints of panic now, "the chance of him killing someone who doesn't get the word about the water or ignores the warning isn't zero, right?"

"Right," Colin had to admit but didn't like it.

"The risk of him taking my life to save others is something I might have to do, if it comes to that."

Colin clenched his hands. "A decision we'll all make together and find a way to protect you."

"If he wants to see me in person, I can't imagine that he'll let you all come with me." She gripped her hands together and fidgeted with them.

"We'll figure that out." Colin had no idea how, but he wasn't going to let Brooklyn risk her life.

"And we'll provide official support as well," Sheriff Day said. "No one is getting hurt on my watch."

Colin couldn't let it go at that, and he eyed Brooklyn. "But, and hear me, Brooklyn. Hear me loud and clear. You'll have nothing to do with him unless we approve it first."

She lurched back from him.

Fine. He'd done it. Spoken more sharply than he intended, but hopefully hurting her, which he'd obviously done, would have the result he needed. She had to stay away from Tarver if she was going to stay alive.

Problem was, could he live with himself if he stopped her from going to see this lunatic, and her parents or other people in her hometown died?

～

Nearing three a.m., Brooklyn stared at her laptop screen while propped up on the big bed in the condo bedroom. She'd put a towel down at the door so Colin couldn't see that she was up and using her computer.

She'd typed her response and just had to hit send, agreeing to the last message from Kane. Then she would need to find a way to sneak past Colin to go meet him. She could tell Colin that she was going down to Nick's lab, but Nick would have to come up to get her, and Colin would demand to see him. He would probably also insist on accompanying her.

So how did she get out? Was she even going?

*Yes.* Yes, she was. That was a given. The DNA results had come back. The gun, bullet, silencer, and casing all matched to Kane, and his DNA was also found on the black box, the burner phone, and on the index finger inside. The finger also matched the skeleton, which was now positively identified as Matteo Albertelli, and AI had matched the partial print on the door to Albertelli as well. So Kane was likely a killer. A killer of Matteo Albertelli. And also a man who would snip another man's finger off for his own motives. Probably took pleasure in it.

So yeah, he would gladly kill again, and she couldn't risk a single person losing their life due to her fear of meeting with him. Blake had already warned the water management division in her hometown about the potential threat. They'd inspected their facilities, found nothing amiss, and decided at this time not to notify the public.

The local police had put an officer on duty twenty-four/seven at the treatment plant and another one at the water tower for a potential in-person threat. She and the team believed he'd already been to either the plant or the water tower, and the biological agent was in place. But they'd failed to find it, and the threat was going to be released electronically from a distance.

Still, she would go. Meet the killer. Because Kane would outwit the local officials. He was cunning. Seeming even more so these days. What good would it do her to save her own life only to be plagued for the rest of her days over the loss of a life that she could've prevented?

*None. No good at all.*

She peeked out the door into the living room. Spotted Colin on the sofa. His head was back, his eyes closed. Had he fallen asleep? Could it be that easy for her to leave? She would be shocked if he was asleep, but he had to be exhausted. He'd stayed up the night before to stand watch for her and had worked very late the night before that.

She eased back into the room. Sent a message to Kane telling him she would try to sneak out now, and she would meet him at a parking lot a few miles away that he'd requested.

His immediate reply came in.

*Don't bring a phone or any electronic device or a weapon. Come alone. Anyone comes with you and they will die on the spot.*

# 19

Brooklyn hopped off the bus and stepped into the unlit parking lot. The stars and moon had ducked and run under heavy clouds, leaving the space dark and gloomy. But then, what had she expected from a closed-down strip mall? Not lights, but maybe a street light? No such luck, of course. Things had not gone her way so far with Kane. Why start now?

She was beginning to think God had turned His back on her. In her situation, that was easy to believe. It was much harder to believe that a loving God was still there walking alongside her and yet allowing all the problems, stress, and suffering in her life. He had a purpose for it, she just didn't have a clue what that purpose was yet. Might never know. But it was only human to want to know.

On the far side of the lot, the powerful engine on a taller-than-normal pickup truck rumbled to life, and the truck rolled her way, lights out. As it crunched over the crumbling asphalt, the lights flashed on, blinding her.

She was a sitting duck right now. Couldn't see. Could be run over and flattened by the giant tires. Colin would be so mad at her for coming here, but she couldn't let helpless people suffer. Die. Hundreds. Maybe more lose their lives all so she could live. No. That was the one thing she was certain of. She couldn't live with herself if she allowed that to happen.

The truck stopped. The engine revved. The wheels jerked forward a few feet. Brakes slammed on. Repeated. Another time.

Okay, he was playing chicken with her. Trying to scare her. She wouldn't falter. She planted her feet and resisted shouting at him and calling him a coward for not exiting the vehicle.

The truck roared a few feet closer. Brakes squealed, and it jerked to a stop. It rocked and rocked on the heavy-duty suspension, but then it finally stilled, and the door opened.

A man unfolded his body and stood on the running board. "Step over here, and turn your back to me."

She didn't want to do as asked, but she knew he would want to search her for that phone he'd told her not to bring and any other electronic tracking device or weapon. She took her time though, as if she had a semblance of control left.

As she passed, she hoped for a good look at him to see if he changed or if she'd missed seeing the monster that he was, but the darkness shrouded his face. Oh, well. There was plenty of time for that when she had enough light to take in the nuances of a madman.

His footsteps as he plopped down onto the parking lot from the truck sounded in her ears.

"Arms out," he said, his voice deeper than she remembered. He was probably trying to sound like a tough guy to scare her.

She lifted her arms and gritted her teeth.

He ran his hands over her as if he had a right to touch her wherever he wanted. She clamped down tighter on her teeth. To endure the embarrassment, she thought about her family's uncontaminated drinking water and their safety.

"Good. You listened," he said. "Didn't bring a phone or gun. I figured you would try to get away with something. Now get in the truck."

"No. I'm not going anywhere with you."

"Suit yourself." His steps sounded as he landed on the running board. "I'll just get that program started to flood the drinking water with poisons."

And he would—and could—kick off such a program from his phone. He could easily have designed an app or easily connected to his system via the internet.

She couldn't call his bluff. "Wait. I'll get in."

Keeping her eyes downcast to protect them against the light, she marched around the front of the vehicle until she reached the side of the truck. A monstrous vehicle. Perfect choice for a monster. The tires came to her waist. She had to go up on tiptoes and stretch to reach the door handle. After opening it and releasing the overpowering odor of marijuana from the cab, she climbed onto the running board to get in.

If the strong smell of pot didn't make her hurl, she suspected her first look at Kane would have her tossing her dinner to the floor.

She swiveled on the seat. Took a long look. Blinked. Blinked again. The man sitting behind the wheel didn't have Kane's blond, almost white, hair or piercing blue eyes that she'd once somehow seen warmth in.

No, this guy was dark. Swarthy. Deep-set eyes. Mean eyes.

"Hello, Brooklyn. Not who you were expecting." He smirked and slid his jacket aside to show her his holstered gun.

Thoughts raced through her brain, but she didn't know this man. "Who are you?"

"Luka Albertelli."

*Albertelli? Wow, oh wow.* The head of a huge organized crime family. The one who'd killed before. Dangerous. Deadly. And he was sitting right next to her, a gun at his side.

He couldn't poison the water, right? She should flee. She reached for her door.

He clamped hold of her wrist and jerked her arm. "You just arrived. Don't be in such a hurry to go."

She shook off his hand and rubbed her wrist. She had to get him talking so she could try to get away again. But what did she say to him? "You're Matteo's brother."

"Ah, so you know about my deceased brother?" He eyed her. "Were you in on his death?"

"In on it?" She gaped at him. "How could you think that? No. Of course not."

His eyes narrowed. "You're Tarver's girlfriend. Not a stretch to believe you'd help him."

"Hah!" she said. "I'm not his girlfriend. Far from it. He's been stalking me for three years. Trying to kill me."

Luka snorted. "Not what he's told my men."

"He's lying then." She took a moment to process this information, but it made no sense to her. None at all. "Why did you want me to come here?"

"Tarver took something very valuable from me, and I want it back." He rested his hand on his weapon. "He's refused to return it. We'll use you as leverage to make him talk."

She laughed, but it held her panic at the thought of what was coming for her. She wasn't here to reason with Kane, but to be tortured to make him talk. "Then you're wrong. Hurt me all you like. He'll love it. Likely even cheer you on."

"If what you say is true, he may still not want us to hurt you." He locked gazes, and the perverse darkness in his eyes gave her no doubt he would hurt her if he thought it would get back his missing item.

"Then you don't know him at all."

"But I know his type." He let his gaze dig deeper. "He may want to do the hurting all on his own."

He could very well be right, but she had to try to change this to be in her favor. "But you won't let him, will you? You'll never free him. Not after he killed your brother. Or at least I assume he did."

"He did indeed, and your assessment is most accurate." A cunning smile crossed his mouth.

"So why keep me? I can go now, and no one has to know I was here."

"*I* will know, and I will always know you could report this conversation." He scrubbed a hand over his jaw, covered in a thick five-o'clock shadow. "Besides, I think you can still be useful to me."

She would give in for now, but would continue to look for a way to escape. "What happens now?"

"Now, as long as you listen to everything I say, your family and their town will be spared death."

She eyed him. "You expect me to believe you have the skills to create a program to poison a water system?"

"No, but I expect you to believe I have access to Tarver's program to poison them." He grinned. "Yeah, your boyfriend already had it all set up. I just had to take over. One tap of the app he created on my phone, and it's done."

Defeated for now, she slumped in the seat. "What do you want me to do?"

He tipped his head at the door. "Start by closing the door and buckling up. Wouldn't want you to get hurt before it's time to hurt you."

228

He laughed, low and sinister, but she had to ignore him or fear would eat her alive. Deep down, part of her had thought Kane wouldn't hurt her, but the head of a huge organized crime family who had likely dissolved a witness in a barrel would without blinking an eye.

∾

Something woke Colin. He'd dozed off and jerked to his feet. How had he fallen asleep? Rookie mistake. Big, huge mistake. He should probably have had either Reid or Dev join him, but he didn't figure there was any point in two men losing sleep. Too late now, and hopefully no damage had been done.

So what had woken him?

He glanced around the condo. At the rooms, with the moonlight filtering through the linen drapes and across the room.

Nothing odd.

Both bedroom doors were closed. No lights coming from beneath.

He went to the main exit to check the security of the lock. Found the deadbolt open.

*What?* Had Reid or Dev gone somewhere?

He jogged across the large space to their room. Pushed open the door.

Both men came to a quick sitting position.

"What is it?" Dev asked.

"The front door's unlocked," Colin said.

Reid swung his legs over the side of his bed. "And Brooklyn?"

Colin didn't wait for Reid to get out of bed but turned and bolted down the hallway to the other bedroom. He knocked and waited for Brooklyn to answer. She didn't respond.

His brain started imagining the worst, but she was probably just soundly asleep. He flung the door open. Ran his gaze over the room.

Her bed was empty. The adjoining bathroom door stood open, no lights on.

Was she in there?

"Brooklyn," he called out.

No response. He raced across the room to the bathroom. Flipped on the lights. Searched. She wasn't in there.

She wasn't in the condo.

He scanned the bedroom again. Spotted a cell phone sitting on the nightstand. Hers? Who else's would it be? He had to confirm. He dialed it. The ringer trilled in the quiet. His heart sank.

Reid and Dev joined him at the door.

He turned to look at them. "She's gone. She's not here. I don't know where she is."

Panic invaded his body. His legs were like rubber, and he could barely remain standing.

Reid took a step closer. "She has to be in the building, right? She doesn't have the ability to access the fingerprint scanners at the exit doors, and the security is set up to require prints to enter *and* exit."

"Yeah, yeah," Dev said. "Maybe she went somewhere with one of the partners. Like with Nick. He's likely up at this time of night, and they could be working on something together."

"I would've heard him come up to get her," Colin said.

"Not if she wanted to be quiet to let you sleep."

"Okay, right. She's likely with Nick." Colin said the words, but they rang hollow even to him. Phone still in hand, he dialed Nick.

He answered, his voice deep. "Yo. What you need?"

"Is Brooklyn with you?" Colin fired into the phone like the sharp report of a bullet.

"No, why?" Nick asked.

"Because we're in the condo, and she's not here. She's missing, and I'm afraid she's in danger."

"I'm still in my lab," Nick said. "I'll be right up, and we'll find her together."

Colin hoped Nick was right, but for some reason, he didn't have a lot of confidence in the guy. Not that Nick wasn't a superhuman when it came to computers, but if Brooklyn had left the building, it wasn't likely a computer issue, and Colin had no idea how they might find her.

No idea at all.

Brooklyn had tried to get Luka to tell her where he was taking her, but he just kept smirking at her and saying, "Wouldn't you like to know." She expected a higher maturity level for a man in his fifties who gave out life and death orders every day.

They'd driven for about an hour, heading over the Oregon Coast Range toward the ocean. They were just nearing the Tillamook State Forest when he suddenly turned off the highway into a narrow driveway that led to a home overlooking the river. Completely secluded. At least, from what she could see with the truck headlights, which he killed when he killed the engine.

"Kind of a funky house, but Tarver rented it to meet his special needs." He used his fingers to show air quotes over special needs.

"He has special needs?" she asked.

"He does, and you'll find out all about them soon

enough. But for now, get out and let's go into the house." He glared at her. "And before you think about running, you should remember I've taken control of Tarver's program and can end your family's life with a tap of my phone."

She didn't need him to remind her. She knew full well what Kane had planned for her family if she didn't cooperate with him. She opened the door and slid down to the running board and then to the ground, covered with a thick layer of gravel.

She slammed the truck door in hopes it might be heard somewhere by someone, and they would come to her rescue. But what were the odds? Not good at four in the morning that someone in the area would hear a truck door slam and think someone was in need of help. Minuscule odds, that was what it was.

No, she was on her own, meaning she had to take in every single detail she could.

She swept her gaze over the property, slightly illuminated by the partial moon peeking out behind heavy clouds. A large man, arms crossed over his barrel chest, guarded the front door of a single-story ranch house. To the right, she spotted some sort of structure. Not big enough to be a barn, but larger than what she would expect from a storage shed. To the left, a boat sat on a trailer. From the sound of the river rushing behind the house, this home sat directly on the riverfront. Would that in any way help someone find her?

Someone like Colin. If he'd even woken up to discover she was gone.

"Quit wasting time and get in the house." Luka fired an angry look in her direction. "You better believe I'm not bluffing when it comes to the water treatment plant."

"Don't worry." She headed for the door. "I don't think you're bluffing."

"Keep alert, Rocco," Luka said to the guard, then opened the door.

The man with inky black hair nodded and widened his stance. Not a man to fool with.

She slipped past Rocco and followed Luka into a home that hadn't been updated since the sixties. Orange shag carpeting covered the living room floor, and a light glowed over the stove, giving her a glimpse of green-and-orange-flowered wallpaper in the kitchen, along with avocado green appliances.

"I'd never rent a place like this that requires so much work." Luka shook his head. "But Tarver? Guy said he didn't care as long as it suited his needs."

"Needs you haven't yet mentioned."

"First thing he said was privacy. Which also suits me quite well too. Secluded. No one will see you here or ask any questions, so don't bother calling out. It's a waste of your breath." He flicked on a brass light hanging over a small dining table outside the kitchen. A half wall with wooden spindles on the top divided the small dining area from the living room.

The light flooded the space, and she blinked to adapt, then looked at him. He was studying her as if the change from dark to lightness didn't bother his eyes. Which it should, as he was the kind of guy who lived a lot of his life in the dark, and the bright light should impact him.

"It'll be dawn soon. I want to grab some sleep before we start. But before you settle in for the night, I'd like you to meet Tarver's best friend and his special need, so you can think about tomorrow." He laughed, the deep, almost other-worldly tone cutting into her.

"Follow me." He headed through the kitchen to a side door and pushed it open to a garage.

A low growling noise that sounded more like a deep

male snore than anything filled the space. But she knew it wasn't a man snoring. The growl came from an animal. A large one, by the sound of things.

Luka flipped up the light switch, illuminating a large cage sitting on a trailer. A majestic jaguar paced inside the metal bars. His golden brown coat was covered with black rosettes, and he had a white snout. He snapped at them, revealing large teeth that could cut through a human like taking a bite of soft butter.

"This guy's tired of being in this little cage. He had to hang out at my compound for a week. When I gave him back to Tarver, he took off from his other house, trailer in tow. But there's a nice enclosure for the kitty cat here. Tomorrow you and Tarver can move him. Oh, and did I forget to mention, we'll offer you as his plaything to get Tarver to talk? I know the cat will want to keep you, but we won't let him until we have the answers we need from Tarver. Then you're all his."

Her knees lost all feeling, and she thought she might sink to the floor. *No. Get control. Keep him talking.* "And if Kane doesn't talk?"

"Then he'll join you in the enclosure with the pretty jaguar. But only piece by piece until he does confess the location of my item."

All breath left Brooklyn's body, and she had to grab on to the wall so as not to drop to the ground. She'd imagined Kane had something awful planned for her, but would he have fed her to his jaguar like this guy wanted to do? If so, it couldn't get much more horrific than that. Or maybe going body part, by body part like Albertelli had planned for Kane was worse. So much worse.

## 20

Colin couldn't stop pacing. Stop beating himself up over his last conversation with Brooklyn, when he'd spoken harshly to her. Did she think he wouldn't support her, and his words somehow encouraged her to leave? He couldn't live with himself if anything happened to her. Not only from knowing he'd been harsh, but because he really did care for her and couldn't imagine not getting a chance to get to know her.

A pounding on the condo door had him racing to fling it open. "Nick. Good. Please tell me you can help."

"I don't know." Nick, wearing a scowl and carrying his laptop, rushed past Colin. "But I aim to try."

"You'll need to do the best work you've ever done." Colin trailed after him.

He went straight to the dining table and opened his computer. "We first need to determine if she's left the building. I called Pete on the way up. He hasn't seen her, and she didn't exit through the lobby."

"But you have security camera feeds that you can look at for other exits, right?" Reid asked as he joined them at the table.

"Pulling them up now." Nick's fingers flew over the keys,

the clicking sound grating on Colin. "We have three exits. Front door. Parking garage. And one rear door."

"No matter which exit she took," Colin said, "your doors are tied to fingerprints for entrance and exit. Her prints wouldn't match your database, so how could she leave and not have set off an alarm?"

"Good question." Nick paused typing and looked up. "We haven't changed over the garage to a print reader yet. It's still a number keypad. She might've gotten the code somehow."

"But how?"

Nick tilted his head and tapped a finger on the table. "She could've watched Blake when he let you in."

Was that what she'd done? "But that would mean she was planning to leave before she even got the news from Tarver."

"Not likely then. So maybe she hacked our database and copied a keycode."

"Your system is locked down tight, right?" Dev asked. "Wouldn't you know if she did that?"

Nick frowned. "Normally I would, but she's a super hacker and knows how to hide her trail. Still, I think I would've gotten an alert. But when she toured my lab after dinner and used one of the lab computers, she could've gotten the garage keycode without kicking off an alarm."

"So check that door first then." Colin moved behind Nick to look at the screen. Reid and Dev joined him, there to support him.

If there was a way to find Brooklyn, these guys would help him. He should take comfort from that, but his brain kept shouting *if* there was a way, and his nerves were too fried to even begin to feel a hint of comfort.

*Pray. Yeah, pray. Please. Please, let her be okay and let us find her. And if she's afraid right now, give her comfort.*

As Nick brought up the computer feed for that camera, Colin waited for some comfort of his own to come, but it didn't. Was he not trusting God to have Brooklyn's back? Were his old issues blocking it? His inability to trust at all. Was he just going through the motions of trusting but not really believing it?

"I'll fast forward until I see some action or reach the current time." Nick clicked the arrow. Time flew by, but movement made Nick stop at the timestamp about an hour earlier. Brooklyn appeared in the hallway and approached the door.

"No. Oh, no." Colin's heart fell. "She really did leave."

She peered up at the camera and mouthed the words, "Sorry. My family."

"She knew we would see this." Colin's throat closed, and he could barely speak the words.

He watched as she tapped in a code, and the door opened. She slipped outside and disappeared into the lot.

"Switching camera feed to the parking entrance." Nick's voice was choked with the same emotions threatening to swamp Colin.

The feed filled the screen. Nick moved it ahead at two times the speed, then slowed when she appeared on screen, leaving the garage on foot.

"Going to the parking lot feed," Nick announced.

The third camera came online. She exited the lot on foot and then moved out of camera range.

Colin couldn't move. Brooklyn was out there. On foot. Alone. Maybe unarmed. Vulnerable.

"Run them again to see if we can tell if she's carrying," Colin demanded.

"You do that, Nick. I'll go to her bedroom to see if I can find her Glock." Dev bolted from the space, dodging the long leather sofa on the way toward the other end of the room.

Nick opened each window, and they moved through the feed in slow motion, Nick enlarging her waist so they could look for the telltale bulge of her gun through the denim shirt she wore over a T-shirt.

"Doesn't look like she's carrying," Reid said. "Does she have an ankle holster? We didn't look carefully for it."

"No need." Dev joined them, Brooklyn's Glock dangling from his finger and a phone in his other hand. "Found it in the nightstand and the phone on top."

If stress could make Colin's heart quit beating, it would. Right now. Immediately. Brooklyn, the woman he'd come to care for far more than he'd known until now, was out there. Not only alone, but unarmed. She needed him, and he failed to be there. To see the signs that she would take off. If anything happened to her, he could never forgive himself.

"Okay, my next play is to check that phone and her laptop to see if she's been communicating with anyone." Nick held out his hand to Dev.

He plopped the phone in Nick's palm. "Her laptop was on the nightstand too. I'll go get it."

Nick swiped the phone up. "Password-protected, just like I figured it would be."

"Do you have any idea what password she might've used?" Colin asked.

Nick frowned. "I wish I did. But I'm sure some random bunch of characters that have no meaning. We're all pretty careful like that with our phones. Don't want anyone to be able to connect them to us."

Colin got that. His was random too. Most IT professionals operated that way. "I assume you have a password cracking tool in your lab."

Nick nodded. "Gonna take time though. It would be easier if I thought I could use a dictionary attack."

Colin knew that wasn't going to cut it. "It's likely going to take a passport brute force guessing attack."

"I'll pretend I know what you two just said." Reid gave a wry smile.

Colin understood it all just fine from his years at the FBI, but he didn't like it.

"Doesn't matter if you understand, just matters that you know if I fail at the dictionary attack and have to go to brute force guessing it will take longer. The same will be true of her laptop."

The very reason Colin didn't like it. "So that's our only play, and we'll just have to wait for you to accomplish that?"

"No," Nick said. "One of my guys is still working in the lab, and I'll have him handle the password cracking while I review the network to see if she left a footprint of any computer access."

"Could she have even been on your network?" Colin asked. "I wouldn't think with evidence information in your network files that you would allow an outsider to access it."

Nick scowled at Colin. "I wouldn't and don't. The evidence network isn't connected to any other network. But we have a condo and guest network and an administration one."

"So you might be able to track her movements, like seeing if she accessed the internet for example," Reid asked.

Colin knew the answer to that would be yes and wasn't surprised when Nick nodded. But this lead, like looking at her phone and computer, were only leads if she used them and left breadcrumbs for them to find. But if she didn't want to be found, she had the skills to make sure that she wasn't. Her dodging the super hacker, Tarver, for three years was proof enough of that.

~

Luka had won. Got his way. Brooklyn couldn't sleep. Not at all. She laid in the lumpy bed, wide awake for hours, imagining the fate that she would endure in the morning. She turned to her side and tucked her knees to her chest. Rocking. Rhythmic. Moans deep inside wanting to escape, but she wouldn't let them out and let Luka have the satisfaction of hearing her deep-seated fear.

Was this God's will for her? To be put in front of a wild animal and somehow find the faith like Daniel had exhibited in the lion's den? Would she be saved? She doubted it unless she could have the faith to believe she would be saved. And honestly, she couldn't dredge up that much faith right now. Maybe she would by morning, but the sun was already rising, casting a reddish glow in the window, and she doubted that Luka would leave her be for long.

And then there was Kane. Where was he, and when was she going to see him?

Didn't matter. None of it did at the moment. All that mattered was that she found a way to get this debilitating fear under control so she could concentrate and figure out a way to escape.

She couldn't lay around any longer. Not a moment. She got up and silently padded out to the living room. The wide glass patio door revealed the miraculous sunrise reflecting off the river.

God's beauty. God's creation. God's evidence of His all-powerful being.

He could save her today. She could be saved.

She dropped to her knees and raised her face. Flung out her arms and prayed like she never prayed before.

# 21

Colin paced behind Nick in the small lab where he was still reviewing log files. Reid and Dev had gone out to canvass the areas around the building to see if anyone had seen Brooklyn, and if so, which direction she'd headed.

"Here. This." Nick jabbed a finger at his screen. "It could be just the thing we're looking for."

Colin stopped behind him and stared at the screen. "A bus schedule?"

"She looked it up. Leaves from outside our building, and she could've hopped on it."

"Okay, say she did." Colin dropped into the chair next to Nick. "Buses have security cameras on them. We need to see the feed from this bus, but I doubt that there's anyone at TriMet who'll let us look at it."

"No problem," Nick said. "I can access it."

"How are you going to do that?" Colin stared as he waited for the answer.

"Better you don't ask, but let's just say, hypothetically, I could get such information by accessing the TriMet security system."

"Ah, right. Not exactly legal. It would've been problematic when I was an agent, but if it helps us find Brooklyn, I don't care what records you access." Colin thought about it for a moment. "But can you do it and not get arrested?"

"I've done it before. I can do it again." Nick's eyes narrowed. "The arrested part I don't know, but Brooklyn's worth the risk."

Colin couldn't be more thankful for this guy than right now. He was risking everything for her. "Hey, thanks, man. I'll owe you big time."

"Then let me get to it so I have something to hold over your head." Nick grinned and started typing. "It's most obvious you have a thing for her."

"No point in denying it."

"I'm glad." He continued to type. "She deserves to have someone in her life."

"I agree but don't know if that's me." Colin wished he could say it was. With Brooklyn's sweet goodness in his life he could let go of the vile things he'd seen at the FBI. Even could imagine having children with her, but that wasn't the only issue standing in his way. "I have my mom to take care of right now, and that's got to be my top priority."

"A guy can have more than one priority, and I'm sure she would understand how important it is to you."

"I couldn't ask her to take on such a responsibility just to be with me."

"Have you seen her with your mom? They seem to get along just fine, and Brooklyn has a big heart. Huge."

"But that was when she was thinking it was a part-time job. I don't know if she'd feel the same way if it was a till-death-do-us-part kind of thing."

"I've known her for a long time, and I can tell you if she loves you, she will do anything she can to help you. That includes caring for your mother." Nick glanced up. "She wants a family of her own, too, and once we have Tarver behind bars for good, she'll be free to pursue that."

Could Colin hope it would work out okay? Trust that if God meant it to be, it would happen? Maybe. "We have to find her first."

Nick changed his focus back to his computer. "Cool your jets. This isn't an instant thing, as you should well know." His fingers crawled over his keyboard. "I'm almost in. Give me a minute of quiet so I can finish faster."

Colin stood back, but it was pure anguish to just wait, so he texted Dev.

*Any luck finding someone who saw her?*

*Not yet.*

Another lead that wasn't panning out. Colin paced. Back and forth. Back and forth. His mind racing with horrible possibilities of what might be happening to Brooklyn if she was with Tarver.

"Okay, got it. She took a bus all right, and I've got the details." Nick jumped up. "Let's move."

They raced for the garage and Colin's SUV. As soon as he had the vehicle heading for the exit, he used the infotainment system to text Dev and ask their location so they could pick them up. Dev replied immediately with corner streets.

Colin turned in the direction of the guys and found them exactly where Dev said they would be. They climbed in the back, and Colin updated them on their progress. They continued down the road to the bus stop.

Colin peered around at the decaying neighborhood. "Not the kind of area I would like Brooklyn to have gone alone at night."

"And why here?" Reid asked. "Nothing but an empty lot and run-down convenience store."

Colin peered out the window. "Looks like the convenience store has a security camera. We might be able to see if she met someone or where she went."

He killed the engine. "You guys wait here. Don't want to overwhelm the clerk."

He slid out into the sunshiny morning and caught a whiff of fried bacon. His stomach rumbled as they hadn't taken the time to eat. He followed the smell across the road to the store and pushed the door open. A bell above tinkled.

A customer stood at the counter, the man behind the desk was short and dark-skinned. Perhaps of Spanish descent.

"Thanks, Antonio." The customer picked up the bag. "Can't start my day without your breakfast burrito. Only guy I know who puts fresh bacon in a burrito."

The customer left, and Colin approached the counter and forced himself not to bombard the guy with questions. "Your burrito as good as he says?"

"Better." Antonio laughed.

"Then give me four of them, and I'll grab some coffee too." Colin went to the coffee bar to pour the cups, his hands shaking as he did. Not only did they need to eat, but buying something could help him convince Antonio to show him the video.

He put the paper cups into a holder and took it to the counter where Antonio had laid the generously sized burritos.

"I didn't come in for the food," Colin admitted.

"Didn't figure you did." Antonio cocked a thick black eyebrow. "You a cop or something?"

Colin wasn't surprised by the question, and he would tell the truth as he suspected this guy was sharp enough to see through a lie. "You have a good eye, but no. Former FBI."

"Yeah, you have that cop look about you."

"Is that a problem?" Colin kept his gaze pinned on the

guy when he wanted to jump over the counter, grab him by the throat, and force him to help, instead of spending valuable time getting to the answers he needed.

"For me, nah. Not in this neighborhood. Good to have protection around. Unless you need me to snitch on someone. I ain't no snitch."

"No snitching, but I was hoping I could see your video for the wee hours of the morning." Colin continued to play things down, but his insides screamed to move this along. "A woman under our protection has gone missing, and we think she got off a bus across the street at around three a.m."

"Oh yeah. Yeah. I was here. Saw her." He set his jaw and challenged Colin with it. "But how do I know you're not some crazed boyfriend trying to find her or some other nut trying to do her harm?"

"You only have my word for it and that I was former FBI. My colleagues in the car are former law enforcement, too, and one guy works with the Veritas Center. You ever heard of it?"

"That fancy, schmancy lab that no one in the neighborhood knows what they do?"

"Do you want to know?"

He shrugged. "Depends on what they do."

"They mostly process DNA for private individuals and crime scene evidence for law enforcement."

"DNA, huh." He planted his hands on the counter. "Always wanted to do DNA for me and my family to see if we could find missing relatives who entered the country from Mexico."

Could Colin use the lab for leverage to get to see the video? "If I arrange for a tour of the facility and free DNA for your family will you show me the video?"

"Sure."

"Then consider it done."

"I need some proof of the Veritas thing first. Still don't know you're not bluffing."

"While I pay for this, I'll get my friend to come in." He ripped his phone from his pocket and fired off a text to Nick to come inside and bring some evidence of his employment at Veritas.

Antonio tapped his cash register, and Colin swiped his credit card. As Antonio was bagging the burritos, Nick pushed inside.

"You better be buying whatever is making my mouth water." He laughed.

"I am." Colin gave him a pointed look, asking him to play along and not push this guy to shut him down. "Apparently, Antonio here likes to put bacon in his breakfast burritos."

"Something I can get behind for sure." Nick pulled out his wallet and drew out a business card to hand to Antonio. "I'm a partner at the Center. Work in computers." He flipped open his wallet again and displayed an ID card.

Antonio nodded. "And are you the one who can authorize free DNA tests for me and my family?"

Nick looked at Colin. "Guess you struck some sort of deal to see the video."

"I did."

"Then if free DNA tests are what it takes to see the video, I'm your guy." Nick smiled.

"I mean no disrespect." Antonio slid a paper and pen across the counter. "But I'd like that in writing."

"No problem." Nick grabbed the pen and noted the information, then signed it. "Call or email me tomorrow, and I'll get the process started."

Antonio snatched up the paper and shoved it in his pocket.

"Where's the video?" Colin asked, losing patience now.

"In the back. I'll have to lock up to show you." Antonio came around the counter, clicked the deadbolt on the front door, then made a sharp pivot toward a door on the back wall which he had to unlock. "Gotta keep things secure in this neighborhood. Wish we could move our business somewhere else, but the landlord is saying we signed for ten years when I know we didn't. Can't afford a lawyer to help get us out of the lease."

"Maybe I can help with that once we've found the woman we're looking for," Colin offered.

"Yeah, me too," Nick said. "I know a really great lawyer."

"For real?" Antonio gaped at them. "Why would you do that?"

"Why would we not if we can be of help?" Colin said.

Antonio shook his head as he stepped into a small storage area with shelves filled with merchandise lining the walls. "No offense again, but ain't used to white guys like you."

"Then we need to change that," Colin said.

Antonio led them into the dark and dank room that smelled like mold or mildew to a small office that was also locked. He opened the door and dropped into a squeaky desk chair to wake up a computer.

He pulled up the right file, and it captured Brooklyn stepping off the bus and heading into the deserted lot.

"What on earth is she doing?" Colin mumbled as he watched her enter the dark lot and just stand there.

"Yeah, I kinda thought that was odd, too, when I seen her do it. But then the truck appeared, and the guy got out to search her, so I figured it was a cop, and she was okay."

"Truck?" Colin asked, feeling his stomach go queasy again.

"Hang on, and you'll see."

And he did. The jacked-up pickup pulled forward.

"I think it's the same vehicle that the guy who tried to break into the compound drove," Colin said. "But without plates I can't be sure."

"Would make sense if it's Tarver," Nick said.

A man slid down. She backed up to him, and he skimmed his hands over her body in an intimate way that said he thought he had a right to be touching her.

Colin gritted his teeth.

"Can you zoom in on the guy's face?" Nick asked.

"Can do." Antonio enlarged the picture.

Nick stared at the screen. "It's not Tarver."

"Not Tarver." Colin gaped at the image. "But who then?"

Nick cast a horrified look at Colin. "Luka Albertelli."

"The organized crime boss?" That panic threatened to take Colin down again.

"Yes," Nick said.

Colin's mouth dried, and he couldn't say a word.

"You should be able to enlarge it and get the license plate," Nick said.

Antonio did as directed, and they had a clear shot of an Oregon plate.

"I'll need you to email that video to me," Nick said.

"I'm not sure I know how to do that."

"Then get up and let me drive this thing." He nearly shoved the guy out of his chair and took control.

Nick was thinking clearly, where Colin had allowed the shock to take control. He shook his arms to get his blood flowing and get rid of his brain fog. He couldn't determine if Brooklyn was in more danger with this crime boss than if she'd gone to meet Tarver. And why would she meet Albertelli anyway? Did it have something to do with the death of his brother? If so, what?

"Done." Nick got to his feet and looked at Antonio.

"Thanks, man. This woman is one of my best friends, and your video is the best lead we have in finding her alive."

Antonio's forehead creased. "So that guy who frisked her isn't a cop, then?"

"No," Colin said. "He's the furthest thing from one, and we have to find her before he hurts her."

*Before he hurts her.* The words kept pounding in Colin's head on the way to the SUV. He had no appetite and could barely stand the smell of the burritos now. He only hoped and prayed that Nick had a quick way to track down that jacked-up pickup, as Colin was fresh out of ideas on how to find the man before he hurt Brooklyn.

God's peace covered Brooklyn like the sun warming her body, and she flung out her arms to let more of the rising sun's warmth caress her skin. To aid in believing in a great God who could bring the sun up every morning. Surely, if He could do that, He could protect her from the monster-sized jaws of a jaguar. She drifted into a lovely warm trance of God's love.

Something slammed into her back. Shoving her toward the floor. She whipped her hands down just in time to prevent face-planting. She hit hard. Her breath evaporated.

"I don't abide praying in my presence." Luka's acerbic tone came from behind.

His foot. That's what hit her. He'd kicked her as if she were a piece of garbage. He cared so little for her as a human being, she was certain he would toss her in with the big cat.

"Get up," he demanded. "We have work to do."

She didn't move as she panted to catch her breath.

"I said get up." He kicked her in the side with a heavy booted foot.

She screamed in pain and rolled to her side to pull her knees to her chest. Nausea assailed her, and she breathed hard to stem it off.

"Quit being such a big baby." His tone was much like that of the jaguar that was reacting to the yelling with low warning growls. Threatening and intimidating. "Now get up or you'll get another one to the back."

Certain he would follow through, she slowly moved, the pain in her side like a hot poker, ripping through her skin. Her insides. Had he done internal damage? Maybe not, but she would surely bruise from it.

She staggered to her feet and clutched the wall to remain upright. At least mostly upright. She couldn't fully straighten.

He took a step closer and shoved her. "Get some shoes on. We're going out to move Sumo."

So the cat had a name. Sumo. Fitting as she suspected he would wrestle for his life, and she remembered reading once that the speed and suddenness of an attack by a jaguar were almost as important as their weight and strength. Appropriate for the cat too.

"I said go." He shoved her hard.

She stumbled but righted herself and moved toward the bedroom she'd been in. She sat on the hard bed. Luka followed and glowered at her. She wanted to rest until some of the pain subsided, but she had to keep moving or he would hurt her again. She reached down to get her shoes. Tears stung her eyes. She ignored them. Got her feet in the shoes and tied them.

Luka took a step closer to her, his gaze tight and threatening. "Get up and head for the hallway."

She rose, pain sending bottomless waves of nausea

roiling in her stomach. She took as deep of breaths as the pain would allow, hissing the air out silently to stop giving him any satisfaction for hurting her.

She entered the hallway.

"Stop by the last door," he commanded.

She paused, leaning a hand against the wall and taking shallower breaths while he pushed the door open.

"Time to move the cat, Tarver." Luka disappeared into the room.

Kane stepped out, his face bruised and cut. His lips and eyes swollen.

She gasped.

"What's wrong?" Luka said from behind Kane. "Don't like my handiwork displayed on your boyfriend?"

She didn't bother correcting him on the boyfriend comment. "Hello, Kane."

"I never expected someone to serve you up to me on a platter, but I guess I should thank Luka for that." He laughed, a mixture of anxiety and pleasure.

She'd never heard this tenor in his laughter before. Had he just developed it, or had it been there all along, and he'd kept it under control? Or maybe she just didn't notice it. Didn't matter really. It was here now, revealing his true nature.

"Get moving, Brooklyn," Luka said. "To the garage."

She had to work double-time to get her feet moving, but she did and took the route through the house to the garage and opened the door. The jaguar ran to the metal bars and growled at her. "It's okay, kitty. I won't hurt you."

Kane laughed. "Like he's going to listen to you."

She looked around. Rocco stood just outside the garage door. Someone had hooked the cage up to the pickup she'd ridden in last night.

"Get in the truck, and we'll take Sumo to his new home," Luka directed.

She moved around the cage, Sumo following along, slinking low to the ground and growling. She caught her foot on wood tucked under the tire and fell against the cage. She grabbed the bar. Sumo lunged at her hand. She snapped it back just in time.

He spit and hissed at her.

"C'mon, kitty, give me a break," she whispered. "This wasn't my idea."

"Just shut up and get in the truck before I pick you up and shove you in there myself." Luka eyed her. "And I won't be gentle on your busted ribs." His grin revealed his great pleasure in hurting her. "You too, Tarver. In the truck."

"Or what?" Kane lifted his chin and pointed it at Luka. "You'll break the only rib I likely have that's still solid after you and your goon there railed on me?"

"Or your sweetheart here will become kitty food."

Kane shrugged. "Go ahead and feed her to Sumo. That was my plan once I got her here."

"Just get moving. Now!" Luka frowned and reached past Kane to shove her.

She stumbled, then started walking. Slowly. Dragging her feet, she glanced back at Kane. "Did you want to hurt me like this when we were together or only after I took off?"

"Honestly, each time we made out and you pushed me away before we got very far, I wanted to smack you. Being a virgin at your age is an embarrassment. I'm a catch, and you were lucky I wanted you." He stopped at the refrigerator and took out a large plastic bag.

She swallowed down her snort before she made him madder and climbed into the truck, her side screaming with every move. She feared Luka was right and he'd broken a rib or two with that sharp kick. Kane climbed in after her, but

252

he really had to struggle. His face was contorted with pain. Not that she took comfort in his suffering. He might be a bad person, making bad decisions, but she still didn't relish seeing another human suffer.

Luka fired up the diesel engine, and Sumo thundered with a deep reverberation. Not a roar like a lion, but more like a rumble of distant thunder mixed with the intensity of a primal roar. Scary. Very. Her palms started sweating.

Luka pulled out of the garage and turned right onto a narrow dirt drive that ran along the river. The picturesque waterway was lined with dense forests of majestic, native evergreens so typical of the Pacific Northwest. The river was known for salmon and steelhead runs. Great fishing. Maybe food for Sumo. If cats ate fish. She had no idea. All she knew was the rapidly rushing water prevented her escape in that direction.

Kane and Luka started talking about unloading Sumo, but she kept her eyes on the verdant landscape. On more of God's beauty, trying to calm her nerves. It no longer worked. Fear was creeping in like a snake slithering into his den.

*Oh, Father, please, if it's Your will spare me such a horrid death, send help. Send Colin.*

# 22

Colin turned into the parking lot for the Veritas Center and aimed for the ramp to the garage. He hadn't wanted to go back to the lab, but they had to regroup to find Brooklyn. Dev had called one of his buddies at the Clackamas County Sheriff's office to see if he would run the jacked-up pickup's plate, but his buddy didn't answer, and Dev had to leave a message. If the deputy didn't call back by the time they reached Nick's lab at the Veritas Center, he would hack the DMV database to search for the license plate.

Colin's phone rang. "It's Micha. Maybe he has something on the gun we recovered."

He pulled up to the barrier and answered his phone. "Tell me you have something to help."

"Boy, do I." The excitement in Micha's tone sent hope growing in Colin. "I finished calling local gun dealers."

"And?" Colin almost snapped out as he was eager to hear the news and didn't want to wait.

"And I found the dealer who sold the Sig to Tarver. Of course, that's not the name he used to buy it." He paused, and Colin wanted to push him more but waited. "He went under the name of Lionel French, and the address matches the house that burned down."

"The name doesn't mean anything to me." He looked at Nick. "What about you?"

He shook his head. "But I can get a search going right away. See what we can learn."

"He likely assumed a deceased individual's identity," Dev said.

"Good lead, right?" Micha asked.

"Maybe," Colin said.

"C'mon, man. You have to admit it's the best thing we've found so far."

Colin shared the license plate number for the truck.

"Oh, man, the crime boss has her? Well, yeah, you should be able to track that plate down."

"I hope so. Having this name is great, but if it's tied to the address Tarver bailed on, and even if we find information on Lionel French, we're probably already too late for it to help bring the guy in."

More importantly, too late to save Brooklyn from the terrible fate Albertelli had planned for her.

They all piled out of the truck near the enclosure. The space didn't surprise Brooklyn, except for the size of the fenced area. She estimated it to be thirty-by-thirty. Way larger than the kennel-type structure at the house that had burned. The grassy area held two large maple trees and a big water trough. Kane had surrounded the area with heavy metal panels, much like she'd seen with cattle fencing. But unlike the type used for cattle, this fencing was two sections high, making it ten feet tall or taller. She assumed that jaguars could jump high, and of course, he wanted to keep the cat inside.

Kane stroked the fencing as if it were a favorite pet as he gazed at her with a mixture of hatred and admiration. "Took me weeks to build this. When I wasn't trying to find you, I was here."

She wasn't stepping in that enclosure if she could help it, and maybe she could delay by questioning him. He'd always liked to brag about himself, so hopefully, he would go along with her and Luka would let him talk. "You were never one for pets. Not that I guess Sumo is a pet, but why a jaguar?"

Kane leaned against the fence, his face still holding a great measure of pain. "I didn't plan to keep him. Got into wildlife trafficking as a side hustle and bought Sumo to sell to a big-time drug dealer. Before I could deliver him, the dude got himself arrested and sent away for twenty years. He obviously couldn't take Sumo to prison with him, so he was out as my buyer. I tried to find another one. Didn't happen right away, and I started to like having the stupid cat around. Found out when I went out to feed him that I could talk to him."

Wow, and a personal thought she never expected he would share with her. "You could make a human friend to talk to. That would be a lot easier than keeping—what?—a two hundred pound cat alive?"

"He's closer to three hundred, but yeah, he does eat a lot and require some care. But he doesn't talk back. Humans do. Sumo just grunts and growls. I can handle that."

"But you must've been talking to a human too, right? I mean the guy who died in the fire."

"Ah, that's where you're wrong. The fire didn't get my brother." Luka scowled and thumped Kane on the head. "He did. Popped him in the head using his stupid little Sig."

"Loved that gun." Kane's words were said matter-offactly, like he was talking about the weather not killing a man. "Gonna have to get another one like it."

Luka let his fist fly into Kane's face. "You're going to respect my brother and feel remorse for what you did before we finish here, so help me."

Brooklyn agreed. Not to the point of violence, but she didn't care if Kane missed his gun. He'd killed a man with no regret. "Why do it? Why kill him?"

"Not my fault. They made me." He glared at Luka. "I accidentally stepped on his toes. Apparently, he's big into wildlife trafficking. My bad. Should've done better research, but the money was too good." He chuckled, but then it faded as fast as it came and morphed into a scowl. "They stole Sumo and warned me to back off."

"And you couldn't let it go at that," she said, knowing him. "Sumo belonged to you, and you had to get him back. Like you think I belong to you."

"You *do* know me, don't you?" He laughed but grimaced and stopped. "And you do belong to me. Time you start realizing that."

She wouldn't go there. "So what happened?"

"Luka took something of mine, so I took something of his. Maybe a little more important, but still his." That wry smile came back, but he stopped and touched the wounded corner of his mouth.

"What did you take?" she asked.

"Not what. Who." Luka glared at Kane. "My brother."

Ah. That made sense. "Matteo."

Kane flashed her a wide-eyed look. "So you figured out his ID, huh? I thought the fire would've taken care of obscuring it. Or did Luka here tell you?"

"Not Luka, and the fire did make things difficult, but my new friends at the Veritas Center lifted his print from the finger you left behind."

He cursed and slammed a hand on the fence, then held it close to his body as if he'd hurt it more. "I ran out of time. Couldn't grab the box after I'd worked out a deal with Luka to trade Matteo for Sumo."

"A deal you reneged on." Luka cuffed Kane across the face again.

"Well, yeah. Did you really expect anything different?" Kane stared at him as if he couldn't believe someone would do the right thing.

"So what happened?" she asked.

Kane faced her. "Luka's thugs were breathing down my neck, and I had to leave fast. Figured no one would find that box under the floor until I could get back there for it. But, of course, you would remember that I hid things in a crawl space in the past."

She remembered far more than she would ever admit to him. "But you weren't planning to release Matteo, then?"

"Not hardly." He eyed her, passion burning from his eyes, then he shifted to face Luka and raised his shoulders. "Can't let someone treat me that way and get away with it, now can I?"

Luka roared and plowed into Kane with his shoulder to the ribs, knocking Kane to the ground. "You'll pay for this insubordinate behavior."

Kane clutched his abdomen and curled up. "I don't have much to lose at this point."

Luka fisted his hands but held them at his side. "Time to start thinking of your sweetie here. Next time you give me any of your guff, she gets it."

Kane shrugged but locked gazes with her. "No skin off my nose. She's not going to get away with bailing on me. Either I give her to Sumo or you do."

His sudden glazed anger directed at her sent fear coursing through her body again, but she resisted letting it take hold, swallowing hard and not letting him know he was impacting her. "But you got Sumo back."

"I did. Luka here sent two goons to bring him to me." Kane sat up. "I dragged Matteo out on the porch as proof of life and had them unhook Sumo's trailer from their SUV, then go wait at the end of the driveway for Matteo."

"And then you killed him and started the fire."

"Well, yeah, but first I hooked Sumo up to my truck so I could drive out the back way. But I had to hurry before the goons came looking for Matteo and I got into a shoot-out. I couldn't clean up any evidence of my being there, so I grabbed a spare can of gas and set the place on fire, then bolted to come here."

She shook her head, not sure what to say. "All for the love of money."

"Is there anything else worth loving?" He smirked.

"Not even Sumo?"

"This stupid cat? Nah. After he takes care of you once and for all, and you fatten him, I'll be selling him to the highest bidder."

"Not if you're not alive to sell him to anyone," Luka said.

Her mouth fell open over the man's blunt statement. Just a day ago, she had one man wanting to kill her, and she thought that unbearable. Now two men wanted her dead, and a three hundred pound wild cat would likely be used to end her life. Her odds of survival got less by the minute, and she needed a miracle to get out of this dire dilemma alive.

Dev's buddy didn't call back. Of course not. That would've been too easy, and Colin could have already been on the road to where Brooklyn was being held. Instead, they'd wasted thirty minutes while Nick hacked into the system.

Thankfully, he was skilled, or the database wasn't as secure as everyone would like to think. Either way, he'd just plugged in the license plate number.

"Vehicle's registered to a Danny Newton with an address in Tillamook," Nick announced from behind his computer.

"You think the truck belongs to one of Albertelli's guys?" Colin asked. "Or could it be another alias for Tarver and somehow Albertelli is driving his vehicle?"

"We can find out soon enough." Nick's fingers ran over the keyboard. "I'm searching for a corresponding driver's license to get a look at the photo."

Colin leapt to his feet and moved behind Nick. The computer churned through records in the DMV database until it landed on one and opened. The photo displayed.

"It's Tarver all right," Nick said. "And the address matches."

"C'mon, let's move," Colin said. "Get out there now."

"Hold up." Nick lifted a hand. "I'll bring up a satellite photo so we know what we're up against."

"And now that we know we're dealing with Albertelli," Reid said, "we'll need additional weapons and surveillance equipment that we don't have with us."

Colin couldn't waste more time. He just couldn't. Not with Brooklyn needing him right now. But could he afford to rush off? Could they take Albertelli with just handguns?

No. He had to listen. "You're right, but no way we have time to go back to Shadow Lake for them."

"Call Grady. " Nick kept his attention on the computer. "Extension 126. Have him round up what we might need. We'll stop by to pick it up on the way out."

"I'll do it," Reid said.

"Hey, thanks, man," Colin replied as he was too frazzled to think straight to request what they might need. "Make sure we get a semi-automatic rifle that we can use to take Tarver or Albertelli out from a distance if needed."

"Roger that," Reid said.

Colin looked at his brother. "Without Micha here, you're our best marksman. Be ready to take a long shot if needed."

"You got it." Dev's enthusiasm for the job shone on his face. He wouldn't want to kill another human being, but he would want to be able to use his skills to help, and if Brooklyn's life was in danger, he would take the shot. After all, law enforcement officers were trained to protect innocent lives at all costs, and that meant taking the hard shot when necessary. As a former deputy, that training would never leave Dev, and he would man up if needed.

"Okay," Nick said. "The place is on the Wilson River. Tree canopy too thick to really see anything else."

Colin looked back at Dev. "With the river, we might need your water rescue skills too."

Dev gave a firm nod. "Glad to help."

Reid hung up. "Grady will have the supplies ready in five. He also offered to come along if we need him."

"The four of us have it covered," Colin said, and prayed he was right. "Let's move."

Nick grabbed his laptop. "It's about an hour drive. I can do additional research on the property on the way."

Colin hadn't been coherent enough to think about the fact that they had a long drive outside the metro area. At least they were on the west side of town right now, putting them closer to Tillamook. A helicopter could get them there faster, but there wasn't any place in the area where one could put down other than on the road. Besides, it would draw attention to their arrival, and if they were going to take on both Albertelli and Tarver, Colin and the guys would likely need the element of surprise.

Still, they were an hour away from taking anyone down.

They raced for the elevator, their footfalls pounding on the tile floor. Inside, Colin looked each guy in the face. "No matter what we do, we need to pray that Brooklyn has an hour to wait for us to get to her."

～

Brooklyn was trying to stall. Move slowly but not anger Kane or Luka. A fine line to balance as Kane had snapped at her a few times while they got Sumo ready to move. Sure, she was simply putting off the inevitable. Her fate appeared to be sealed. Death by Jaguar. Unless God intervened in the last minute. He could still decide to rescue her. Like He saved so many people in the Bible.

Luka went to the truck and took out a soft-sided red case that held a tranquilizer gun. "Rocco and I'll be over here. Try to unleash the animal on us, and we'll take him down, then you both will follow."

Rocco drew his handgun as if for emphasis that Brooklyn didn't need to be made clear. Though honestly, death by a bullet would be preferable to dying by a jaguar attack. So maybe she should be thinking about how to make that happen.

"Now get to it." Luka waved the red case.

She wanted to get her hands on it in the worst way. She could use the tranquilizers on both the four legged beast as well as the two legged ones.

"Okay," Kane said from where he stood near the pacing cat's crate door. "When I get Sumo into the enclosure, Brooklyn, you close the door behind him."

She looked dubiously at the door that swung inward into the enclosure. Kane had backed the trailer up to the wide gate, leaving zero space between the crate and the enclosure. No way she could close the door without going inside. Maybe that was Kane's plan, but she doubted it as he would want the cat to be safely inside when he attacked her so he could watch from the outside where he would be protected.

"And just how do you suggest I close it?" she asked.

"Use the rope I tied on it. I'll open the crate, prod Sumo out, and keep him from coming back in the crate. Then once he clears the gate, you tug it closed. Grab the rope now so you're ready." He stared at her until she picked up the heavy rope.

"Be ready because he's not going to like me prodding him and might fight to stay in the crate."

She nodded, looking at the big animal pacing the small space as if he knew they were planning to irritate him.

"Ready?" Kane asked.

How did she answer? Was anyone ever ready to try to slam a door behind a wild and irritated jaguar?

"I asked if you're ready," he snapped.

"Ready." She twisted the rope around her hand.

He grabbed the plastic bag he'd gotten from the refrigerator and took out large steaks. He placed a thick slab of red meat near the crate door and then tossed a few on the ground in the enclosure, each further out than the next. A perfect trail for Sumo to follow.

The jaguar pounced on the one at the mouth of his crate. Kane pushed up the door latch with a long metal pole.

Sumo grabbed the steak and dragged it to the corner. *Yes, stay inside, Sumo. You don't want to hurt me, do you?*

She resisted pumping up her fist as the jaguar did just the opposite of what Kane and Luka might want.

Kane cursed and tossed another steak in the doorway, then stood back. Sumo gobbled down the first steak and went for the new piece of bloody red meat at the door.

Kane got behind the big cat and jabbed the tip of the pole into his back.

He turned and roared at Kane.

He didn't back down or even look afraid, but he crouched in pounce mode. Kane stood his ground and tapped the floor by the meat, redirecting the jaguar's attention as a parent might do with a toddler.

Sumo clamped his monstrous jaws on the steak and leapt out into the enclosure with the meat dangling to the side of his mouth. He stopped in the gateway to consume the steak with sloppy, noisy chewing, then promptly snatched up the next one. And the next one. And finally, the one that had him clearing the gate.

She had to force her mind not to imagine him chomping down on her in the same way.

"Close it now!" Kane yelled.

She pulled and dragged the heavy metal toward the trailer. The edge caught on the ground, and she had to dig deep to get it moving again. She planted her heels and jerked hard until it inched forward, then broke free. Her injured ribs screamed, and she had to pant to breathe, but she jerked the latch side to the pole.

Kane flipped down the heavy-duty hasp and settled an equally strong padlock on it, then tugged.

Brooklyn sagged with relief. Not only had she done her job, but Kane had locked the enclosure, which meant he didn't think anyone was going to toss her in with Sumo right now. But then, he had no idea of Luka's plan, right?

If Luka hadn't arrived, what would Kane be doing with her? Would he torment her with the thought of being consumed by a jaguar so she was even more terrified by the time it occurred? Sounded like something he would do. Especially if he was super confident that no one could find them.

"We'll head back to the house, now," Luka said. "First to give the two of you a chance to tell me where my missing item is located."

"Not happening." Kane tried to cross his arms but winced and let them fall.

"No worries." Luka grinned. "It'll also give Sumo time to work up an appetite again. Then we'll come back here, and your girlfriend will be the main attraction."

"I can hardly wait." Kane grinned.

She obviously didn't share his sentiment. She could wait and would use the time to pray and try to figure a way out of this deadly situation.

# 23

---

Brooklyn had sat on the couch in the dark and damp living room for an hour under the watchful eye of Rocco while Luka hung outside making phone calls. Kane was seated on the far end of the sofa, not at all looking worried. Well, he should be. If he didn't give up the missing item, Luka would torture him until he did.

"What does Luka want from you?" she asked.

"Ah, yes. That." A snide grin crossed his face. "When Matteo came to stay with me, he happened to have a flash drive with their client information on it. Enough info for me to either steal their business or turn it over to the police and have them all arrested."

"And which one were you going to do?" She looked at Rocco to see his reaction. A muscle jumped in his cheek, but nothing else. Was he going to go tell Luka that Kane admitted to having the drive, or did Luka already know for a fact that Kane had it and was simply refusing to give it to him?

"Don't look so worried." Kane leaned back and lifted his arm on the back of the sofa as if he hadn't a care in the world. "I'm not saying anything they don't already know.

They knew Matteo had it, and I would've been foolish not to search him. We all know I'm not foolish."

"Aren't you? Because look at the position you're in. Only a foolish man would end up about to be executed by a big organized crime boss."

Rocco snorted. Apparently he found that funny.

Kane not so much. He slammed a fist into the arm of the couch and glared at her. "Talk about foolish. You're about to be fed to Sumo if I don't talk, and you're insulting me. I would call that the ultimate in foolishness."

"Really? I think the ultimate would be to believe that you wouldn't put me in Sumo's enclosure anyway, even if Luka wasn't in charge here, regardless of what I do or say. It's your plan to get revenge for me leaving you." She drew in a ragged breath. "Also foolish? You bragging about me being your girlfriend when I hadn't seen you in years. Why do that? What was the point?"

"Stupid small talk to gain Matteo's trust. All my time is spent on the web, so I couldn't think of anything else to say. And I don't regret it because Luka found you, and here you are. Ready to feed Sumo." He rubbed his hands together. "If that's a result of foolishness, then I'll be as foolish as you want me to be."

"Where did you hide the drive?" she asked.

He eyed her. "As if I'd tell you. And if I did, I sure wouldn't do so in front of this goon."

Rocco widened his stance, stomping a foot when he did. He *was* a goon, but apparently he didn't like being called one.

The door opened, and Luka strode in. "You ready to talk?"

Kane lifted his chin. "Nope."

"Then she's toast. "

"Can I help?" Kane asked.

267

"You're bluffing."

"No." Kane's expression turned hard as if wearing a stone mask.

Luka looked at Brooklyn. "I'll give you one last chance to tell me where it is."

"I wish I knew so I could end this all without anyone getting hurt," she said, though she knew he would never let them live, even if they gave up the drive.

Another snort from Rocco.

"Then let's go." Luka looked like he didn't believe her or Kane, and that he would soon call their bluff at Sumo's gate to find out where his flash drive was located.

She stepped out the door, blinking against the bright sunshine belying her potential fate. She was still believing God for a miracle, as she had found no answer to her dilemma. None. Zip. Zilch.

Luka shoved Kane ahead. "Get her inside."

"My pleasure." Kane pushed her down the dirt road toward the enclosure.

She dragged her feet, but he just shoved her harder, and she couldn't stop her forward progress.

Unfortunately they reached the enclosure's gate far too soon. Panic greeted her and took hold. She glanced back at Kane. "You could just give them what they want, and they would let us go."

He scoffed. "Naive as usual, I see. They're going to kill us no matter what happens, and this will buy me time to get away."

She glanced through the metal to see Sumo at the back of the enclosure. He was crouched down in knee-high grass, his eyes ever watchful.

Kane unlocked the gate. Drew it open. Gave her a shove. She bolted backward. He shoved her again. Hard. She lost her footing and fell. Sumo raised his head.

She thought to get up. *No.* Stay low. Small. Be less threatening to Sumo. She crouched, ready to spring up if needed,
and wrapped her arms around her body, ignoring the pain
from her potential broken ribs.

Sumo stood. Locked those ferocious eyes on her and
started forward.

*Don't panic. Stay still. And whatever you do, stay close to the
gate so you can get out if it opens.*

~

The vehicle was still rolling when Colin exploded out the
door with a backpack full of surveillance gear. Dev charged
after him, his rifle over his shoulder, ready to take Tarver out
if needed.

Colin plunged into the ditch by the road and then back
up, slowing when he got close enough to the property for
his movements to be heard. He signaled for the others to be
as quiet as possible from this point on, then crept forward
until the house came into view. He stopped and got out the
high-powered binoculars.

Lifting them, he ran the lens over the clearing, noting
the same jacked-up pickup from the almost breach at their
compound. "Same truck that I saw outside Shadow Lake's
gate holding the guy who tried to break in."

"Can't get a read on the plates," Dev said from beside
him. He'd dropped to his knees and was using the scope on
his rifle to see in the distance. "But we can probably assume
it's the truck from the parking lot that Brooklyn got into too.
No movement on the property, though."

"They're likely in the house," Reid said catching up to
them along with Nick.

Nick squatted and put his laptop on his knees. "Still no
internet traffic, or network traffic for that matter, so if they're

inside, they're not using the internet. And odd that there aren't any surveillance cameras so far either."

"He might not have had time to install them yet," Reid said.

"He could have a second vehicle and not even be here," Dev said.

"Nothing registered in DMV to the same name." Nick suddenly grabbed his phone from his pocket. "Call coming in from Sierra."

"Could be important," Colin said. "Find out what she wants."

"You have something for us?" Nick asked and listened. "Okay. Get them to my team to image, and I'll be back as soon as possible to decrypt them."

Colin looked back. "What is it?"

"Sierra was storing the black box in evidence and found a false bottom. Kane had taped two small flash drives to the lid. They're likely encrypted, but my team will get started on imaging them right away, then I can work on cracking the encryption."

"Could be what we need to put him away," Reid said.

"That's all well and good, but first we have to find him and get Brooklyn back." Colin couldn't sit here talking about evidence when Brooklyn could still need him. They had plenty of time to discuss that after she was free.

A low, threatening sound rumbled through the air.

"The jaguar?" Dev asked and mocked a shudder. "I've never heard one, but it sure sounded like a big cat."

Colin looked at Nick. "Is the guy sick enough to use that jaguar to hurt her?"

Nick swallowed hard. "Unfortunately, yes."

The growl came again, this time louder. Lower. Angrier.

"Sound came from my left beyond that small outbuilding." Dev nodded toward the direction.

"We have to get over there," Colin said. "But we split up in case they're in the house. Reid, you take the house. Don't breach, but keep an eye on the exits and keep us updated on the comms. The rest of us will take the big cat. Any questions?"

The men shook their heads and split off. Colin led Dev and Nick through the understory of massive Douglas firs so common in the Pacific Northwest. They trampled ferns, hostas, and low-growing ground cover to reach the other side of the clearing. He advanced forward.

The animal cried out again, the tenor of his call changed as if aggravated now. Was Tarver provoking it?

Colin kicked up his speed, reached the outbuilding, and used it as cover to take a look ahead.

*No. No.* His veins froze as if injected with ice water.

Brooklyn was inside the gate. Crouching and hugging herself, her body trembling.

The gate was closed. The cat was advancing her way, one giant paw in front of the other. Low. Stalking. Licking its mouth.

"Tell me where the flash drives are, Tarver," a man standing next to Tarver said, "and I'll let her out."

Tarver cocked an eyebrow in a swollen and bruised face. "Ah, no, you won't. I know that."

"Fine. Open the gate, Rocco," the guy said. "Time for Tarver to join his sweetheart."

"You got it, Luka." The big burly man took a few steps closer.

So Rocco and Luka. Had to be Albertelli and one of his guys from the organized crime syndicate, and they had to be looking for the drives Sierra had just located.

Tarver held up his hand. "You can put me in there, but if Sumo kills me, you won't ever find the drives."

271

"I'll have to take that risk and hope no one else finds them either."

Kane looked back at Luka. "You're willing to risk your client list getting into the hands of the cops."

"How will they find it?" Luka asked.

"Maybe I left the drives in the house. Maybe they didn't burn, and they'll find them."

"Nice try." Luka shook his head. "We searched. Nothing there. And they're done with forensics on the house, so they won't likely go back."

"Maybe the cops already have them, and once they decrypt them, they'll be coming your way."

"Then there's no point in keeping you alive, is there?" Luka looked at Rocco. "Get him in there now."

Rocco lifted the gate latch and shoved Tarver into the enclosure. Sumo stopped moving forward and stood to watch, his big eyes not missing a thing.

Luka held up a red case. "If you decide to talk, I have the tranquilizer gun right here and your precious jag can go nighty night while we let you out."

"This is crazy," Dev said. "I don't want to shoot that cat, but we might have to."

"We're better overpowering Luka and taking the tranquilizer gun from him." Colin didn't have much time, and Brooklyn's life could depend on what he decided. "We have the element of surprise on our side. Dev, you stay here and take a stand. If the cat gets close to Brooklyn, you take it out. Nick, you have Rocco. I have Luka. We overpower them. Either one goes for their sidearms before we get to them, we take them out. Understood?"

"Roger that," Dev said, already squatting to take a stand.

"Understood," Nick said.

"Then we move now." Colin held his weapon in hand and waited for Nick to come alongside him.

The cat was on the move again. Slinky. Low. Stalking. Brooklyn or Tarver his prey. Brooklyn started crying, but she seemed to be working hard to keep it under control.

"Stop sniveling," Tarver said. "You're making me mad."

"That guy's a real piece of work." Colin continued to inch forward.

Luka stood, watching. Dispassionate. Rocco leaned against a trailer as if he couldn't even be bothered to care. The cat looked past Brooklyn and Tarver, eyeing Colin and Nick. Sumo stopped. Watched. *Good.* As long as Rocco and Luka didn't realize who the cat was looking at, they were golden.

Nick signaled that he was splitting off to go for the big goon. Colin nodded and moved to the right to slide up on Luka from behind. He glanced back at Nick. Saw him bring Rocco to his knees with a gun at his temple.

Colin marched ahead. Reached Luka. Shoved his gun in the creep's back. "Don't move."

He jerked but remained still.

Brooklyn pivoted. "Colin, is that you? Really you?"

"Yes. Just stay low until I can help." Colin assessed the situation. The jaguar was too close to the gate to open it. The animal's speed would allow him to be through the gate and free to roam the countryside and kill people or other animals. Colin couldn't let that happen. "I'll tranquilize the cat and get you out."

Luka hugged the case to his chest. "Good luck with that."

Colin saw the cat start to move again. His heart could barely beat. He had to act. Now. He shoved the gun barrel into Luka. "You're risking a bullet in the back."

"Hah, you're one of the good guys," Luka said. "The calvary. They never shoot an unarmed man in the back."

*Maybe not, but I'm not above disabling you.* Colin kneed the back of Luka's knees, bringing him to the ground. He shoved him down and hoped the guy would reach out to protect himself and the case would come free.

No such luck. He took a tumble and rolled to his stomach, burying the case under his large body.

Luka gave Colin no choice. He holstered his weapon and dropped down on the man. He flipped him and tugged to take the tranquilizer gun away. Luka held fast. His strength beyond what Colin expected.

"Colin, hurry," Brooklyn cried out. "Sumo is so close."

As if hearing his name, the jaguar roared.

"Stop!" Tarver's voice was high and terrified now.

Colin dug deep. Coldcocked Luka. His arms fell to the ground. Colin grabbed the case and rolled free to get an eye on the big cat. He was nearing the pair. About five feet away. Colin ripped the zipper open. Pulled out the gun. Loaded it. Aimed. Fired. Hit the cat.

He raised up on his back legs and ran across the enclosure, then curled back to try to get the dart out of his flank. Angry now. Still moving. Not sleeping from the drug, he eyed them again.

"Does he need a second dart?" Colin called out as he reached into the case for another one.

"One is enough," Tarver shouted, cowering low to the ground. "A second one will kill him. It takes time. Could be up to five minutes."

Then Colin would have to risk opening the door while the cat was on the other side of the yard. He started for the enclosure. Luka grabbed his ankle, dragging him back. Colin had to toss down the case to get free.

They scuffled. Tumbling over each other.

Luka clamped his hands around Colin's neck. He tried to pry them off, but Luka suddenly had the strength of ten men.

Dev fired a warning shot next to Luka's body.

Luka snapped back, his panicked gaze seeking the source of the bullet.

Colin dragged in air and rolled free.

He staggered to his feet.

Went for the gate. Opened it.

Tarver lurched to his feet and pushed Brooklyn down to run toward Colin.

The cat started moving. Coming fast now.

"Run for the gate, Brooklyn," Colin yelled and charged Tarver, tackling him into the dirt away from the opening so Brooklyn could squeeze through. "Close the gate behind you."

She got to her feet and slid outside. "I can't close it with you in there."

"You have to." Colin strained to hold Tarver back from blocking the gate. "We can't risk the cat getting free. Killing others."

She started sobbing and latched the gate.

Colin prayed for help.

His strength seemed to double, and he rolled free of Tarver to scramble up the chain-link fence, clinging for safety near the top. Sumo could likely drag him down, but Tarver was an easier prey right now.

A bullet struck the dirt in front of Sumo. Then another and another. Had to be Dev trying to warn the cat off without killing him. Sumo skidded to a stop, his eyes dazed.

*Please, God, say the dart is finally starting to work.*

Sumo roared, then lunged at Tarver, his mouth wide open. He came down, his mighty jaw clamping around Tarver's leg. The man screamed in agony. Colin wanted to look away, but he couldn't. Not when Sumo could come for him next.

# 24

Brooklyn screamed, feeling as if she were out of her body in a nightmare.

She didn't like Kane, but she didn't want him to be mauled by a giant cat. And she sure didn't want him to move on to Colin.

"Stop! Stop!" She waved her arms and charged the gate.

Sumo looked up at her, his eyes rolling back, and he suddenly collapsed, releasing Kane's leg. Kane glanced at her, his face contorted in pain. He doubled up and moaned.

"Calling an ambulance and we're in Sheriff Day's jurisdiction, so I'll give her a call too," Dev yelled from somewhere nearby, but it sounded like he was moving their way.

While Brooklyn was focused on Sumo, Nick had come forward, gun in hand and had Luka pinned down. She looked around for Rocco. The giant of a man was tied up next to the trailer, with the rope she'd used to pull the gate closed as his restraint.

She continued to the gate. Lifted the latch to let Colin out.

He dropped to the ground. Went to Kane.

"How long does the tranquilizer work?" Colin asked.

"Not sure."

"Then let's get you out of here, but it's gonna hurt." Colin scooped under Kane's armpits and dragged him out.

He screamed in anguish with each step. Brooklyn's stomach roiled, but she got the gate closed. Locked the cat in. She took a long breath, then turned to stare at Kane's mangled leg as it bled into the soil.

Colin whipped off his belt and secured it above the wound. Kane screamed and writhed in pain.

She felt bad for him. She really did, but he'd brought this on himself. Still, as her thoughts started to be more coherent, she offered a prayer on his behalf.

"We need a first aid kit or some bedding or towels to pack the wound," Colin said.

"Got a first aid kit in the car," Nick said, "but you need more than the little bit of gauze it contains." He looked at Dev, who'd joined them. "Take over guarding this loser, and I'll check the house."

Dev stepped up to Luka and held his rifle at the ready. Overkill? Likely, but Brooklyn had to admit to finally feeling safe.

Colin whipped his shirt over his head, revealing a white undershirt. He turned his knit shirt inside out, balled it up, and pressed it on the wound. It was soon saturated with blood, but then the bleeding seemed to stop.

"Looks like the tourniquet is holding," she said. "Is there anything I can do?"

Colin glanced up at her and searched her face, concern etched in every inch of his expression. "Just tell me you're okay."

"Shook up, but fine." She didn't bother to tell him about the ribs from Luka's earlier mistreatment.

"So who are these two thugs?" he asked.

"Matteo Albertelli's brother, Luka, and his associate

Rocco." She glared at Luka. "He and Kane were so sure they were going to kill me that they were very free with admitting their crimes. With the info they gave me, they'll all be serving many years."

Colin nodded at Kane. "If this guy lives."

She took a look at his tortured face, pale and clammy. "Looks like he's passed out from the pain."

"He's still losing some blood, so not surprising."

Nick raced across the lot, towels in hand.

"Reid's going to the road to signal the ambulance so they don't miss the drive." He tossed a towel to Colin, and he swapped it for his shirt. "You mind trading places with me?"

Nick dropped to his knees and took over pressing the fabric on the gaping wound.

Colin wiped his hands on another towel and stood. He moved to Brooklyn, placed his blood-stained hands on her shoulders, and ran his gaze over her. "You're really okay? They didn't hurt you?"

As much as she didn't want to worry him, she couldn't lie. "Luka might've broken a few of my ribs."

"He what?" Colin spun to glare at Luka.

"It's okay. Everything will be fine now that Kane will be arrested for trying to kill me, and of course, these guys for their crimes too."

"We'll get you to the ER right after the police and ambulance arrive." He brushed a hand over her hair and straightened out a few strands. "And you should know Sierra found flash drives taped in a false bottom in the black box you located."

She raised her chin and stared at Luka. "Guess the police are going to get your client list after all. How many of them will roll over on you? You'll never get out of prison." She resisted gloating and explained to Colin.

He gently ran his hands down her arms and took her

hands. "I'd like to hug you, but not until those ribs are checked out."

"Just be careful, and I'm good." She didn't wait for him to agree, but released her hands and slid them around his neck. Pain stabbed into her side. So what? It might've hurt to lift her arms, especially after waving them at Sumo earlier, but it would hurt more to miss this hug.

He still looked uncertain.

"It might be better if we kissed instead of hugging," she said. "They didn't hurt my lips." She giggled.

He crushed his mouth to hers, silencing her.

His lips were warm and insistent. Everything she remembered from the first kiss and more. He deepened the kiss, and it went on and on and on until she was breathless and had to break free to gulp in air.

"You're right," he said and grinned. "Your lips were most certainly not damaged in any way."

"Gagging here," Nick said drolly.

She looked at her good friend. "You always said you wanted me to find a guy."

"Yeah, but not on my watch." Nick laughed.

She would've kissed Colin again, if for no other reason than to keep annoying Nick, but sirens sounded in the distance.

"I'm with Nick on this," Dev said from where he stood still holding his rifle over Luka. "I'm glad you two finally are admitting how you feel, but no need for me to see or hear it."

Colin gently circled his arms around her waist and drew her head to rest on his chest. "I don't know what we're going to do about these feelings, but I want to figure it out."

"Me too," she said, glancing at a pale Kane who would once and for all be out of her life. "More than anything I've wanted in years."

Two days later, Colin wished he were alone with Brooklyn and free to talk about a future with her, but they were in his dining area with the whole team, along with Nick and Sheriff Day, crammed into the small space. His mom sat on the couch, pretending to watch *Casablanca* when he knew she was listening in to their conversation. Brooklyn had gotten his mother hooked on the classic movies, and they'd been watching this one together until Sheriff Day arrived.

The sheriff stepped to the head of the table and scrubbed a hand over tired eyes. She wore her usual uniform, badge at her waist, but even at eight in the morning, her pants were wrinkled, and she looked a bit disheveled. She'd been working nonstop due to staffing shortages. Looked like that meant overnight.

"I won't take much of your time," she said, "but wanted to confirm that, thanks to Nick here decrypting the flash drives, we were able to arrest twenty-five wildlife traffickers and break up a huge ring."

The group started applauding.

"Way to go, friend." Brooklyn put out her fist to Nick for a bump.

He grinned and tapped her fist gently, likely out of respect for her remaining rib pain. "You really should hold your applause until she mentions the charges Kane is being brought up on."

"He's right," Abby said, her tone uplifted. "The other drive in the box gave the FBI and DA enough information to bring Tarver in on twenty-nine counts of mail fraud, wire fraud, bank fraud, money laundering, and aggravated identity theft. All of this is in addition to first-degree murder. Plus, we matched the gasoline from the fire to a local station, and they had a video showing him purchasing it. So we've added abuse of a corpse for Matteo Albertelli and arson charges."

She paused and took a long breath. "And if that list isn't long enough, the FBI is still investigating the stalking and attempted murder charges as relates to you, Brooklyn. The footprints outside this compound were a match to his shoes, putting him here when the alarm went off. And of course, you have the video with him at your home doorbell. The FBI has found other information on the drive, and they're sure additional charges will be forthcoming."

"Wow," Brooklyn said, sounding the happiest Colin had ever seen. "Will he ever get out of prison?"

Abby rested her hands on the chair back in front of her. "If convicted of all of these charges, it's unlikely."

Brooklyn's face split in a wide smile. "So I'm free, then? Able to go on with my life?"

Abby nodded. "Even though his leg had to be amputated, he's under guard in the hospital. He'll be transferred to lockup when he's well enough. Bail has been denied, so he won't be getting out. He can't hurt you now. Oh, and Sumo has found a home in a wildlife refuge."

"Now that deserves applause," Nick said. "For all the work done, not just what I accomplished."

"Amen to that." Brooklyn started clapping and it traveled around the table.

"That's all I have," Abby said when the applause died down. "I'll continue to keep you updated as time allows."

Dev leaned forward. "Does this mean my time as your deputy has come to an end?"

"It does." She eyed him. "But only if you want it to."

"Sorry. Not that working with you hasn't been great, but I need to go back to my real life now, where the biggest excitement is whether to have hot dogs or hamburgers on a client campout."

She smiled. "Sounds real good right about now."

Colin wouldn't be surprised if she didn't seek reelection when it came up in the fall. That she might go the private route to get her life back, too, like so many law enforcement officers were doing these days.

He stood. "So unless anyone else has anything to add, this meeting is over, and our involvement in the investigation, other than testifying, is over."

"My only thing to say is, what in the world smells so good, and can we have some of it?" Dev asked.

Brooklyn laughed. "Chocolate chip cookie bars that I just took out of the oven, and let me get a plate."

She slowly eased to her feet and went to the kitchen.

Colin followed her to help. She shouldn't be baking for them when she should really be on bed rest. "You don't have to cater to everyone."

"I'm glad to share so I don't eat half the pan myself." She cut into a cake-pan-sized slab of browned cookies. "This is one recipe I can hardly say no to."

"They're that good?"

"Wait and see." She lifted out the first inch-thick bar and handed it to him.

He took a bite and moaned. "What's that unique flavor?"

"Vanilla. Lots of vanilla. There's a tablespoon in here when most recipes call for about a teaspoon in a similar bar."

He took another bite, and the flavor seemed to explode on his tongue. "I take it back. Go ahead and cater to all of us all the time."

She laughed and finished filling the plate. "It feels good to be living a normal kind of life. I forgot what it was like not to have to worry."

"I'm glad Tarver is in custody. It makes me happy to see you happy."

She picked up the plate and a napkin that she'd placed a single bar on. "Then follow me. Cooking for others is my love language, and I am about to love all over your brother and team."

She laughed and the joyous sound trailed her out the door. She handed the bars to Dev. "Share with others, but don't eat too many if you want to stay fit."

He chuckled and took one, then passed the plate to Nick, who was on his computer. He grabbed one, but she doubted he would even taste it.

Dev swallowed. "Oh, man, there goes my girlish figure. I'm going to need another one. Give me the plate back. Or that one in your hand."

"It's for your mom." Brooklyn jerked her hand back. "You'll have to fight the others for one."

She went to the living room and sat down next to Sandy. Colin followed to sit in the leather chair. He only hoped Brooklyn didn't think he planned to follow her like this every day, but he couldn't get enough of being with her. Of seeing her happiness and relief.

She handed the bar to his mom. "I'm sure you heard everything."

"Oh yeah, but I had to turn the TV down to do so." She laughed and took a bite of the bar. "Oh, Dev is right. This is wonderful. You are spoiling us, but you know that's not really part of the job, right?"

"I do, but it's my pleasure." She smiled at Colin's mom, and his heart filled with gratitude.

His mom held the bar but didn't take another bite. "And you're really going to stay here for a while?"

Brooklyn gave an enthusiastic nod, warming Colin clean through. "I contacted my favorite company I worked for in the past three years, and they'll let me work remotely. So unless things change, I'm good to be here for you and still do some hacking."

"I promise not to be too needy." His mother took another bite of the bar, then set it and the napkin on the table.

Brooklyn took his mother's hands. "That's not possible. And don't hide things from me just because I am hacking. Hacking can wait. You can't."

"But I—"

"But nothing. Promise you won't hide things from me, or I can't stay. I need to know I'm taking care of you in the way you deserve."

"I promise." His mother's eyes filled with tears, and she gently drew Brooklyn into a hug. "I don't know what I've done to deserve you, but I am most blessed."

Colin understood her emotions. He could get teary-eyed, too, if he let himself. He hated that Brooklyn had gone through such a terrible situation with Tarver, but it brought her to him and his mother, and for that he was forever grateful.

No matter how bleak things looked—like facing a jaguar that wanted to chow down on you for a snack—God could and would work everything for good. Colin just had to remember that. Let go of any residual issues from his time at the Bureau. Release his need to let his mother's health consume him. Allow himself to follow these feelings for Brooklyn and fall for her.

No matter the situation, God would work it out. He always did.

# 25

---

The Saturday before Father's Day, Brooklyn took a deep breath of the glorious sun-warmed air. She kept one eye on Shadow Lake Survival's driveway and one on Colin, where he stood on the other side of the lakeside pavilion. Picnic tables covered in dishes of food filled the large structure. The Shadow Lake Survival team members and their families gathered around, the children were running and playing without a care, adding to the festive event. Just outside, a smoking grill held hamburgers and hotdogs that Reid had charge of grilling.

Brooklyn didn't think she would ever see this day. They'd done it. Had Kane in custody. Her life was her own again. And as a bonus, they'd done it before the big Father's Day gathering. Just barely. But in enough time for her to call her parents and invite them to today's celebration. Her mom just texted that they were turning into the driveway.

Brooklyn's heart pounded. Her palms were moist. She was both excited and nervous about seeing them again. Three years was a long time to be separated. They would both have changed. What wouldn't have changed was the love between the three of them, and that could overcome anything else.

A white SUV drove up and parked. Ah, she was right. Change had occurred. The first one—a new car. Life had gone on for them. For her. Didn't mean they didn't miss each other. Just that they'd lived their lives as she would expect them to, and hopefully, they were happier than she'd been.

The doors opened, and her dad slid out from behind the wheel, and her dear, sweet mama out the passenger side. She retrieved a casserole dish from the back and handed it to Dad. Brooklyn had told them not to bother bringing anything for the potluck, but she knew her Southern-bred mother could never come to a potluck empty-handed.

They hurried down the driveway, and Brooklyn started off to greet them, but her legs went weak. Rubbery. Her mind blurred. She felt lightheaded. Like she might drop. Strong hands came to lift her up by her elbows from behind before she fell.

"Don't worry." Colin's strong voice whispered in her ear. "I've got you. I'll always have you."

"I don't get this," she said. "I'm so happy to see them. So what's wrong with me? Why do I feel like I'm going to drop?"

"I'd suspect it's excess adrenaline over expecting your parents than a crash of relief when you actually saw them."

She wanted to fling herself into her mama's arms and hold her for hours, but when she tried to take a step, she still felt weak.

"Why not sit on the bench for a minute?" He helped her to a nearby picnic table.

Her mother frowned. Looked hurt.

*No. Oh, no.* Brooklyn didn't want to hurt her mama.

Colin rushed to them and held out his hand to her dad.

"Colin Graham." He shook her dad's free hand, then looked at her mama. "The excitement got to Brooklyn, and she felt weak, but I know she's eager to hug you."

"Mama, please," Brooklyn called out. "I'm sorry. I...I want..."

Her mother charged across the open space like she did when Brooklyn was young and had hurt herself. She dropped onto the bench and scooped her into her strong arms. She held tightly, hurting Brooklyn's ribs, but she didn't care. The pain was so worth it. Her mama smelled like her flowery jasmine perfume that she'd always worn, and Brooklyn couldn't hold it together any longer. The tears she'd released ramped up to sobbing.

"It's okay, sweet pea," her mama said and stroked her hair. "We're back together, and we'll never be parted like this again. That's all that matters."

Brooklyn leaned back and drank in the sight of her mama, slightly older looking but still fit, with regal posture learned from her mama as she'd said all good Southern girls knew. Her nose was pointed much like Brooklyn's. Her smile, a joy to behold. Brooklyn suspected that even though they knew why she had to go into hiding and was probably safe, that they worried the whole time and that beautiful smile might not have been so readily present.

"Let me take that dish over to the food table for you, Mr. Hurst," Colin said.

She caught sight of him and gave him a smile of thanks.

"Oh!" her mama exclaimed. "Oh my." She took Brooklyn's hands and lowered her voice. "When did this happen? When did you fall in love?"

Brooklyn stared at her. "I didn't know I did."

"That smile said it all. You love this man. Who is he? Where did you meet him?"

Brooklyn gave a quick overview.

"So he works here at Shadow Lake?"

Brooklyn nodded.

"Isn't that wonderful?" She clapped. "You'll be living closer to us then."

"Mama," Brooklyn warned.

"Yes, Geneva." Her father sat next to Brooklyn and put his arm around her. "You'll have her married off in less than five minutes here, and she hasn't even said she loves the guy."

"She doesn't have to say it. A mother knows. That's good enough for me."

"And if Colin doesn't love her back?" her dad asked.

"He does," Colin's voice came from behind her. "But he hasn't had a chance to tell her yet."

Brooklyn fired a look over her shoulder, seeing in his eyes what her mama must've seen in Brooklyn's. So they were in love. What did that mean?

"Gather around everyone," Reid called out. "The burgers and hot dogs are ready. We'll eat while the girls put on the special show they've planned for us."

"To be continued," Colin said.

"Yes." Her mother winked. "To be continued. And if it's okay, I believe I need to sit between you and Colin for lunch so I can get to know him."

"It's okay with me," Colin said.

"Of course," Brooklyn said, but wasn't really ready for her to get to know Colin all that well, when they hadn't even talked about dating or a long-term future.

Colin offered his hand to help Brooklyn up, and the four of them started for the food table. Brooklyn had gained a bit of strength in her legs again, but eating would help chase the remaining weakness away. She would need all of her strength for her part in the afternoon's program that eight-year-old Jessie, Reid's biological daughter, and seven-year-old Ella, his stepdaughter, had planned.

She introduced her parents to people as they passed them and when they got in line for food. They filled their plates with casseroles, salads, fruit, coleslaw, and more before getting a burger from Reid at the grill. Colin then led them all to a table with his brother and their mom, who were already seated on the long bench. He introduced them to her parents.

"You have a very special daughter." Sandy moved her cane so Colin could sit next to her. "She's been helping with my health issues, and I couldn't ask for a better companion."

Brooklyn's mom beamed. "It all started with her baby dolls. No pretend mother ever took better care of her babies."

Sandy smiled. "Something you miss out on when you have boys."

"Mom just doesn't want to embarrass Dev here." Colin grinned. "He loved his baby doll."

Dev socked him. "I did love Luis, and I'm proud of it."

"And let's not forget that Luis was a hand-me-down from you, Colin," their mom said with a smile. "And he was well loved by then."

"Yeah, well, he was more like a stuffed toy than a doll."

Brooklyn loved how her big, tough guy wouldn't admit to loving a doll when he was little.

Colin also introduced her parents to Russ and his wife Sydney, along with her teenage sister, Nikki, who sat across from them. Sydney glowed with happiness, but Nikki's frown and slumped posture said she wasn't all that eager to be there. Still, the sisters resembled each other, but Sydney had blond hair while Nikki had dyed hers a wild shade of blue.

Chatter and laughter filled the afternoon as people ate

and got to know each other until Jessie and Ella, wearing matching pink party dresses, climbed up on a makeshift stage. A large, colorful banner fluttered in the breeze where they'd strung it across the back, and it read, '*First Annual Father's Day Celebration.*'

Jessie grabbed a karaoke microphone. "Attention. Attention. We're going to start our program. Each kid—well, me and Ella together cause we only get one song—chose a Christian song that was a hit the year our dads were born, and we're gonna sing it. Sorry. We didn't realize when we decided to do this that some are really old and a little bit lame." She rolled her eyes.

The others laughed.

"How adorable." Brooklyn's mom leaned over to whisper. "Reminds me of Father's Day banquets we used to have at church when I was young. The kids always did a program. I wonder why we ever stopped having them."

Brooklyn suspected it was just a sign of the times when kids were too busy to do one more activity, but she didn't say that. She squeezed her mama's hand. "Sounds nice."

People quieted down and gave the girls their attention.

"Dad, we love you," Jessie said, looking at Reid. "And we wanted to go first. I mean, it was our idea to do this and it should be fair that we start, but it's getting close to naptime, so we're going to start with the youngest." She gave a pointed look at Ryan's wife, Mia, who was holding their seven-month-old son, Austin.

Mia flipped her mousy brown hair, still holding hints of a former black dye, over her shoulder. She got up, kissed a surprised Ryan on the head, and took the baby to sit with her in a chair on the stage. "Sydney, you should be up here, and I really shouldn't be going first, but I guess we can wait until the baby's born."

"Five months down and counting." Russ beamed at his

wife and put his arm around Zach, his six-year-old son from a previous marriage. "Then we'll have Mini Me II."

Zach looked confused but still beamed up at his dad with pride.

The crowd laughed, then settled down.

"I first want to apologize for my lack of singing voice, but Austin loves his daddy, and I wanted to be sure he knew it." She locked gazes with Ryan, and the air was fairly charged with electricity between them. The same electricity that sparked in Brooklyn when she looked at Colin.

"Hey," Reid called out. "Cool the looks. This program is only approved for G-rated content."

Another outburst from the crowd, and Russ socked Reid in the arm.

"So, if Austin could choose a song to dedicate to his daddy from the year he was born, it would be *In a Father's Heart,* by Kathy Troccoli."

Brooklyn wasn't familiar with the song, but as Mia sang it, she learned it was a song of hope and love, joy and family.

She watched Ryan, the tough guy, tear up as he listened. He kept clearing his throat. Mia stepped down, and he jumped up to envelop her and his son in a hug.

"Looks like a sweet family," Brooklyn's mom said.

"They do," Brooklyn said as she hadn't spent any time with them but the vibe was obvious.

Jessie raced up on stage, Ella right behind her.

Jessie passed the mic to Ella, who stubbed her toe and looked down. "We chose *I Will Be Here,* by Steven Curtis Chapman."

Jessie took the mic and slung her arm around her sister's shoulders. "Ella's a little shy, but she sings really good. Better than me. And she loves my dad a whole bunch, and I know he loves her too. We're adopting her. Dad *and* me, and then we'll be official sisters."

Jessie hugged Ella, whose happiness beamed from her adorable little face, and the crowd clapped.

The music started, and for the first time, Brooklyn noticed Reid's wife, Megan, operating a sound system from just off stage. She proudly beamed at the girls as she started the music.

The lyrics told of our Father being there for everything and in every time. Always. In all ages.

Reid had a similar reaction to Ryan, except the moment the last word was sung, he raced to the stage and grabbed the girls up in a hug.

"I love you both." His voice came over the speaker.

"Ouch, Dad," Jessie said, still holding the mic. "You're squishing me."

"You should've thought of that before you sang me such a pretty song." He laughed and released them.

Jessie stepped back. "Zach and Nikki are next, but Zach says singing stupid songs is for girls, so it's just gonna be Nikki."

Russ flashed a surprised look at Nikki, then knuckled Zach on the head. "Didn't I say he was my Mini Me I?"

Zach looked up at his dad. "You're not mad?"

"'Course not. I don't need a song. I just need to have you here with me."

"Hey, thanks, Dad. You're the coolest."

"Don't I know it." Russ blew on his fingers then brushed them against his chest.

The crowd groaned and laughed.

Not Nikki. She dragged herself up on the stage as if she were going to her execution and took the mic. "I didn't really want to do this either. I mean, you're not my dad, Russ. Not at all. You're just married to my sister, but you've been cool. Like a dad. Helping me out. Kicking my butt, too, but that's okay. I usually deserve it. Okay, you only do when I do deserve it." She eyed the crowd from eyes lined with heavy liner and thick mascara on her lashes. "And if anyone speaks of this again or tells other people, I'll get all up in your face."

Sydney groaned and blushed, but Russ puffed out his chest. "If I could have a Mini Me daughter, this girl would be it."

Nikki lifted her shoulders a fraction. "So I chose *Place in This World,* by Michael W. Smith. He talks about finding his place in the world, and Russ is helping me do that. You know, like a dad would do." She looked down at her feet. "So, yeah, I love you. Now let me get this song over with."

Russ's smile evaporated, and he swallowed hard as he took Sydney's hand.

Tears formed in Brooklyn's eyes. She'd been so blessed to have such an amazing dad when Nikki didn't have one at all. He'd taken off when Sydney was a teenager and Nikki a little girl. Then their mother turned to booze to drown her sorrows, and Sydney ended up raising her little sister.

Despite Nikki's angst, she sang with enthusiasm. When she sang about needing his light to help her find her place in this world, her voice broke, and she swiped the back of her hand over her eyes.

The song ended, and she almost tossed the mic at Jessie, then marched back to her table. Russ got up and held out his fist for her to bump. "Love you too, kid."

She awkwardly threw her arms around his neck and held on tight. Sydney smiled up at them and was bawling openly.

Nikki jerked back and pointed at her sister. "Now see what we did. She's pretty much been crying over nothing almost nonstop since getting pregnant. Man, I don't know if I can survive another four months."

"Not just four months," Russ said. "There's all the after having the baby hormones to deal with."

"Are you kidding me?" She pretended to faint into her chair. "Just kill me now."

Laughter rang out, and Brooklyn shook her head. She hoped she and Colin did get together for so many reasons, but it would be fun getting to know this blended family too. Never a dull moment, she suspected.

Jessie got up on stage again. "So this was supposed to just be for kids, but Brooklyn said she wanted a turn, and Dad said I had to let her."

Laughter returned, and Jessie looked bewildered, so Brooklyn hurried to the stage to help with her unease. She took the mic, and Jessie went to sit on Reid's lap.

Brooklyn looked at her dad. "I haven't met everyone here yet, but for those who don't know, I've been away from my family for three years. I had to go into hiding and couldn't have one bit of communication with them. Not a word. So when the girls told me about the program, I asked if I could choose a song for my dad. I cheated a little and chose one that was a hit in the year I was born. I picked *I Will Be Here For You,* by Michael W. Smith."

She smiled at her dad. "It basically talks about being there and being able to trust in you. And you always were there. Will be again, now that we're free to see each other. Mama too, but this is your day. And there's not a more trustworthy man I know. So be patient with me while I butcher this song. But know that it comes from a place of complete love."

She sang the song, trying her best to remain on key and more importantly, not lose it in front of everyone. She left the stage, and her dad gripped her in a fierce hug. "Love you, too, daughter, and I will always be there for you. No matter the physical distance between us."

He released her, and she sat, looking upward to keep her tears at bay. Colin scooped up her hand in his to hold it tightly.

Jessie announced that Brooklyn was the end of the program. The crowd got up cheering and shouting. Reid took the stage and drew Megan up with him. "A special thanks to our daughters for arranging this event, and to my lovely wife, Megan, for running the sound. I am the most blessed man on earth, and this right here tells you why. There're still burgers and dogs and lots of food, so dig in. And what say we do this again next year?"

The rapt applause spoke to the crowd's agreement.

Colin leaned over her to look at her mother. "Do you mind if I take Brooklyn for a walk?"

"Mind?" her mama asked. "I can see you have something special planned, so go for it."

He tugged Brooklyn to her feet.

She smiled at her parents. "Be right back."

"Take your time, sweet pea," her mama said and turned to look across the table at Russ and his family. "We have all the time in the world to catch up, and I know getting to know this lovely Nikki is going to be fun."

Colin moved at a rapid clip, leading Brooklyn through the crowd, who were complimenting her on her song. Once he reached the edge of the pavilion, he ducked into the trees, drawing her with him.

"Alone, at last." He grinned and circled his arms around her waist.

She leaned in to him. "I'm glad to be alone with you, but I really shouldn't leave my mama and daddy for too long."

"I get that, but I thought we needed to talk about me declaring my love." Unease darkened his eyes. "I don't want to scare you away. It's really fast, I know. You didn't have to say it if you don't mean it."

"I do mean it."

"Oh. Oh, right. Good. Great." His broad smile sent chills through her.

"What would you think about dating, then?" His timid tone was back.

"You're sure you can continue to care for your mom and start dating?" She searched his gaze. "I mean, Dev told me that's why you're not dating now."

"He's right, but yeah. I guess I just needed to find the right person to know when it's the right time to forget about all of that nonsense and trust God."

"Your mom told me your dad was a firefighter, and I've never gotten a chance to tell you my dad is too."

He arched an eyebrow. "What are the odds of that?"

"Long, I imagine. But I only mention it to say I understand what it's like to have a parent go to work each day, wondering if you might lose them."

"Until you do." His eyes closed, and he swallowed.

"I'm so sorry for your loss, Colin. And for bringing this up now when we were talking about such happy things, but I thought you should know."

"No, it's good you did. My trust issues stem from that, but I really think I can let them go." He took a long breath. "If I fail, now I know you understand."

She touched his cheek. "I do and will be there for you."

His gaze searched hers. Maybe he was wondering for how long she would be there.

"I was hoping I might talk to you about continuing to care for your mom," she said. "Not just for a few weeks like we discussed, but indefinitely."

His eyes widened. "You don't want to go back to Portland and your hacking career?"

"No, I do, but she doesn't need that much care yet. More like just having someone with her in case she needs help.

And maybe to encourage her to rest more. I can hack from anywhere and take care of her in my downtime." She knew he might balk at the next bit, but she had to say it. "No need to pay me. I just want to do it for you and her. Dev too."

He tilted his head and studied her face. "You really want to do that?"

"I do. I'm sure. And as my parents said, this is closer to where they live, so that would be good for all of us too."

A broad smile crossed his face. "Well, then I accept, as I'm sure Mom will too."

"Wow, convincing you was easier than I thought. Is this the new Colin speaking?"

"I guess so." He laughed.

"I suppose if we'll be living under the same roof, we'll have a crash course in dating." She batted her eyelashes at him.

"We're bound to get to know each other pretty quickly." He smiled. "So maybe it won't be too many Father's Days before you can sing to me."

The thought of someday having children with this fine man sent a tingle through her, but she'd had far too an emotional day to discuss this in the way it deserved.

"I don't know," she said. "I might have used up all my cred with Jessie this year, and she'll never let me on stage again."

"Don't worry about it." He tucked her hair behind her ear. "I was once an FBI agent. I can take out an eight-year-old girl. No problem."

A feeling so indescribably delicious after her three years of fear and exile took over her that she tossed back her head and laughed, but it soon was silenced by a demanding kiss.

Something she would take over laughter anytime, and God willing, she had many years ahead of being silenced in this very way.

## SHADOW LAKE SURVIVAL SERIES

When survival takes a dangerous turn and lives are on the line.

The men of Shadow Lake Survival impart survival skills and keep those in danger safe from harm. Even if it means risking their lives.

Book 1 – Shadow of Deceit
Book 2 – Shadow of Night
Book 3 – Shadow of Truth
Book 4 – Shadow of Hope – April 8, 2024
Book 5 – Shadow of Doubt – July 8, 2024
Book 6 – Shadow of Fear – November 4, 2024

For More Details Visit -
www.susansleeman.com/books/shadow-lake-survival

## STEELE GUARDIAN SERIES
### Intrigue. Suspense. Family.

A kidnapped baby. A jewelry heist. Amnesia. Abduction. Smuggled antiquities. And in every book, God's amazing power and love.

Book 1 – Tough as Steele

Book 2 – Nerves of Steele

Book 3 – Forged in Steele

Book 4 – Made of Steele

Book 5 – Solid as Steele

Book 6 – Edge of Steele

For More Details Visit -

www.susansleeman.com/books/steele-guardians

## NIGHTHAWK SECURITY SERIES
Protecting others when unspeakable danger lurks.

A woman being stalked. A mother and child being hunted. And more. All in danger. Needing protection from the men of Nighthawk Security.

Book 1 – Night Fall
Book 2 – Night Vision
Book 3 – Night Hawk
Book 4 – Night Moves
Book 5 – Night Watch
Book 6 – Night Prey

For More Details Visit -
www.susansleeman.com/books/nighthawk-security/

## THE TRUTH SEEKERS
People are rarely who they seem

A twin who didn't know she had a sister. A mother whose child isn't her own. A woman whose parents lied to her. All needing help from The Truth Seekers forensic team.

Book 1 - Dead Ringer
Book 2 - Dead Silence
Book 3 - Dead End
Book 4 - Dead Heat
Book 5 - Dead Center
Book 6 - Dead Even

For More Details Visit -
www.susansleeman.com/books/truth-seekers/

## The COLD HARBOR SERIES

Meet Blackwell Tactical- former military and law enforcement heroes who will give everything to protect innocents... even their own lives.

For More Details Visit -
www.susansleeman.com/books/cold-harbor/

# ABOUT SUSAN

SUSAN SLEEMAN is a bestselling and award-winning author of more than 50 inspirational/Christian and clean read romantic suspense books. In addition to writing, Susan also hosts the website, TheSuspenseZone.com.

Susan currently lives in Oregon, but has had the pleasure of living in nine states. Her husband is a retired church music director and they have two beautiful daughters, two very special sons-in-law, and three amazing grandsons.

*For more information visit:*
www.susansleeman.com

9 781949 009507